CAGED
ANGEL

CAGED ANGEL

Anne-Marie Vukelic

ROBERT HALE · LONDON

ISBN 978-0-7198-1699-4

Robert Hale Limited
Clerkenwell House
Clerkenwell Green
London EC1R 0HT

www.halebooks.com

2 4 6 8 10 9 7 5 3 1

Typeset in Palatino
Printed in Great Britain by Berforts Information Press Ltd.

ACKNOWLEDGEMENTS

My thanks go to Mr Roger Flavell (Oxon) for access to his library, with grateful thanks for editorial advice and for suggested titles. Your support as always was invaluable. Also to Chris Nichols for contributions to the diary of Richard Dunn. Lastly to my extended family who always inspire me with their own talents.

For my nieces, Beatrice-Lee, Ella Grace and Ellie Louise and remembering Hannah Victoria Carter.

AUTHOR'S NOTE

Angela Burdett-Coutts lived 1814-1906 and was heiress to part of the Coutts bank fortune. This novel is a fictionalized account of her life and the misery which was caused her by the persistent and unwanted attentions of Richard Dunn, barrister-at-law.

BOOK ONE

PROLOGUE

21 February

> *My heart is the glass to your window's soul*
> *Inside within where pieces remain whole*
> *Your life is my sadness*
> *My kiss is your taste*
> *I'm alone in your dream*
> *Your laugh is my embrace*
> *I'm awake and sleeping to the silence of sounds*
> *Your hurt is my pain to the clarity of clouds*
> *The face of your woman is my girl in your eyes*
> *Your colours are the sharpness to the lights in my skies*
> *Your eyes are my jewels*
> *Your body is my love*
> *The beauty you brought me my angel from above.*

Piccadilly
London 1838

FROM THE UPSTAIRS window of the Gloucester Coffee House Hotel, Berkeley Street, the view was perfect. A hand held back the dark, velvet curtains, and a pair of searching blue eyes scrutinized the sash windows of the house opposite, lit by candlelight. His eyes were set deep and darkly encircled, as if he had not slept well in months.

He allowed himself the pleasure of imagining what the young woman who lived there might be doing at that precise moment. His preferred image was that of her standing in front of a mirror, brushing her hair. He had decided that when she finally became his, it would be his privilege alone to take the brush in his hand and to pass it through those silky locks.

Wondering about the sound of her voice, he imagined it to be soft and light. He had often heard her playing the piano when the window was open, and had imagined her slender fingers running up and down the keys. He glanced at the carafe at his bedside and smiled at the thought of her taking a sip from a glass of water, watching her neck tense and relax as she swallowed.

He remembered the time when he had first become aware of her existence: he had been reading the newspaper. The day had probably been a Thursday; he knew it couldn't have been a Friday, he never took a paper on that day as he didn't like Fridays. The report in *The Morning Chronicle* had spoken of the impressive inheritance of Miss Angela Georgina Burdett-Coutts, but his interest in the young lady was not motivated by money; he had an ample private income of his own.

A flattering sketch of her had accompanied the newspaper headlines and he remembered the feelings which had crept over him as he took in the features of the fascinating young heiress. With intensity her innocent eyes had looked into his and seemed to appeal:

I am young and inexperienced, sir, and without your assistance I shall surely fall into the hands of those who wish only to take advantage of me. Please come to my aid soon.

He had been shaken by the force of his emotions and looking back into those angelic eyes, he had promised her then, 'Yes, I will protect you, my love. Wherever you go, I will always be with you, watching over you and acting as your guardian.'

And so he stood now, as he had done since the first moment he had taken the room at the Gloucester Coffee House directly opposite her house, watching. He let the curtain fall, and on the glass remained a smear where his face had been.

'Angela ...' he whispered the name to himself. '*Like an angel....*'

CHAPTER ONE

Stratton House
Piccadilly
A Year Earlier

For THOMAS COUTTS, banker, the bustle of the world had ceased. His body lay on a couch in the sitting room. His eyes were closed and his hands folded in satisfaction that the business of his life had been conducted with kindness, friendship and integrity. At eighty-six his strength had been failing for some weeks; his death had not been unexpected. His daughter, Lady Sophia, married to the politician and baronet, Sir Francis Burdett, had stood at his side, crying quietly at the sight of her father and slightly troubled that her black French gown jarred unfashionably with the red wallpaper.

She did not like death, it upset her social plans. How could she dazzle in black crêpe? Her mother and both her sisters had all died in the last three years, and now her father. It annoyed her that her husband would not be inconvenienced by such visible displays of grief; a dark jacket and a black-bordered handkerchief would be all that society expected of him. But then she called to mind the fashion plate in this month's *La Belle Assemblée* and was cheered at the remembrance of an evening gown in dark lavender.

A hearse and four black horses took the body from Stratton Street and made a slow, dignified procession to the parish church. The coffin was swathed with a black cloth embroidered with the Coutts family crest, and a simple inscription embellished the brass

11

plate on the lid: 'He hath done what he could.'

Following were three coaches, carrying the partners in the bank and two generations of the Coutts family. The Dukes of York and Clarence had sent carriages and so had many other noble heads who had confidently placed their money in the principled hands of Mr Thomas Coutts, banker. Even in his final days while he was still able to write, his business correspondence had spoken first of family, the weather, and the health of his customers before turning to monetary matters. His wealth had been the consequence of his kindness, not the purpose of it. To the family mourners in the carriage following immediately behind the hearse, there was a particular matter of business which was weighing on their minds and that was the question of inheritance.

Sir Francis Burdett MP, baronet, had decided that he wanted nothing from Thomas Coutts: no bequests, no annuities, or deeds. He was still irritated that he had allowed his father-in-law to purchase his seat in north Yorkshire at a price of £4,000. The very essence of Sir Francis's political career had been centred on electoral reform. He had admired the revolutionary downfall of French aristocrats decades before, expressed indignation at injustice for the poor, and yet here he was, a man who had campaigned for justice, allowing his wealthy father-in-law to purchase his parliamentary seat. Thomas, always with an eye turned to family, had done so to discourage Sir Francis from moving his family to Europe, which was at that time a very dangerous place for an Englishman to be but Sir Francis still wrestled with his conscience. No, he wanted nothing more from his father-in-law and if an inheritance came his way, he would soundly reject it.

Seated at Sir Francis's side in the carriage was his son-in-law, John Bettesworth-Trevanion, husband to his eldest daughter, Susan. Trevanion's hair was curled in the fashion of the day and – along with his neatly trimmed whiskers – was a little too oily, which was indicative of a man who was himself rather too slick. Unlike Sir Francis, Trevanion had no scruples as to where his own advantages came from. There had been his education at Winchester and Eton, obligatory for a man of his background. A commission in the army, purchased at the hand of his father; and the house in

Northamptonshire, a wedding gift from Sir Francis.

Seated in a carriage, Trevanion reflected how fortunate it was that his wife's grandfather should end his life of opulence at this very moment. Trevanion had argued with his father recently and there had been all manner of threats, namely that he would be excluded from his father's will. He had already sold some of the plate from the house in Northamptonshire to settle the most pressing of his debts, but with the death of Thomas Coutts, there was sure to be a handsome gesture shortly to come.

The seat opposite had been reserved for Sir Francis's son, Robert, but the boy had snubbed the family by failing to return from his post in the army without any word of explanation. Sir Francis had written to him and advised him that he was expected to attend the funeral of his grandfather and to conduct himself with a measure of sympathy for his mother's sake. Robert had written a terse note of reassurance that he would arrive shortly; however, the vacant seat in the carriage reminded Sir Francis that the future of the Burdett baronetcy was not in the hands of a sympathetic man but in the hands of a cold, military machine.

To ease the boredom of the journey, Trevanion thought that he might enjoy the diversion of seeing Sir Francis turn blood-red at the mention of his absent son, but he reasoned that it was best not to upset a man upon whose pocket he may need to call someday.

In the following carriage sat another of Thomas's grandsons, Lord Dudley Coutts. Lord Dudley knew that any hopes of an inheritance had vanished upon his marriage to Christina Bonaparte, niece of Napoleon. His grandfather had told him in no uncertain terms that no relative of that foreign adventurer would benefit from a penny of his money, which Dudley thought a damn inconvenience as his lovely wife was a hopeless spendthrift. Seated with the other women of the Coutts family, paying quiet respects at Stratton House, was Dudley's sister, Frances. Already an heiress, she hoped simply to be remembered with a small token.

The partners in the bank centred their concerns on the worthiness of the intended heir. Seated alongside them in the carriage was Edward Marjoribanks, Thomas's most trusted friend and associate. Unknown to anyone else, Majoribanks had in his pocket a document at which the grey-haired men making that slow, digni-fied procession to the parish church of St James would salivate and that was the will of Thomas Coutts. The partners had asked him of its existence, had questioned him repeatedly of Coutts's plans for a successor, but Marjoribanks had remained loyally silent upon the subject. The time to speak was shortly to arrive.

Reaching the parish church, the mourners stepped down from their carriages to the sound of a tolling bell. Marjoribanks adjusted his cravat, put on his hat, and glanced idly at a gravestone at his feet.

COME YOUTHFUL FOLLY, AS YOU PASS BY,
AND ON THESE LINES DO CAST AN EYE.
AS YOU ARE NOW, SO ONCE WAS I;
AS I AM NOW, SO MUST YOU BE;
PREPARE FOR DEATH AND FOLLOW ME.

Marjoribanks looked away abruptly and, with a shiver, drew his topcoat across his chest. At the sound of another toll, he joined the mourners who followed behind the coffin, their hands folded in front of them, their faces turned to the ground.

Hearing little of the service, Edward Marjoribanks had his mind not on heavenly matters but on matters of the earth. He knew that the contents of the document which he carried in his jacket pocket were soon to cause the most spectacular of scenes. Many hopes were founded upon this document, yet no man in that church could imagine for one moment that Thomas Coutts had proposed the most unlikely of heirs.

A psalm was read, a prayer was offered and the mourners filed to the chancel where a tablet had been erected on the wall. Marjoribanks wondered if the men gathered beneath it were expecting a finger to appear and write upon the marble precisely how and when the kingdom of Thomas Coutts would be divided. The coffin was taken into the vault below and the mourners bowed their heads for the last time and made their way out towards the waiting carriages.

They talked in a low hum and the gentlemen's topic was that of luncheon. Death made a man hungry to stay alive. Marjoribanks declined his place in the carriage in favour of a stroll. He had yet to fix a date for the reading of the will and he wished to settle this matter as quickly as possible.

Coutts and Co. had been in existence for almost 150 years and could claim to have conducted business with both monarchs and dairymen. Under the respected headship of Thomas Coutts, profit margins had increased each year but without a living son, Thomas had pondered endlessly on who could safely inherit his vast fortune. It was not just the future of one of the great banks of Europe which had been at the heart of his concerns. He desired that the name of Coutts continue, and that the kindness which had always marked his dealings with others remain linked to that name. Neither Robert nor Dudley was equipped for such a responsibility.

Marjoribanks had not broken the seal on the document in his pocket, but nevertheless he knew its contents. He had drawn it up and had been present when Thomas had signed it.

'We are sure to set the cat among the pigeons, are we not, Edward?' Thomas had remarked with a chuckle.

Marjoribanks had questioned his friend's sanity. He was taking the most unprecedented gamble. He was sending the name of Coutts – and by extension the business that was Coutts and Co. – into uncertain waters, and if the name of Coutts were to sink into disrepute, then the partners were sure to go down too.

With a lot on his mind, Marjoribanks stopped to eat at an inn in the village, to ponder over this great matter. Should he make known the contents of the will to the partners before the reading? Should he destroy the will, denying all knowledge of it? He had to believe that the man who had steered the bank to greatness and had gained the respect of so many important men had made this vital decision with customary deliberation.

As Marjoribanks had kept faith in his friend over so many years, he resolved to show that same faith now. Finishing his meal, he moved his empty plate to one side and, draining the contents of his wine glass, he settled his mind to gather the Coutts family at the London home of Sir Francis Burdett in two days' time.

CHAPTER TWO

St James's Street
Piccadilly

NOTIFICATIONS HAD BEEN sent to the partners and to all members of the family to attend the reading at St James's Street at ten o'clock, on 24 February. Lord Dudley Coutts, who had just opened a bill from his wife's milliner, had glanced at the remaining letter lying on a silver salver. He was reluctant to open the correspondence which he guessed had come from Marjoribanks. When he finally slit open the envelope he hesitated, imagining the scene that was sure to unfold at St James's Street; and he promptly threw the invitation into the fire. Lord Dudley Coutts was not about to be publicly snubbed over what had been to him the most satisfying, if not expensive, of marriages. If his grandfather had had a change of heart, he was sure to be informed of it in due course.

Sir Francis had been pleased to see that the reading was to be held at his London home. With his own wealth about him, he could confidently reject any bequest that might come his way. Lady Sophia had worried about what to wear. Black was so unflattering in the grey of a February morning. She had, however, just taken receipt of a stunning hairpiece. The thick plaits, looped and fastened on the top of her head, were set off with a large tortoiseshell comb ornamented with jewels and flowers. She would look just like her heroine, the tragic Marie-Antoinette, a name not to be mentioned in the company of her egalitarian husband.

Edmund Antrobus, partner in Coutts and Co., had complained to his colleague, James Campbell, that he did not see why the reading could not be held at the bank. The bank was created for talk of business, its mahogany coffers hewn for pounds, shillings and pence. Nevertheless, they were anxious to know what Thomas Coutts had directed and they sat together, beneath the portrait of Sir Francis Burdett, fifth baronet.

Seated side by side in a pair of quarrelsome chairs were Susan and John Bettesworth-Trevanion. Trevanion, his hair and whiskers shining with oil, complimented his mother-in-law on her stunning headpiece and she inclined her head, giving a little laugh. The boy was in love with her, it was plain to see. Trevanion privately thought that she looked absurd but if the woman was about to become a major beneficiary in the will, then what did ringlets, curls and tortoiseshell combs matter to him? In fact, he should've complimented her on her gown too.

Sitting by the writing bureau, Angela Burdett, Sir Francis's daughter, reflected soberly upon her grandfather's death. Of Thomas Coutts's grandchildren she was most like him in appearance: dark-haired, an oval face and a slender figure. She knew that she was not considered pretty but she did not care. She had determination and intellect; the two qualities which had made her grandfather a very rich man. She recalled that Thomas had once asked her what she would do if ever she were to become wealthy in her own right and she had answered, without hesitation, that she would do something for the poor. The same question was posed to her two younger sisters and the answer had centred on hats and trousseau.

Angela's thoughts were interrupted by her mother's sharp whisper. 'My dear, was it really necessary for you to wear that dark, grey gown?'

'But it is with respect for Grandpapa.'

'Ah, but you are so young. No one expects a grandchild to fully mourn a grandparent. The old are destined to die, my dear. It cannot be helped.'

Angela cast a glance at her sisters, Clara and Joanna, arrayed like cakes in a patisserie shop and engaged in a game of draughts.

How could they be so trivial?

Mr Marjoribanks, who had been warming himself in front of the fire, took out his pocket watch and noted that it was ten o'clock precisely. He nodded to Sir Francis, who had been quietly rehearsing his refusal speech. The baronet knew exactly when and how he was going to decline his bequest.

Sir Francis rose to his feet and spoke. 'It seems that Mr Marjoribanks is ready for us now, ladies and gentlemen.'

He indicated to his footman that the servants of Thomas Coutts, who had been asked to wait in the library, should be called in. Sir Francis attempted to greet them with a smile but he was thinking about his Turkish carpet and hoped that they had wiped their feet before entering the house.

Marjoribanks, seeing all eyes upon him, began to read out the contents of the will. There were annuities of up to thirty pounds for Thomas's longest-serving staff, and smaller amounts for the outdoor staff. Two of the groundsmen were given a lifelong tenancy on the farm land; and to friends Thomas had bequeathed books, works of art and other articles of property which they had admired when visiting his home.

Marjoribanks, who had removed his spectacles to pinch his nose, put them on again, his white, bushy eyebrows arching above, and cleared his throat before continuing in his sonorous voice.

'To my ... ah, daughter, Sophia, I leave the sum of £20,000, the mahogany grand piano which she loved as a child, and jewellery to the value of ... ah, £2,000.'

At the mention of jewellery, Sophia adjusted the arrangement upon her head and wondered if a tiara might be among the collection. She recalled a portrait of Marie-Antoinette wearing a pearl tiara in her hair and thought how much she would like that. Sir Francis stood behind her, his hand resting on her chair, and Marjoribanks cleared his throat once more.

'To my son-in-law, Sir Francis Burdett ...'

The baronet's hand tensed on the back of his wife's chair and he tried to remember the refusal speech that he had rehearsed. Did he want to say that his father-in-law had done so much for him in life and therefore he neither wanted nor expected anything more? Or was it that he had a worthy body in mind to receive a bequest in his stead? Ah, yes, a contribution to the preservation of the Countess of Derby's alms houses, that was it.

'... I leave him the sum of £5,000 that he might continue to purchase for himself a seat in parliament.'

Sir Francis opened his mouth and closed it again. After all, he could do so much good for the people as an MP, and was he not a man for the people? He looked at his wife and suddenly noticed how much like Marie-Antoinette she looked.

Marjoribanks continued, 'To my eldest granddaughter, Mrs Susan Trevanion, I leave the sum of £500 on the condition that it is not used to clear her husband's ... ah,' Marjoribanks hesitated before saying a word which was most disagreeable to his palate, '... debts.'

The partners in the bank shuddered and Susan's eyes narrowed with disdain. Her husband jumped to his feet immediately. 'It is an outrage!'

Marjoribanks raised an aged hand. 'Mr Trevanion, let us not forget decorum, sir.'

Trevanion resumed his seat at his wife's side and the couple joined hands in matrimonial protest.

'To my granddaughters, Clara and Joanna, I leave a trousseau each of Indian shawls, bonnets, gloves, lengths of muslin, satin and lace, as well as jewellery to the value of ... ah, £500.'

Lady Sophia Burdett smiled and nodded with approval.

Marjoribanks took a sip from a glass of water upon the table at his side and then continued.

'My grandson, Robert, will inherit as his father's heir under the terms of his father's own will, and therefore I leave him nothing.'

Sir Francis turned blood-red, wishing that Lord Dudley Coutts had been present so that the shame of an omission had fallen upon him, and not drawn attention to the unworthiness of his son alone. Marjoribanks folded the document, put it down on the table momentarily, while he retrieved a linen handkerchief from his jacket pocket and blew his nose.

Whispered protests rippled through the room. Sophia looked at Clara and Joanna, who were still whispering with delight over their trousseau, and then to Angela, disbelief crossing her face.

'And my father left nothing for Angela either, sir? It makes no sense. Not that she wants for anything, as you can see. But he was so fond of her, as you know, Mr Marjoribanks, I thought he might leave her some small token.'

Angela, who had found the topic of money so distasteful when her grandfather was not long beneath the ground, had been about to say that she had no want of anything. She had her memories and those were precious to her.

'On the contrary, Lady Burdett.'

Returning his handkerchief to his jacket pocket, Marjoribanks picked up the document once more. After observing that everyone was paying full attention, he recommenced the reading.

'The bulk of my estate which consists of my share in the bank, my homes at … ah, Stratton Street and Holly Lodge, their contents along with silver plate and jewellery to the value of £40,000, I leave …' Marjoribanks paused, knowing that all eyes were upon him, '… to my granddaughter, Angela Burdett, on the condition that she append the name Coutts to her surname.'

Trevanion swore beneath his breath and shouted, 'This is an insult!'

Susan turned on her sister. 'You are nothing but a hypocrite! Snaking your way into the old man's favour and sitting there as if you had no idea at all as to what was in his will.'

Sir Francis shook his head and demanded, 'But my son has been overlooked; how can this be?'

'And a woman on the board of the bank, it's unheard of!' chorused the partners.

Sir Francis requested sight of the document in Edward Marjoribanks's hand, and quickly saw for himself the plain truth of the matter: that his daughter, the newly-styled Miss Angela Burdett-Coutts, had been chosen as the major beneficiary to the vast fortune of Thomas Coutts, banker.

CHAPTER THREE

The Gloucester Coffee House
Stratton Street

15 April 18—

I did not believe that I would ever find love again but when I least expected happiness, I stumbled across the most heavenly creature. However, I fear that she is at great risk from opportunists and I have taken a room at the Gloucester Coffee House where I can keep her under my watch continually.

Sometimes my desperation to make her know of my existence almost overwhelms me. But I tell myself to be patient. I have decided to reveal myself to her by degrees, and make her believe that I am worthy of her love....

PUTTING DOWN HIS pen and closing his journal, he set it aside. He glanced at the letter on his desk which he had written earlier, and smiled. Picking it up, he tapped it lightly against his lips, deliberating what he should do. He nodded and decided that it was time to deliver it. He hoped that his words would create within his angel a feeling of excitement and anticipation. A sense that something more was about to unfold.

He pushed back his chair from the desk, stood up and returned to the window, where he resumed his constant watch.

*

She chose the front room with the Chinese carpet and a view of Green Park as her study, and the smallest bedroom directly above would be more than adequate for her modest personal needs. Marjoribanks had allowed her time alone to walk in the extensive gardens, quietly thinking over the enormity of her new responsibilities, and there she remembered what she had once proposed to her grandfather. She would use an inheritance wisely: she would turn her hand to charity.

On the ground floor, in a room with tall sash windows flooding the room with light, Angela Burdett-Coutts now worked diligently at her desk, her long fingers examining each piece of correspondence with deliberate care. Three piles of letters were arranged before her: the first collection being made up of applications from a variety of causes requesting her patronage; the second architectural designs for a number of building projects which she was sponsoring and the third relating to matters connected with the family bank.

The door to the study opened and an elegant figure in a brown woollen dress entered the room.

'As you didn't come in for breakfast, Miss Angela, I took the liberty of bringing you something.'

Angela glanced at the antique French clock on the mantelpiece, once a favourite of her grandfather's, and noticed that it was mid-morning already.

'I'm sorry, Hannah, I've lost track of time. My mind is quite taken up with all of this correspondence. I never imagined that there could be so many people in need of assistance. Had I been left twice as much, I don't think I could begin to do what is needed.'

'Why don't you rest and take a moment to eat, or you'll have little strength to do good for anyone.'

The girl looked so thin. She appeared to find no pleasure in food.

'Bringing you to live here, Hannah, was the wisest thing I could have done.'

Hannah placed the tray on a nearby side table.

'When I first came to be governess to you and your sisters, I thought that I wouldn't last the week, and yet it seems that I am set to become your companion in old age.'

'It *was* good of you to postpone your marriage to Dr Brown. But don't worry, once I am equal to my new role I promise to let you go.'

Hannah Meredith recalled that her young mistress had been promising this for the last year, yet there had been no mention of a precise date. She found that her loyalties were becoming divided. How could she leave the girl so vulnerable and alone in this huge house? There had been all manner of men calling, some of whom had not even the decency to commence a courtship before they came out with a proposal.

Thankfully, Miss Angela had had the good sense to refuse them all so far. But now Hannah had a chance for happiness of her own. Dr Brown had proposed and it was typical of his goodness that he had promised to wait until she was free of her duties. But the man might not wait for ever, and neither could she. She would have to tell Miss Angela that she had come to a decision: she would be leaving at the end of the month.

The governess placed the cup of tea in front of her mistress, who nodded abstractedly, focusing her attention instead on the correspondence in her hand.

'This is most interesting, Hannah. I have received a letter here from a Captain Elliot who is seeking funds for the staffing of a newly established seaman's office. He says that there has been little done to protect sailors from press gangs, and he wishes to open an office to recruit men for the ships in a more legal manner.'

'I'm very glad to hear it. Your tea is there.' She gestured.

'Captain Elliot says that there is an excellent spot for premises in Well Street, but he requires the advance on the rent. And he says that already some of the India ships have approached him for crew ...'

Hannah fetched the breakfast tray from the side table and placed it on the desk, hoping to tempt her mistress with the smell of food.

'... and if the office becomes a success, he believes that he can run a post-office system for the men's letters, and a banking system for their wages. That would certainly improve things for the men.'

'Your breakfast is going cold, Miss Angela—'

'In London, there are far too many men whose labour is only good for the summer – brick-makers, the ground labourers – men who can only earn a living while the ground is yielding and the weather good. Even the sailors and dockmen rely on the winds to support their work.'

Hannah picked up the knife and fork and held them out to her mistress. Angela took them indifferently in her free hand and then continued to read the letter.

'Captain Elliot also mentions the Asylum for the Homeless. Do you know, Hannah, that even though it offers nothing but dry bread to eat, and straw to sleep on, hundreds flock there when the temperature reaches freezing point ...'

'Your knife and fork are in your hand, miss....'

At the mention of them, Angela absent-mindedly put them down.

'... and he says that even though it is a place of misery, suffering and squalor, it is seen as a haven to those who have nowhere else to go. I think that I must find out its location, Hannah, and see what can be done with a donation.'

'I don't think that your father would want you—'

A knock at the door interrupted them and Mrs Mills, the house-keeper, entered the room with a letter in her hand.

'Miss Angela, this was left on the doorstep, wedged beneath the bars of the iron balustrade. It's for you.'

Hannah took it from Mrs Mills and handed it to her young mistress.

'On the doorstep you say, Mrs Mills. Are you sure?'

'I am not in the habit of lying, Miss Meredith,' the housekeeper replied.

'No, I'm sure you're not, but why would someone do that? It could have blown away.'

'The doorbell rang, Miss Angela, but when I opened the front door there was no one there. I was just about to close it when I noticed the letter. I took another glance up and down the street but there was no sign of anyone.'

Angela turned the envelope over and examined the hand-writing.

'Thank you, Mrs Mills.'

'Shall I take the tray, miss?'

Hannah interjected, 'The mistress has yet to eat, leave the tray be!'

Mrs Mills gave a curt nod and left the room. She disliked that woman. She acted far above her station.

Angela stood up from the desk and wandered to the sash window. She frowned at the writing; it was not a hand that she recognized. The strokes of the pen were tall and thin, the letters written with little spacing between them. The address on the envelope was clearly legible, as if the writer wished there to be no doubt as to who was the intended recipient. She tore open the envelope, and as she read the letter her eyes began to pass over words which were shocking.

'Who would say such things!'

As the governess sought to take the letter from her hand, Angela went immediately to the fireplace and threw the vile insult onto the flames.

'Hannah, it is the most indecent of proposals!'

Hannah encouraged her mistress to take a seat by the window.

'Shall I call the police, Miss Angela?

'No, Hannah, that won't be necessary.'

'Your father, then?'

'Certainly not my father.'

Noticing the discarded envelope on the floor, Angela rose and crossed the room to pick it up. She examined the writing once more and returned to the window overlooking the street.

'Do you think it was some kind of indecent joke, Hannah?' She pressed her face to the window, peering up and down the length of Stratton Street, which was, by now, busy with carriages, horses and all manner of pedestrians. Anyone could have delivered the note.

Angela withdrew from the window and a feeling of unease crept over her. Uninvited callers at her home were nothing new. The fame of her wealth had filled newspaper columns. She had since been left a cascade of calling cards from complete strangers and received all manner of marriage proposals in writing. She was often recognized in the town, and Hannah frequently broke off uninvited conversation with curious passers-by who had recognized the young heiress; but never had she been addressed in such an intimate manner.

'I really do think you should call the police.'

She felt sick.

'Perhaps I will go away for a few days, Hannah.'

As she got up from the window seat, a face came into view at the top-floor window of the coffee house on the opposite side of the road, and raising a pair of opera glasses, focused them on the study of Miss Angela Burdett-Coutts.

CHAPTER FOUR

30 September 18—

Each night, as I sleep, a voice from a dream far away screams in the night, it is the sound from a place in my dream, a dark dusty landscape full of lost love and lost souls to go with it. Her eyes are closed, her lashes bat with her heart and her body is swathed in the sheets with longing and expression, her mouth is open, speaking words she dare not say when awake.

My dream calls once again and she answers with sleep, she is deep and diving in its misty-coloured clouds, flying in its wings. Her lover calls and she responds, he is flying and she is with him, their arms locked and they are naked in the winds, though no coldness or weather affects their dreams. Love has tempted them from their given lives; they are lost in its feeling and need no map to guide them, and she is his ...

SIR FRANCIS BURDETT, Fifth Baronet of Foremarke, was sitting in his library reading in a wing chair. He crossed his booted leg first this way and then that, having scanned the same paragraph in the newspaper three times, each time instantly forgetting what it was that he had read. News of *The People's Charter* dominated reports in *The Morning Chronicle*. The aims of the Chartists were to secure votes for every man over the age of twenty-one whether he was rich or poor, propertied or otherwise. Throughout his career, Francis Burdett had campaigned tirelessly for such a cause, had been imprisoned for such a cause and had never ceased to hope that each minor victory he won in the name of this cause would one day result in votes for all men; but although political reform was on the horizon, it was not politics which was on his mind that morning. He folded his newspaper with a sigh and set it on the table at his side.

The day before, his daughter had arrived from London by carriage with a small trunk and a carpet bag. In the year since her inheritance, she had maintained her distance from her family in Derbyshire. She had declined to take part in the London season, and had only seen her parents when they visited Stratton House to advise her that her absence was not in keeping with her position. Now she had arrived at Formarke completely unannounced. Angela was not given to acts of caprice, her father mused, and her manner had been almost too cheerful. He sensed that something was troubling her.

He acknowledged that Angela was wilfully independent and despite his efforts to guide her in her new life, she had been determined to find her own way. He admired her resolve but he did not like the idea of her living in that huge house in London with no protector. Marjoribanks had been of some use to her but the man was on his last legs. She needed a person of good influence upon whom she could depend. Not so young that he could not advise her well but not so old as to be rendered useless in the coming years. If Sir Francis had known that his daughter had already received a number of unsuitable proposals from fortune-seekers, then he would have ordered her return home immediately.

The baronet stood up, left the library and headed out into the large reception hall where he found one of the maids.

'Have you seen Miss Angela, girl?'

He could never remember names.

'Why yes, sir, she is talking to the mistress out on the lawn.'

Sir Francis nodded his thanks, 'Very good, very good....' He substituted her name for a cough, and headed out towards the back of the house.

Lady Sophia Burdett, her black hair piled up high in ringlets, was sitting in a garden chair, her daughter at her side.

'Now, my dear, why are you wearing that awful gown? It does your figure no justice at all, and the wool is so shabby. With *your* great means you should have an ample wardrobe of fine clothes.'

Angela looked down at the grey woollen day dress that had served her very well and was, she felt, most practical for walking in the garden.

'I have no interest in clothes, Mama. You know that I never have, and my purse is in far better use for causes which really matter.'

'My dear, no one would try to dissuade you from your good deeds for the disadvantaged, but there is no sin in looking after yourself. After all, if you are going to find a husband then you have no choice but to pay attention to matters of appearance. Why don't you let Mary-Ann do something with your hair? Pulled back in that manner, it looks so severe. It makes you look far too serious, my dear.'

'Mama, perhaps I prefer to be serious. And as for attracting a husband, I hope that when I do find someone to share my life with, he has more depth to him than an interest in my wardrobe and plaits.'

'How about something in pink or lilac, instead of brown or grey?' her mother suggested. 'Your sister, Clara, has just had the most delightful length of silk made up in a pink day dress.'

'If I were to choose a colour for a gown, it would certainly never be pink, Mama. I would choose something in olive green, with a plain ribbon trim. That would be much more to my simple taste.'

'Oh, not green, Angela! The colour would make your complexion too pale.'

Angela was becoming exasperated at such a pointless conversation and was just about to excuse herself from her mother's company, when her father appeared through the French windows onto the terrace. Lady Sophia turned and addressed him.

'Francis, will you tell your daughter about her appearance? Don't you think she looks a little too thin and pale? And I was telling her—'

'I wish to steal our daughter away from you for a while, Sophia,' he interrupted. 'I need some assistance with my correspondence and I would like to speak to Angela alone.'

'Very well, my dear.'

As Lady Sophia rose to her feet she said, 'By the way, your late arrival yesterday evening, Angela, did not give me the chance to tell you that your father is holding a ball this evening. We did not write to invite you because you always refuse such occasions, but now that you are here we want you to join us, don't we, dear?'

'But I've brought nothing suitable for a ball!' Angela objected.

'Well, I'm sure that Clara or Joanna will be able to find something for you to wear. I'll go and see to it. Susan and Trevanion are expected shortly, so I must ask the cook to prepare them a light lunch.'

Lady Sophia returned to the house, and Angela stood up immediately, her face colouring with anger.

'Papa, you cannot expect me to keep company with Susan and Trevanion after the terrible things they have said about me! The begging letters that Trevanion sent to me the months following Grandpapa's death were incessant. I cannot possibly stay. You know that there is sure to be an unpleasant atmosphere when we meet again.'

'Yes, there are matters to be considered in connection with Susan and Trevanion, I agree, but there is something of greater importance which I want to speak to you about.' He indicated that his daughter should sit down again, and she wondered anxiously if Hannah had told him about the indecent correspondence.

'I am concerned for you, Angela. You look as if you have not slept or eaten properly for months. This life you are living is not natural for a young woman …'

He raised his hand as she tried to interject.

'I'm not saying that charitable duties are unworthy – not at all. Am I not a man of the people myself?'

She inwardly remarked how easy it was for her father, sitting in the shade of his ancestral home, surrounded by acres of land, to identify himself with the struggles of the working man.

'But shutting yourself away in that vast mansion,' he continued, 'benevolence dinners your only society, and a spinster governess for company and conversation is most irregular, Angela, and I don't like it. Your mother and I are concerned for your welfare.'

'Papa, you were in London for the entire season and you visited me almost daily. Miss Meredith is a well-educated woman, as you know. Her conversation is not to be equalled, and she is most particular about whom she permits in the house. And since you and Mama returned here, Mr Marjoribanks looks in on me every Friday. So I am not without guidance and protection entirely.'

Her father grunted, 'And you think that your papa believes that you tell him everything?'

'Papa, if you can trust me to survive the society of Susan and Trevanion, then you can trust me to manage my new life and all its snares.'

'Your singular circumstances are not a matter to joke about, Angela. It is not fitting for a young woman to live as you do. When you're in London a husband would be a great asset to you. Now the ball this evening will be the perfect opportunity for me to introduce you to some very eligible fellows. Young Mr Disraeli, Mr Gladstone and the Duke of Devonshire—'

Sir Francis was interrupted by his greyhound running from the stable courtyard and barking, darting furiously at the high hedge and growling.

'Dagwood! Leave off, boy. What is it?'

The dog ran to his master's side but continued to bark loudly. As Sir Francis marched in the direction of the gate, a figure dashed from a concealed place inside the hedging and began running in the direction of the copse, which edged the grounds of the hall. The dog began to chase after him as the figure ran with some agility through the trees ahead.

'Bring him down, boy!' Sir Francis shouted.

The greyhound, however, was more interested in the intruder's cloak, which was dragging on the floor behind him, throwing up leaves and snagging on branches. The dog grabbed at the material and began tearing at it, and the figure, whose hat was set in a manner so as to obscure his face, snatched at a heavy branch on the ground which he quickly raised and brought down on the dog's skull like a club. The dog fell to the ground with a yelp and, throwing the weapon behind him, the intruder disappeared into the dense woodland.

'Dagwood!' Sir Francis ran towards the injured animal, followed by his daughter and a stable boy.

31

The dog whimpered, his body and legs twitching.

'Can he be saved?' Angela stroked its wounded head, unaware of the blood on her hands.

'I doubt it.' Sir Francis turned to the young stable hand, hovering with uncertainty nearby. 'For God's sake, fetch a gun, boy! And call Frith to quickly gather some of the men together to sweep the grounds. We cannot risk the man returning when we have a house full of guests expected later.'

The baronet reached for the torn cloak which had been discarded by the intruder and drew it over his dying pet. Angela noticed a scrap of paper which had fallen from the pocket of the cloak as her father had moved it. She picked it up and as she smoothed it flat so that she could read it, the dog's blood on her hand streaked across the paper. A simple map of the grounds of Foremarke had been sketched out in ink. The entrance via the French windows where she had been sitting with her mother was marked with a cross, and beneath it – written in a tall, thin hand with little spacing – were inscribed the words *My Angel*....

CHAPTER FIVE

DAGWOOD HAD BEEN buried in the copse not far from where he had fallen. Sir Francis had warned the stable hand to say nothing of the day's events to Lady Sophia; the news would unsettle her nerves. The baronet had ordered a search of the immediate grounds. He had never been in favour of mantraps and he accepted that some poaching was an inevitable consequence of his wealth, but never before had a poacher turned to violence on his land. What worried him further was that Frith had not found evidence of any game caught. So what other purpose had this intruder in mind?

In a bedroom with views across the estate at Repton, Sir Francis, his cravat half-tied, absently inspected his reflection in the looking-glass. His thoughts had turned to his tempestuous political career of earlier decades. He had made enemies, yes; but there could be no one who wished to confront him over politics now. His fervour was ebbing. He had passed on his fight to be continued by men much younger.

The figure looking back at him was a still a respectable one. That was Sir Francis's opinion, and would be the opinion generally held amongst almost anyone who knew him. He was tall, had retained his upright bearing of former years and although his hair was not as thick as it had once been, it had turned to a striking shade of silver. He gave his cravat a final knot and decided to ask Frith to stay on hand at the stables, with his gun loaded. There would be Members of Parliament and aristocracy in the house this evening, and as host he had a duty to protect them.

In the room adjoining, Lady Sophia was admiring her reflection also. She was satisfied that she certainly looked much younger than both Countess Beaufort and Countess Moncreiffe, and that even her close contemporary Susannah, Lady Forbes, did not have hair as black as hers; forgetting for a moment that it was not her own. Her eyes moved from the looking-glass to the portrait which hung on the adjacent wall. It had been painted just prior to her marriage and showed a young, dark-haired woman holding a straw bonnet, the pastoral scenery as natural as her own simple beauty had once been. Nothing stayed the same, Sophia reflected soberly.

Hearing her husband in the next room she turned and hesitated, before calling his name.

'Are you there, Francis?'

There was no reply, as if he had frozen, hoping she had not heard him.

Deliberating, Sophia then crossed to the connecting door and tapped it lightly.

'Francis?'

After a moment's hesitation he answered her.

'Sophia?' He nodded at her stiffly as she entered, reluctant to ask that she adjust his cravat.

She took in his appearance: he looked magnificent but she faltered at telling him so. They were not often on their own together.

'Are you …'

They spoke at the same time.

'… I'm sorry …'

They apologized in unison.

Silence followed and the discomfort of the moment was broken when Sophia noticed a handkerchief stained with blood on the dressing table.

'Oh, what have you done, Francis?' She began to fuss. 'Have you cut yourself?'

'A gash sustained in the woods, Sophia. It's of no consequence.' He wanted her to leave.

'That valet of yours is witless. Why hasn't he—'

'As I said, it's nothing.'

'I'll call Mary-Ann, she can—'

'There's no need, Sophia. Please don't agitate yourself. I don't like it when you—'

'—bring a bowl of water and a bandage. Now let me see it—'

'Sophia—' he warned.

'I can see if—' She reached for his hand.

'SOPHIA!'

Sir Francis closed his eyes to calm himself for a moment before lowering his voice again. 'I am quite all right. Thank you for your concern. Now please return to your room and I will see you shortly at the reception.'

He held out his hand, gesturing that she should return to her to her own apartments, and she obeyed.

CHAPTER SIX

FLICKERING TORCHES LINED the driveway leading to the portico steps. The strains of an orchestra floated from the house as the guests stepped down from their carriages and made their way up the steps of Foremarke Hall, the ancestral home of the Burdett family since the last century. A glass chandelier hung from the ceiling of the reception hall, which was already filling with an assortment of magnificent moustaches, splendid sideburns and daring décolletages. Guests flitted between potted palms and marble pillars, talking trivialities and drinking champagne. Standing at the foot of the staircase which led to an impressive balcony was the bachelor Duke of Devonshire. At almost fifty years of age, he was still unmarried and his presence at the ball had sent ripples of excitement among both spinsters and widows. The ladies whispered behind their fans.

'His hair is receding a little, I grant you, but he still has a handsome figure, wouldn't you agree?'

'Yes, and although his chin is rather large, his eyes are most intelligent.'

Angela was bored by the conversation which seemed so inconsequential in light of the earlier incident in the woods, and she was brooding. Who had sketched out that map and with what purpose? And from whose hand had it come? She had not dared to tell her father that she believed the presence of the intruder to have had some ominous connection to her. She had come to Foremarke to distance herself from the upset of that vile correspondence and now she felt under threat here too.

Her father had repeatedly offered her his support in her new life and had sometimes seemed a little disappointed that she appeared to need him so rarely. She could not afford to let him know, though, that something was troubling her. He was bound to press her to return home immediately and she would lose the independence which had become so precious to her. Worse still, he might insist that the entire family come to live with her instead. Just the thought of her mother's counsel and her sisters' constant chatter induced the beginnings of a headache.

She was relieved that she had managed to avoid Susan and Trevanion so far since their arrival. She had seen Trevanion from a distance earlier in the evening, lingering in the company of the lovely daughter of Lord Carlisle, but she ensured that she did not catch his eye. Lady Sophia was still greeting her guests, and Sir Francis was deeply engaged in talk of politics with the young writer, Mr Disraeli.

'Sir Francis, it would be quite impossible for me to propound any ideas which go contrary to the general measure of reform. I am utterly sympathetic to the majority of the Chartist demands as you know....'

'Of course, Disraeli, but ...' His voice trailed off.

The baronet had caught sight of a woman in a vivid blue ball gown, a Venetian mask held to her face. She hovered for a moment, ensuring that she had engaged his attention, and disappeared into the crowd.

'Sir Francis...?' Disraeli enquired.

The baronet's eyes were anxiously searching the room. The figure was one that had seemed familiar to him.

Sir Francis excused himself from Disraeli's company. 'I'm sorry, Disraeli, I must ...'

Where had the woman gone? Lady Sophia knew that he was not in favour of masked balls. He liked to know exactly who was in his house. So who the devil told that woman to come in disguise? The earlier incident in the woods not far from his mind, he was uneasy at the idea of a stranger in his midst. But that was not what troubled him the most. He threaded his way through dancing couples, his eyes darting from face to face.

Could it really be her? A dread came upon him.

'Ah! Sir Francis, may I say ...' The Duke of Devonshire held out a hand of greeting.

'So sorry, Your Lordship, the champagne is running low. Just on my way to the cellar. Will rejoin you in an instant, sir ...'

Making his way through the guests, he continued to scan the room.

The baronet felt a hand fall softly upon his shoulder and he turned.

'Did you come looking for me?'

An attractive figure, a woman of later years, stood before him and lowered her mask. His eyes filled with alarm at the sight of Lady Oxford.

'Good God, Jane, what are you doing here? I thought you were abroad. Your letters ceased long ago. I thought ...'

'You thought that I was dead?' She smiled. 'Perhaps you would prefer it that way?'

He looked anxiously over his shoulder and, taking her by the elbow, firmly directed her towards the library.

'Of course not, I always hoped that you were happy and well. But when you stopped writing, I believed that it was for the best.'

'Best for whom?' she gibed.

'I mean that perhaps it was best that our lives went on as if the years we shared between us had not occurred.'

'Do you wish that they had not?'

She was trying to free herself from his grip but he persisted until they reached the library door.

'We must not be seen.' He looked over his shoulder, anxious at the whereabouts of Sophia. He closed the door behind them and turned the key.

Loosening her arm he asked with a shake of his head, 'What in God's name are you doing here? Under the very nose of my wife, and in my own house too? Have you lost your senses?'

'No, I have not lost my senses, but looking at your wife I believe that she has certainly lost hers.'

Sir Francis knitted his eyebrows. 'That is spiteful, Jane. Sophia has never been quite the same since she discovered that ... Well, you know what I mean.'

Lady Oxford did not seem to be listening and began to inspect the room with a casual air. She turned and laughed, 'Why Francis, it is just like the old days in Paris, hiding ourselves away.'

She closed her eyes as if conjuring up the remembrance of a dream. 'Ah, the last days of the revolution. It was such a wonderful time for romance, wasn't it?'

Sir Francis was not amused. 'The revolution cost much blood and took many lives. There is little romance in that.'

'You were not always so rational, my dear. I believe that you were willing to lose your head for the cause of political reform once.'

'It was a very young and foolish head, Jane, and I was lucky to keep it. I am not sorry that those days are behind us now.'

''Tis a pity.' She shrugged her shoulders and said softly, '"When we two parted, in silence and tears, Half broken-hearted, to sever for years ..."' She lifted the mask to her face again.

'Don't ...' he appealed.

She moved closer towards him, '"If I should meet thee after long years, how should I greet thee? With silence and tears ..."'

He snatched the mask from her and looking into her eyes for a moment, his mouth was on hers; kissing her as if she were the same beautiful girl of eighteen that he had loved all those years before.

'Oh, Jane ...' he whispered. 'Why have you come back to torment me? Tell me that you are an apparition, a cruel dream.'

She stroked his face. '"Then tell me not, remind me not, of hours which, though for ever gone, Can still a pleasing dream restore ..."'

His face changed. Moving her abruptly from him, he turned away sharply.

'Those are Lord Byron's words, not yours!'

His voice was filled with resentment and he began to walk across the room to the fireplace, standing before it.

She entreated teasingly, 'You have never forgiven him for taking me from you, have you?'

The baronet stared into the flames.

'That libertine only ever wanted what could not be his. I heard that he discarded you as soon as he had won you from me.'

Lady Oxford laughed. 'I am never discarded, Francis, you must know that. But the poet would not follow me, and dear Edward was too amiable a husband for me to leave him.'

At the sound of the orchestra playing and the laughter of guests, Sir Francis was brought back to the present with a jolt: his wife could notice his absence at any moment. He turned to see Lady Oxford walking towards him again in the firelight and acknowledged that although she was still beautiful in her autumn years, he must fight the temptation to relive the past.

'Tell me why you are here, Jane, and then you must leave. You must know that you cannot stay. If Sophia suspects for a moment that you are here—'

'You have become impatient, my love. You were not always so keen to be rid of my company—'

'I am in no mood to be provoked, Jane. What is your business?'

She nodded. 'Very well – my husband, Edward, is getting old, and has been unwell. The doctor in Italy thought that we should come home.' She hesitated for a moment and then continued, 'It seemed wrong that you did not know that *our* daughter, Elizabeth, was married a fortnight ago.'

Sir Francis shook his head, taking in the words. 'Of course, yes, it is only natural that she should be married now. But I can only think of her as a girl.'

He recalled the sketches which Jane had sent him from Italy: a pretty, fair-haired girl, a puppy dangling from her arms; the child taking lessons at her desk, or at play in the countryside.

'She has married Edward's doctor, Henry Bickersteth. He is a good deal older, but she loves him nonetheless. When he recommended our return to England, he made known his feelings for Elizabeth and asked Edward for her hand. They married a fortnight ago at Chatsworth. When Edward stood at her side, almost too ill to give her away, my thoughts turned to you, and reflected that it was your arm she should have been holding.'

Lady Oxford came to the baronet's side and slipped her arm through his, as if recreating the scene.

'The Duke of Devonshire kindly hosted the wedding, and when I asked after you, he remarked upon his invitation to the ball this evening. And now here I am....'

'So I see. Well, you have told me that our daughter is married. What of it? I wish her well, but I am nothing to her, just as we always agreed.'

His eyes tried to read her face which, in that moment, was inscrutable. He knew her to be a mistress of manipulation.

'But I have come to tell you something about Charlotte.'

'Charlotte?'

'Yes, Elizabeth's sister.'

'What have I to do with her sister?'

His voice was edged with mistrust and he removed her arm from his.

'When Elizabeth married, I felt that she should know the truth about her parentage. So on the eve of her wedding, I told her the truth ... that you were her real father. But I did not know that Charlotte was listening at the door and when she overheard, she demanded to know if I had deceived *her* also, and whether Edward was her real father or not. I had to tell her that Elizabeth was her sister in the fullest sense. That you were Charlotte's father too.'

'No, I am Elizabeth's father. Charlotte is Edward's child, not mine!'

'No, my dear, if you remember, there was a time when we were reunited very briefly at Lady Melbourne's. I never saw you after that, but Charlotte is your daughter just as much as Elizabeth, I assure you.'

Sir Francis was silent, and he absorbed her words.

'We have another daughter? But I—'

'Edward has never asked about any of my offspring but has loved each one as if they are his own, and they in turn have adored him.'

'Then why tell the girls something that could only cause them distress?'

'Because Edward is dying, Elizabeth has married a man likely to die well in advance of her, and Charlotte is yet to find a suitable husband. It is my duty to ensure that if my daughters are ever in need of financial assistance, there is someone else who can come to their aid.'

She paused, raising her eyes to his. 'Besides, I heard that there is someone in your family lately remembered very favourably in a will....'

Sir Francis nodded with understanding and pulled a chair towards him, resting his bended leg upon it.

'At last!' He spread out his hands. 'Now the Jane of former days makes her appearance. If there is something to her advantage then she will come to hear of it.'

'It is not *my* advantage I am seeking. I only want the same for my daughters as has been afforded your daughter.'

'You don't understand, Jane. There was a will; it was most specific, even my son did not receive an acknowledgement. And my other two daughters received mere trifles.'

'That is not my concern, Francis. You know why I came and I want to know what you are going to do about it.'

He was silent for a moment. His eyes settled on the ancestral portraits hung about the room. No doubt some of those fine-looking gentlemen had been in similar predicaments.

'And how am I to know that you are telling me the truth? You know that I will not beg off from my responsibilities, but I will not be toyed with, Jane.'

'I have told you the truth.' She shrugged her shoulders. 'And I am happy to share that same truth with your other daughters, if it pleases me to do so.'

His face turning red, he kicked at the chair and grasped at Lady Oxford's wrist. In her words and manner she had not hesitated. Her boldness filled him with rage and yet had it not been this same boldness which had beguiled him years before, and turned him into a man possessed? He thought of his daughter, Angela, and imagined the disappointment etched in her face.

'Damn you, Jane! There was a time when I had no existence or meaning apart from you, when I was miserable and wretched without a moment's happiness away from your company. If that same man was present now, he would take a gun to you, and not think for a moment before pulling the trigger on himself also.'

He threw her from him.

'Thank God for you that I am no longer that man.'

The agitation which had once fired the adventurous radical in his youth had now become prudent conservatism. Sir Francis calmed himself.

'Now, tell me where you are staying and I will make some arrangements.' Hearing the sound of guests nearby he whispered, his eyes on the door, 'You have to go.'

Lady Oxford rubbed at her wrist and made no response.

'Jane! Where can I find you?'

'You can find me through the duke.'

He directed her towards a window leading to the garden.

'Very well, I shall seek you out in a few days.'

He watched briefly as she disappeared across the lawns in the direction of the waiting carriages. He opened a connecting door to the room adjoining and then passed through another into a sitting room. Opening the sitting-room door, he came back out into the whirl of the ball.

Looking back through the columned entrance out into the night, he shook his head in disbelief. He had glimpsed into his past and seen a life which had been careless, wonderful, flagrant, indecent, adventurous, absorbing, inspiring. The baronet became aware of the Duke of Devonshire signalling him and his thoughts returned to the mundane matter of champagne.

CHAPTER SEVEN

ANGELA HAD FOUND a column in the ballroom behind which she could hide and where she hoped that she could pass the majority of the evening unnoticed. There was no one here with whom she felt at ease and if she could slip away unnoticed, she would. She took a step back in an effort to distance herself further from the evening's events, and found herself colliding with a young gentleman who appeared to be attempting the very same thing.

'Forgive me, sir, I did not see you there.'

The gentleman coloured and attempted his own apology.

'Charles Wheatstone.' He made an abrupt bow.

She had often heard her father speak of the talented young scientist.

'Ah, yes, Mr Wheatstone. I know something of your work.' Angela held out her gloved hand. 'Miss Angela Burdett-Coutts.' Mr Wheatstone took her hand and made a brief bow above it.

'Perhaps like me, sir, you do not enjoy these occasions?'

He looked about the room uneasily and she was unsure of what he was most afraid: talking to a woman or dancing.

'I ... I find them completely horrifying.'

'Well, I can assure you, sir, that you are quite safe here with me, as I intend to do everything to avoid the tiresome act myself.' Angela adjusted her gloves.

There was a moment of silence and sensing his difficulty to converse further she enquired, 'May I ask about your experiments, Mr Wheatstone? I have read much about your work in the newspaper.'

Wheatstone – who had been appointed to the chair of Physics at King's College London – was deeply involved in the development of the new telegraph system and forgetting his reticence, his manner eased: he began to enthuse about the experimental line which had been run between the Euston and Camden Town railway stations, and his face came to life.

'Never had I felt such a sensation before as when, all alone in the station office, I heard the needles click. And as it spelled the words, I felt all the magnitude of the invention pronounced to be practicable beyond dispute!'

The young man, his eyes shining with passion for his science, engaged his companion's interest completely and she nodded with delight, forgetting her earlier cares. She was fascinated by the new scientific innovations which were being developed with great ingenuity by the day and Mr Wheatstone, who was now utterly at ease with talk of his favourite subject, was happy to share his vision of the future with the attentive young heiress.

With the passing of the hour, the dances proceeded unnoticed by the two of them, both absorbed in talk of the wider world and its opportunities. Suddenly aware of the passage of time, Wheatstone apologized.

'But I have neglected to offer you refreshments, Miss Coutts. Please forgive me. Let me fetch us some fruit punch, and I will return in a moment.'

Angela nodded and stepping out from behind the column, she observed the floor filling with guests who were about to take their places for the next dance. Across the room, Angela's gaze fell upon her brother-in-law: the brooding and blond-haired Trevanion and the sight of him left her uneasy. Before she had a chance to look away, he caught her eye, giving her an indecorous nod. Raising a hip flask to her, he threw back his head and gulped from it. She had not seen her sister or brother-in-law since the awful scene which had taken place at the reading of her grandfather's will, but given his well-known history, she could only imagine that Trevanion's finances were in as dire a state as ever. As far as she knew, he had no career to speak of since the commission in the army, bought by his father, had ended in disgrace two years before when Trevanion had sold it to pay his gambling debts. Undoubtedly that avenue of familial financial assistance had now been closed off to him.

Unexpectedly, thoughts of the indecent letter she had received entered Angela's mind and she was unsettled by the idea that Trevanion had sent it as some sort of vulgar joke. Worse still, could it have been Trevanion who had hidden amongst the hedges, listening to her conversation? The thought disturbed her and as the orchestra commenced playing, her head began to pound. In need of some air, she headed in the direction of the French doors which opened out onto the lawns, and began to make her way down the stone steps to the gardens.

Sitting down on a semi-circular stone bench, she was relieved to be away from the noise of shallow laughter and the unnerving gaze of her brother-in-law. The breeze gently lifted her hair, and she closed her eyes for a moment, glad to escape the stifling atmosphere. A hand placed itself upon her shoulder and she started at the sensation of it.

'My! How nervous you are, sister. And yet only moments ago, you were eyeing the Duke of Devonshire with the boldness of a common actress.'

Angela turned to see Trevanion behind her. Her cheeks began to burn at the feel of his hand on her shoulder and the tone of his lewd insinuations.

'But then, of course, that is what your grandmother was, a touring actress, was it not? It seems there is no shame in your family, Miss *Coutts*.'

Angela's voice was completely steady but her heart was thudding violently in her chest.

'My grandmother was loved very much by my grandfather, regardless of her background. And I do not think that my sister would appreciate your words or your actions, sir. Please leave!'

Trevanion took no heed of her request. His hand upon her shoulder, he moved himself into position at her side, pinning her to the seat and pushing his face close to hers.

'There is much that your sister does not appreciate, Miss Angela. She does not appreciate the way in which you wormed yourself into your grandfather's favour and the underhand manner in which you have stolen her inheritance and denied her of her rightful share.'

Angela turned her face from his; repulsed at the smell of strong liquor on his breath and aware of the closeness of his body, she tried to hide her fear.

'You are hurting me, sir, and I ask that you remove your hand or I will shout for my father.'

Trevanion moved closer still and lowered his hand. 'I always believed that you were the most beguiling of your sisters, you know. And now you are a little older—'

A new voice cut into the darkness.

'I don't suppose … that … that I could interrupt in order to hand the young lady her drink, could I?'

The young Mr Wheatstone, his fair hair shining in the light of the torches, strolled across the lawn, holding out his hand, an uncertain smile upon his face. Trevanion was silent, wrong-footed for a moment by the unexpected intrusion.

'Your brother-in-law cannot expect to chaperone you out here the whole evening, surely? After all, there are gentlemen queuing up to meet the famous heiress, you know.' Wheatstone's expression was innocent.

Angela felt Trevanion's hand fall to his side, a look of surprise and then anger crossing his face.

'Miss Coutts?'

Wheatstone's hand remained outstretched and, imagining she heard a slight tremor in his voice, she rose to her feet and took it, glad of a means to escape the distressing circumstances in which she had found herself.

As she walked away, Trevanion called after her.

'There is far more to say upon the subject of family matters. I shall seek you out another time, you can be sure of that, my dear.'

Charles Wheatstone felt the tremble of the young woman's hand in his own as they walked back in the direction of the house.

'Thank you, Mr Wheatstone.'

He said with a whisper, 'I think you underestimate, Miss Coutts, what a very vulnerable young woman you are. You should pay more heed to your safety.'

'If you would say nothing of this to my father, I would be most grateful, sir.' And they returned to the house under the resentful gaze of Trevanion.

Lady Sophia was pleased with the success of the evening. There had been several matches in the making, she was certain of it; the young Mr Disraeli had paid particular attention to her daughters Clara and Joanna; the veal at dinner had been good; and she was sure that Lady Beaufort had scanned her figure with renewed envy when they had met. Having now said goodnight to the last of the guests, she strolled the length of the green corridor towards the staircase.

Feeling a draught, she noticed that the library door was ajar. Lady Sophia entered the room, looked about her and saw that the window was open. She moved to close it. Returning, Sophia noticed in the candlelight something discarded on the floor. She bent down to pick it up and found that it was a blue sequinned mask. She had not recalled anyone that evening to whom it might belong and her curiosity aroused, she held it to her face, catching the scent of a woman as she did so.

Sir Francis, also making his way along the green corridor, recalled that the library window had been left unlatched; and did not want to take any chances with security in light of the earlier incident in the grounds. He pushed open the door and caught his breath, startled at the sight of a woman in a sequinned mask.

'What are you doing here?' he whispered with alarm. 'I thought that you had left!'

Sophia lowered the mask slowly: there was pain in her eyes. The baronet stiffened as guilt drummed hard upon his newly awakened conscience, a conscience which had found no place in his younger years.

'Were you expecting someone else?' Distress washed over his wife at the thought of the old days returning.

The baronet had never allowed her to question him, and he had never before felt regret or shame over his affairs. Strangely, though, he felt his wife's torment and for the first time in his married life, regret engulfed him. He had not been a loyal husband and his disloyalty had caused his wife to become a vain and silly woman, anxious for his approval. Of course, she had always known about Lady Oxford and the child. But if she knew that there was now certainty of another child, her bitterness would be renewed.

Should he tell her the truth about Jane's presence that evening and for once be truthful with his wife? Or would the truth prove more painful to her than a lie? Instead he chose to change the subject. He gently took the mask from her hand.

'I was only expecting *you*, Sophia.'

He guided her from the room with his arm about her waist, continuing, 'It ... it was a success this evening, my dear. You were the perfect hostess, as usual.'

She could not recall the last time that he had shown her any sign of affection and was thrown off course by it.

'Thank you, Francis, But I—'

'And I have to tell you that the Duke of Devonshire passed on his particular compliments and admiration for our daughters.'

'Really, well that is—'

'Yes, in fact I am confident that all of the best salons in London will want to receive them if the duke has anything to do with it.'

The baronet's hand remained about Lady Sophia's waist and if there was any lingering desire on Sophia's part to question him about his conduct, it had been extinguished.

The politician sensed it and relaxed.

'I was wondering,' his wife asked as they began to ascend the staircase. 'Can you tell me, who was the young man who engaged most of Angela's attention this evening?'

'His name is Wheatstone. He is a scientist.'

'Heavens above! A scientist. I thought that he did not look like a man of property. She should certainly not have encouraged him.'

'Well, we have an intelligent daughter with an enquiring mind. Mr Wheatstone is a fine man. I don't think we have any reason to caution her.'

They reached the top of the stairs and Sir Francis lingered at the door to his wife's bedroom.

'Sophia?'

'Yes?'

He appeared to be struggling. 'I ... I am sorry.'

It was something he had never said before in all their years together and the words were an utter surprise to her.

'What I mean to say is, I am sorry for my temper earlier this evening. It was uncalled for.'

Had Sophia been an ungenerous woman, she would have reminded her husband that both his temper and his infidelities stretched back long before this evening but instead she opened her bedroom door and said, 'I ... I have completely forgotten it.'

Sir Francis hesitated for a moment, his eyes searching hers. Unexpectedly, he caught sight of someone he had once loved: a young, dark-haired woman holding a straw bonnet, her beauty natural and unspoilt. Sophia lowered her gaze and turning to enter her room, left the door open behind her. Observing the gesture of reconciliation her husband followed, blew out the candle on her dresser and closed the door behind him.

CHAPTER EIGHT

IN THE PALE-BLUE breakfast room at Foremarke Hall, talk across the table had centred on the maiden voyage of the Great Western steamship, the first to cross the Atlantic.

'I think such a journey could be quite hazardous!' Lady Sophia declared.

'Indeed,' remarked Sir Francis. 'In fact, I hear that there was a fire in the engine room before the ship left port, and over fifty passengers refused to continue their journey. Great Western is bound to go bankrupt in a matter of months, mark my words.'

The baronet pressed a napkin to his lips and quietly noted that the seat to his left was empty again this morning.

Trevanion observed the brief glance which Sir Francis had given the vacant chair and seized his moment.

'I see that Angela is not joining us again this morning?' He turned to his mother-in-law and with a pathetic attempt at concern asked, 'Do you think we should call the doctor? She has hardly left her room since the morning after the ball.'

'I think you will find that it is nothing more than a condition of the nerves,' Sir Francis offered. 'I fear that the responsibilities of her life in London have placed too great a strain upon her.'

Trevanion glanced at his wife and raised an eyebrow, giving her a discreet nod.

'I think perhaps, sir, that it is *your* duty to relieve her of that burden. You can hardly expect a woman to be fit to manage such a fortune.'

His father-in-law's face clouded over. 'I'll thank you not to remind me of my duties, Trevanion. I know them very well and …'

Sir Francis's voice curtailed at the arrival of his daughter, Angela, who entered the room and took her usual place opposite her sister, Susan.

'Angela, we were not expecting you. Are you quite recovered?' her father asked, observing her carefully.

'Yes, Papa, I am completely well and despite your fears for my nerves, I can assure you that I am perfectly sound in mind.'

'No one suggested otherwise,' Trevanion replied, a note of irritation in his voice. He had not counted on the reappearance of his sister-in-law this morning, and was not at all pleased by it. 'But you can hardly blame us for wondering at the cause of your unexplained absence. According to the servants, you have barely eaten this past week.'

Angela laid out a napkin on her lap and poured herself a fruit cordial from a jug on the table.

'I had an unexpected bout of toothache. I was not very hungry and thought that I would be poor company at mealtimes. I thought it best to keep to my room until I recovered.'

'I see,' said her papa, unconvinced. 'Then we are pleased to have you join us again, my dear.'

She sipped at her drink and dared not allow her eyes to meet those of her brother-in-law. Trevanion's behaviour at the ball had been a shock and Angela had hoped that if she stayed in her room long enough, then the vile opportunist and her sister would be gone. But each day that she had asked Mary-Ann, she had been told that her relatives appeared to be quite settled with little sign of imminent departure. As the days passed, Angela decided that she could not allow Trevanion the satisfaction of believing he had any hand in her withdrawal and so she had summoned courage that morning and reappeared for breakfast.

'The ball was quite a success, wasn't it, my dear?' Sir Francis asked his daughter, who responded with a quiet nod and placed a tiny portion of fish on her plate.

'And what think you of that peacock, Disraeli?' Sir Francis continued. 'He pretends that his interests are mainly of a literary nature, but I intend to keep a close eye upon him, Trevanion. I'll wager that he has his eye on a seat in the Commons.'

'Yes, so they say,' Trevanion responded with disinterest, putting a bite of salted herring in his mouth and chewing in a manner which Angela found revolting.

'And that young Mr Wheatstone is the genius of his genera-tion, don't you think?' Sir Francis remarked, cooling his tea with a few sharp blows. 'And I think he took quite a shine to you, my dear.' The baronet nodded with some satisfaction in the direction of Angela.

At the mention of Wheatstone, Trevanion had scowled, recalling how the man had annoyingly interrupted that little piece of busi-ness with his sister-in-law.

'The hesitant fool thinks far too much of his ideas for my liking,' he muttered.

Trevanion was aware that he had ventured too far with his conduct that night. His intention had been to win over his sister-in-law, perhaps engage her sympathy so that she might favour him with a cheque, but his drunken attempt and his manner had been all too coarse. He would feign an apology later; there would be plenty of opportunities to make amends. There was a large gambling debt weighing on his mind and his neck would be in the noose if he did not pay it soon.

Clara and Joanna then remarked with excitement upon the wonderful array of gowns that had graced the ballroom, and Lady Sophia turned to Angela to ask why she had not been seen joining in with the dancing.

'It would have been the most perfect opportunity for you to have been observed by the Duke of Devonshire, my dear.'

'Yes,' Sir Francis agreed. 'In fact, come to think of it, you left far too early that night.' He waggled his fork in her direction.

'I was just a little fatigued, Papa, that was all.'

He reminded himself that she had been very upset at the pres-ence of the intruder and the dog's death. But he harboured the belief that something more was troubling her. There was some truth in Trevanion's words about her state of mind, and he was seriously beginning to wonder about his daughter's suitability to manage the immense responsibility of her vast fortune. She looked thinner than ever. Perhaps he should write to Marjoribanks and share his doubts. It was true that to a general observer her measured voice and composed manner was the epitome of a young woman in control, and might be remarked upon as being a quality rare in her sex; but her father sensed that she was hiding something from him.

Throughout breakfast, Susan Bettesworth-Trevanion had remained silent and stony, only lifting her head from time to time to rest her dark-coloured eyes upon Angela. When the meal had finished and the family had left the table, Angela felt the sharp grip of fingers digging into her upper arm as she made to leave the room.

'You may have fooled our father with your excuses of fatigue, but I've got eyes, sister.'

Susan dug her fingers deeper in Angela's arm.

'I have no idea of your meaning,' Angela protested. 'What can I have done to offend you?' She tried to free her arm.

'I saw you in the rose garden with Trevanion the night of the ball. Not content with taking a portion of my inheritance, you seek to further insult me by taking a share of my husband, and then taking to your room in shame.'

'Susan, you're hurting me!' Angela pulled herself free and rubbed at the place where her sister's fingers had been. 'What you saw in the garden was not of my design. I am completely—'

'Let me make it clear so that we understand one another on this point,' Susan interrupted. 'That plain and uninteresting face of yours may hold little attraction except for the most bankrupt of men, but if you are seeking a husband then look elsewhere. Trevanion is already spoken for.'

Angela's voice was incredulous. 'I wouldn't even consider—'

'And, what is more, I intend to tell Papa that you have embarrassed both me and the memory of Grandfather with your conduct. Then he will have no choice but to ask that old fool, Marjoribanks, to review the terms of the will.'

At the mention of the will, Angela grew cold.

'But Papa would never believe you.'

'Where money is concerned, sister, Trevanion will say whatever I tell him to, remember that.'

Angela had watched as her sister ascended the staircase, and began to wonder if her life would be much simpler if she had never inherited at all. Yet, without a fortune this house would be her cage and the opportunities which money held out to her as a single woman would be gone. She could not risk staying any longer and falling prey to the schemes of her sister and brother-in-law.

Angela hurried up the staircase and returned to her room. She began pulling open the bedroom drawers, taking out the few items of clothing which she had brought with her, and reaching under the bed, she retrieved her carpet bag and began to pack. A shadow fell across the doorway and she looked up to see Mary-Ann watching her.

'Is everything all right, Miss Angela?'

'Yes, Mary-Ann, but I'm afraid I will have to leave sooner than expected. I need you to make arrangements for me to be driven to a coaching station where I may secure a carriage to London.'

'Very well, Miss Angela, I will speak to the footman for you.'

'Thank you, Mary-Ann. And if I could ask that you say nothing of my request to any of the family, I would be very grateful.'

'Yes, of course, Miss Angela.' She nodded.

At the end of the corridor, in the bedroom with the chinoiserie wallpaper, an angry exchange was taking place.

'You had the perfect opportunity to win over my sister on the night of the ball, and instead you paid too much heed to the wine bottle and forgot your head.'

Trevanion sat on the end of the bed, pulling on his riding boots.

'You forget, my dear, that it was I who had all the responsibility. What did you have to do that night except look pretty and make pointless conversation?'

He stood and buttoned up his waistcoat.

Seated at her dressing table, Susan put down her hairbrush.

'If you must know, I have been setting another plan in place on the back of your failure. I have implied that I believe my sister's conduct with you to have been improper. Now, if you take an opportunity to find her alone, I will arrange to discover you both together and call for Papa.

Trevanion was not convinced.

'If that idiot, Wheatstone, hadn't come along when he did, then I believe I was already making excellent progress with my own efforts.'

He stood up and walked to the wardrobe, opened the door and found his riding jacket.

'Don't stand there and make excuses for your failure, Trevanion, it makes you seem to be even less of a man than you already are.'

Susan's face was reflected in the mirror and at that moment, he had the urge to cross the room and shatter that face into a thousand pieces; but he knew that if he were ever to be cast out from this family, he would not make his way in the world unassisted. With his temper still burning, he replied quietly, 'Give me time, Susan, and I will win your sister's good opinion before we leave.'

'You had better do so. I will not return to Northampton only to find the bailiffs knocking upon our doors again, nor will I add further embarrassment to our position by asking for my father's assistance.'

'I have said I will win her good opinion!' he shouted angrily, banging his hand against the wardrobe door.

Susan Trevanion was not afraid but a feeling of disgust rose in her stomach, and she wondered how the face which had once won her heart could look so vile and twisted.

A short while later, from his study window, Sir Francis noticed the fly draw up at the front of the house and he frowned. He laid aside the newspaper he had been reading and went outside to ask who had saddled the horse.

'I believe Miss Angela has asked for it, sir,' replied the driver.

'Is she going into town alone?'

The driver hesitated before answering.

'No, sir, I believe that she is going back to London.'

'Back to London!'

That girl was definitely out of her mind. Turning on his heels, he returned to the house and found his daughter descending the stairs with a carpet bag.

'I am told that you are leaving. Is it true?'

'Yes, Papa, I had quite forgotten about a meeting at the bank on Tuesday.'

'The bank? Angela, the bank has done quite well without you over the last hundred years and I am quite sure that it will come to no harm without you for few more days.'

'If I am to be taken seriously in my new role, then I really must not miss the meeting.'

'But you said nothing at all of your plans to leave this morning, Angela. Why the sudden change of mind?'

'I'm sorry, Papa, I am quite determined to go.'

Sir Francis shook his head and lowered his voice to a whisper.

'I know that business with the dog has upset you, but look at it from my perspective. First you arrive here without any word of your coming and, naturally, we were pleased to see you. But your recent behaviour during your stay has not inspired in me any confidence that you are sound in health or mind, and now you propose to disappear just as abruptly as you came. You are hiding something from me, Angela. You cannot fool me.'

'Yes, Papa, you do know me. You know how keen I am to live up to the trust which Grandpapa placed in me. It is that which urges me back to London, nothing more. Although I love the company of Mama and the girls, talk of the ball this morning made me realize how much I miss my work and using my time for matters far more important than talk of trivial matters. I'm bored, Papa, completely bored.'

Her father listened intently and then nodded reluctantly.

'Very well then, at least let me call for one of the maids to chaperone you on the journey and to bring a hamper from the kitchen for you. Some port wine will put the colour in those cheeks of yours. And you must wait while I inform your mother and your sisters of your departure.'

'I will wait in the carriage but please do not alert Mama, she will only make a fuss. I will write to her as soon as I arrive in London and give reason for my unexpected change of plans.'

Angela stepped into the carriage, anxiously eyeing the upper windows of the house and glancing at the hedges which skirted the copse. The baronet returned shortly to bid her goodbye and, with the luggage and hamper finally on board, the carriage circled the fountain on the drive and headed out towards the country road. In the same moment the sound of footsteps caused Sir Francis to turn and see Trevanion run down the front steps and come to a halt, skidding upon the gravel.

'Ah! Going riding are we, Trevanion? What a pity you are too late to say goodbye to your sister-in-law.'

Watching her leave, Trevanion cursed under his breath. What about his gambling debt? How was he to pay it now? He slapped his riding crop against his leg. The solution to his problems had just left in a carriage and was headed for London.

CHAPTER NINE

2 October 18—

> *He tastes the clouds and she breathes the skies.*
> *The heights are scaled and love for ever flies*
> *Horizons are conquered and mountains are felled*
> *Dreams are ignited with fire beheld …*

AT STRATTON HOUSE, a figure sat at the desk, her lips moving wordlessly as she read the correspondence in her hand.

In response to the opening lines she raised her eyebrows.

'Well, if they are going to request a lady's patronage, they could at least attempt to spell her name correctly!'

She shook her head and continued reading.

'We are sure to be reduced to poverty and servitude without your kind assistance. Please send £50 to—'

The governess's hand fell to her lap and with the other, she briskly removed her spectacles.

'How Miss Angela has such patience with these story-tellers I will never know.'

She cast the letter onto the requests pile and reached for another envelope, continuing in the task assigned to her in the absence of her mistress.

It would be wrong to assume that the servants of Stratton House were all equal and without a hierarchy of their own. The order of things below stairs was a very delicate matter, indeed. The housekeeper, Mrs Mills, guarded her position jealously. She had frequently complained to the cook, Mrs Bishop, whenever Miss Angela asked of Miss Meredith, what should rightfully have fallen within the remit of her own duties.

'Miss Angela pays no heed to the natural order of things,' Mrs Mills had protested to Mr Kilburn, the coachman. 'It is *my* job to purchase the food, but when Miss Angela mentions in passing that she would like a rabbit stew, Miss Meredith returns from town with the meat later in the day. These matters should pass through my hands first, Mr Kilburn; it's not how things are done.'

Mr Kilburn had nodded gravely in response.

The kitchen at Stratton House was under the rule of Mrs Bishop, assisted by Anne, a scullery maid. Blossom carried out the duties of chambermaid and Mary, those of a laundry maid. As the mistress had need of only two horses, Mr Kilburn had a boy, John, who assisted with tasks in the stable yard and general household jobs. The walled garden was the territory of Mr Evans, who had been in the employ of Mr Thomas Coutts since boyhood.

Hannah Meredith did not hold the elevated post of housekeeper but she certainly did not consider herself to be a servant. Her mistress, Miss Angela, would have referred to her as a dear companion, although Hannah would never presume to describe herself that way, having once been in the employment of the Burdett family as a paid governess.

It was with this anomaly in mind that Hannah always feigned illness whenever Miss Angela's family chose to visit, and it was the very same reason why she had not agreed to accompany Miss Angela to Foremarke Hall. Without the specific duties of a servant, she felt at a loss with regard to her station in life.

Angela had been twelve when Hannah had been appointed as governess to accompany the Burdett children on a three-year tour of the continent with Lady Sophia. Sir Francis Burdett had been at the height of his turbulent political career and in the throes of his affair with Lady Oxford. Not wishing to compete with either rival, Lady Sophia chose travel as a means of escape. By the time the family returned to England, Hannah had become an indispensable part of the family; retained until the day when Miss Angela requested that she come to live with her as a companion at Stratton House.

The governess turned her attention back to the envelope in her hand. It was marked 'To be opened by the hand of the addressee.' She turned it over to look at the handwriting, having the feeling of it being something familiar to her. The strokes of the pen were tall and thin, the letters written with little spacing between them. Pushing back her chair from the desk, Hannah crossed the room to the door, opened it and called Mrs Mills, who was supervising Blossom in the hall.

'Mrs Mills, did this envelope arrive with the rest of the morning mail?' Hannah's voice held a hint of accusation and Mrs Mills bristled at the tone of it.

'No, Miss Meredith. It was delivered by a gentleman the day that Miss Angela left for Foremarke.'

'Then why has it taken this long for you to hand it to me, may I ask?'

Mrs Mills was reluctant to say that she had distractedly pocketed it when the gentleman's departure had been followed by a loud crash in the library, and she had hurried to find Blossom had fallen from the steps while dusting. The commotion had caused her to forget the envelope entirely, and when she found it again she had hoped to slip it unnoticed with the rest of that morning's mail.

'What did the gentleman look like, Mrs Mills? Did he say anything?'

'He was of good appearance in a black dress coat, slim with dark eyes. A professional gentleman, I would say by his manner. He asked if Miss Angela was at home and I explained that she had gone to Foremarke and that she was expected to return within the month. I asked if he wanted to leave a message and he handed me the envelope. That was it.'

Hannah looked at the envelope and then remembered where she had seen that particular hand before.

'If I've done something wrong,' Mrs Mills said curtly, 'then I apologize. I didn't think the letter was important in light of Miss Angela's absence. When I remembered it in my pocket I put it with the rest of Miss Angela's post, just as I would have done immediately if I had not been distracted shortly by Blossom's fall.'

Hannah had not been listening. She was concerned to know if her mistress was in any danger.

'And when you told him that the mistress was at Foremarke, what was the gentleman's response?'

'Well, I confess, he seemed agitated at the news and he left in a hurry. But beyond that, Miss Meredith, I can say no more. His visit to the door was brief.'

Hannah, still turning over in her mind the identity of the visitor, noticed that Blossom was limping as she crossed the hall with a bucket of water in her hand.

'Are you quite fit to work, Blossom? We don't want any further accidents.'

Mrs Mills cut in sharply. 'That is why in my capacity of house-keeper, *I* am supervising her, Miss Meredith.'

Hannah nodded. 'Very well, then,' and returned to the study, closing the door behind her. She hovered by the fireplace, unsure of what she should do with the letter. With her instincts telling her that nothing good could come from Miss Angela opening the corre-spondence, she tore the letter into pieces and threw it onto the fire. She turned away, and the fragments glowed orange then turned to black. As she took her seat at the desk and absorbed herself in her duties once more, a curl of glowing paper dropped onto the hearth and the heat quickly ate up the words ... *watching you ...*

I have a small surprise in mind for my angel. I have decided that I should be the one to dress her; and no one else....

The bell above the shop door rang and a gentleman in a blue velvet jacket entered Billingham's Drapery and Fine Goods Store on Oxford Street. The man, who was a barrister-at-law, had just com-pleted a very lengthy session at the courthouse in Clerkenwell and his mood was not a tolerant one: the judge had insisted on hearing every piece of evidence in the greatest detail, with certain witnesses being called several times. The barrister had had in mind a personal errand that he was determined to execute before the day was ended, and he had no wish to be delayed by a pedantic judge. He was most relieved when a verdict was finally reached and the session closed.

When he had called at Stratton House with another letter, he had been beside himself with anxiety at the news only to find that his angel was not at home. How could she have disappeared without him noticing? He cursed himself at the idea that he had been too preoccupied with work. The maid had told him that Miss Angela had gone to Foremarke Hall in Derbyshire, and after taking a moment to recover from the shock of her departure, he had begun to make immediate plans to follow in her footsteps. There had been no sessions at the courthouse that week but even if there had been, such was his fervent desire to locate his angel, he would have forgotten his work in a moment and secured a carriage with equal haste.

The journey had been agonizing. What if, upon his arrival, she had moved on elsewhere and he was to lose sight of her completely? How could he watch over her then? But Foremarke Hall in Repton had not been difficult to locate. Taking leave of the coach on the fringes of the estate, he had found it quite easy to draw closer to the house by degrees, ensuring that he was not observed. With his heart thumping in his chest, he had caught sight of his angel sitting on the patio with her mother; and hiding in the garden he drew so close that, it had seemed to him, he could even hear the soft intake of her breath.

If the dog had not ran out of the stables at that moment, he could have left unobserved. He had not intended to injure the animal, and the sight of the blood which had spattered his breeches had brought on an uncommon feeling of guilt when he later removed them. Pushing the thought of the animal from his mind, he had focused instead on the satisfaction that he had seen his beloved. His return to London had been almost immediate but his mind had turned again and again, settling upon an idea. He planned to purchase a small gift to show her that even in her absence he had still been watching over her. It was this very personal errand which had brought him to the drapery store that afternoon.

His leather boots creaked as he walked across the wooden floor of the shop towards the counter, his blue eyes examining the lengths of muslin, linen and lace on the shelves; he was looking for something very particular. A gentleman assistant stepped forwards, smoothing back his hair and then folding his hands together.

'May I be of assistance, sir?'

The man, who was of handsome appearance, looked straight through him and after a long pause, settled his eyes on him and answered, 'I wish to be served by the dark-haired young lady over there.'

He lifted a gloved hand and pointed in the direction of a slender-figured assistant behind the ladies' counter. The gentleman assistant became a little uneasy at the request.

'Ah, it is usual, sir, that our female assistants serve only the ladies, where possible. We find that the very particular needs of our gentlemen patrons can be most ably attended to by either myself or the proprietor, Mr Billingham, sir.'

He turned his eyes very slowly towards the gentleman assistant.

'I require a length of green muslin which I would like made up for my niece. She is of similar colouring and size to the young lady in question.'

Mr Josiah Billingham stepped from behind the well-stocked counter.

'Ah, your niece is a similar size and colouring to young Miss Marchant, here, you say, sir?'

'I believe that is what I said.'

'Very good, sir. Then we will be happy to oblige you.'

Satisfied that all proprieties were being observed, Mr Billingham addressed the dark-haired young woman who had been busying herself with tidying the haberdashery drawers, and pretending that she had been oblivious to the request of the gentleman in the blue velvet jacket.

'Miss Marchant, would you assist this gentleman with a selection of green muslins, please?'

'Yes, at once, Mr Billingham.'

And she began to go back and forth, up and down a set of wooden steps, taking lengths of fabric in varying shades of green from the shelves and laying them out on the counter-top for the customer's inspection.

Eyeing each of the materials in turn, the man's hand went

instinctively towards a dark shade of olive.

'This one. This is perfect. There is no need to bring another.'

The young woman nodded.

'Very good, sir. And do you require anything else?'

'Yes, I need a length of plain ribbon. The dress must be trimmed in a plain ribbon.' A little excitement had now entered his voice.

The young woman set about displaying spools of ribbon taken from the drawers beneath the counter, and hoped that she had not revealed the unease she felt at his manner.

He took off a glove, and ran his finger and thumb along the varying lengths until he found the one he wanted.

'This velvet will do very well.'

'Certainly, sir, I will measure it out immediately.'

'And I need you to arrange the fabric to be made up in a plain and simple style, to your own measurements. The dress is to be a complete surprise. My niece knows nothing of it.'

At the mention of her own measurements, the young woman coloured slightly, but nodded. 'Yes, of course, sir.'

'I wish that it be delivered to this address, but it is imperative that my niece should not know that the dress has come from me.'

The man placed a slip of paper on the counter and the young lady glanced at the address and nodded.

'Yes, of course, sir. The dress will be made up to your requirements and delivered in one week.'

He eyed the spool of velvet ribbon, and noticing his lingering interest the young lady asked, 'Would you care to take a little as a sample, sir?'

He nodded wordlessly.

Taking up her scissors she handed him the cutting, while Mr Billingham took up the matter of concluding business.

'Do you wish to pay on account, sir?'

'No, that will not be necessary. I will settle the matter now.'

'And your name, sir?'

Richard Dunn did not respond. He reached inside his jacket and removing his wallet, he carefully placed the ribbon inside. He then took out several notes and held them out to the draper. He had no wish to identify himself or leave any trace of his purchase at all.

CHAPTER TEN

THE CARRIAGE GENTLY rocked its preoccupied passenger from side to side as the scenery changed unhurriedly from the hills of Derbyshire to the towns and villages of Leicestershire, Northamptonshire, and Hertfordshire. At a pace of only four miles an hour, crossing fields and heaths where the roads were bad, the journey was a tiresome one with little relief from one's fellow passengers. Amongst the men, talk of the weather and road conditions almost inevitably turned to talk of politics; and among the women, gossip of fashion and family.

To pass the time, Angela tried to think over the tasks which she planned to attend to upon returning to Stratton House and she began to number them on the palm of her hand. There was the meeting of the board at the bank in the morning; she intended to check the time in her appointment book. Then there were building plans to inspect, relating to the repair of a disused stable in Kent Street. She had already employed a part-time teacher to instruct a small group of children living in that area. And, of course, there was her correspondence to answer, which she hoped Hannah had been seeing to.

She looked down at the fingers hovering above her palm and tried to recall if that was point number two or three. She found that once again the image of Trevanion's face had crept uninvited into her mind and it disturbed her. As she had drifted into sleep the night before, she had briefly opened her eyes and jumped at a vision of a dead dog lying across the end of her bed. A moment later the beast had gone and she closed her eyes, shutting out the sight of it and willing herself to fall asleep.

Now, looking out at last on the city of London and the bustling parish of St James's, she was grateful that in a few short moments she would take up her life at Stratton House again. She had been mistaken in believing that a change of scene would be good for her; work was the perfect restorative. She recalled that there had been one moment of light relief during her stay which had come in the form of a fair-haired scientist. She had found his company invigorating, and she regretted that there had not been opportunity to thank him in more depth for rescuing her from Trevanion. Perhaps their paths would cross again and afford her the chance to do so.

The driver pulled to a halt in Stratton Street. Blossom opened the door and sent Mary to inform Mrs Mills of the mistress's arrival. Mrs Mills was immediately convinced that Miss Meredith had purposely kept from her the news that Miss Angela was returning sooner than expected. It was just like that woman to make her look like a fool.

'Miss Angela, what an unexpected surprise!' Mrs Mills said, hooking the housekeeping keys onto her apron, and tried to disguise the fact that she was flustered.

'If only Miss Meredith had told me of your return, I would have asked Mrs Bishop to prepare a suitable meal for you.'

The housekeeper nodded to the boy, John, who had come from the stable to bring the luggage into the house.

'My return was quite unplanned, Mrs Mills, I only decided upon it yesterday morning. And there is no need to trouble Mrs Bishop for a meal. I will take tea in my room, and if you would let Miss Meredith know that I have returned, I would be grateful for a moment of her time. Oh, and John, I have only my carpet bag, a small trunk and a small hamper. If you could just see to those that will be all, thank you.'

Pulling off her gloves, she hurried to her office, suddenly realizing how much she had missed Hannah. What a refreshing tonic her common-sense approach would be after the difficulties of recent weeks. She opened the door and saw that the room was empty. On her desk, the correspondence was well ordered and Angela smiled to herself. Closing the door behind her, she made her way up the stairs to her bedroom.

'Hannah, are you there?'

The governess was folding linen and placing it in a large chest at the end of the bed. At the sound of her young mistress's voice, she turned to see Angela standing in the doorway, her face shining.

'Oh, Miss Angela! How lovely to see you. We weren't expecting you today.'

Angela pulled off her straw bonnet, relieved to be free of it. 'I hope that it is a welcome surprise?'

'Of course, dear, the household have missed you. And how was your trip?'

Angela handed her hat to Hannah and answered soberly, 'It was a pleasant change, but I am relieved to be home. There was some unpleasantness with Trevanion and Susan. But I intend to leave all that behind me now and concentrate on my work again.'

'Well, perhaps this parcel will cheer you up. Look what arrived for you this morning. A delivery from the drapery store.'

The governess held out a parcel to her mistress.

'But I didn't order anything from the drapery store. Did you?'

'No, but it has your name and address here on the label. Perhaps it's a gift.'

Angela sat on the bed, and began to untie the parcel, wondering who could have sent it. It could not have come from her parents, for the packaging was labelled by the local store, Billingham's. She pushed back the paper and found inside an olive-green dress, with a plain ribbon trim. Angela held it up with a frown, and saw immediately that it would fit her to perfection.

Hannah nodded. 'If you had described your preference to someone, they could not have matched it in more accurate detail.'

Angela was silent for a moment. This made no sense at all. She searched the tissue paper for a card, but there was nothing. Who could have known the intimate preferences of her toilette? By degrees, she recalled the moment when she had described such a gown to her mother while out on the lawn and shortly afterwards, an intruder had been found in the grounds.

With fear she looked at the garment as if it was possessed, rolled it up with haste and pushed it back inside the wrapping paper.

'Take it away, Hannah, I don't want it!'

'What is the matter, Miss Angela?'

'Get rid of it! Take it out of my sight. I don't care what you do with it or where it goes. I want it gone!'

CHAPTER ELEVEN

THE MORNING LIGHT filtered through the gap in the curtains. Angela opened her eyes and checked the hour on the face of the mahogany bracket clock set on the mantelpiece in her bedroom. She had been found sleepwalking in the night and returned to her room by Hannah, who was concerned for her well-being, but Angela had no remembrance of it now.

There had been no further arrival of correspondence written in that tall, thin hand, nor had there been a delivery of any more unsolicited parcels. On the face of it, her life had carried on in the same manner as it had in the months previous to her troubles. She had tried to focus on the charitable work which she found so rewarding, but she had been left with a feeling of lingering unease. Who had played these cruel tricks, and when would another occur?

The package containing the green dress had been re-wrapped and sent by Hannah to the Magdalen Hospital in St George's Fields, an institution for the reform of penitent prostitutes. By return, Angela had received a letter of gratitude, acknowledging her act of charity and asking whether she might grace the hospital with a visit.

The Magdalen Hospital,
St George's Field,
Southwark

Dear Miss Burdett-Coutts,
*   The hospital is most grateful for the kind donation of the garment*

which you recently sent to us.

It has been given to a Miss Rosanna Mather, a young woman who has been reclaimed from her former life and has been under our care and guidance for the past six months. Having learned the skills necessary for service, she is about to be taken into the employ of a minister and his wife living in Sevenoaks, and the dress will be very fitting attire in which to meet her new employers.

If you would ever consider favouring us with a visit, I would be honoured to accompany you on a tour of our building and show you the chapel where the girls sing in the choir and worship each Sunday. Your own association with the Magdalen Hospital would do much to influence those whose financial support could be of great benefit for our penitents who wish to start out on a new life.

Your humble servant,
Reverend Jonah Dodd

Angela was sympathetic towards the young women living at the Magdalen Hospital. It was not a charity in which her father, or the partners in the bank, would approve of her involvement, but she felt a strong desire to see what was being achieved there and whether more could be done with some assistance on her part. She had replied to Reverend Dodd's letter and a visit had been arranged for eleven that morning.

Sitting up in bed, Angela pushed her dark hair back from her face, climbed out of bed and crossed the room to her dressing table. Catching a glimpse of herself in the looking-glass mirror, she examined her face more closely. Both her cheeks and forehead were flushed with an ugly rash which was rough to the touch of her fingertips. She did not have a fever, nor did she feel in the slightest unwell. Perhaps the sun had caught her face when she had been walking across the park yesterday. Hannah had counselled her to take a parasol.

She would call at the apothecary on the way to the Magdalen Hospital. Mr Hardwick would be sure to recommend something; he had been most helpful when Hannah had had a recent bout of neuralgia.

Angela took a bottle of rosewater from her dressing table and tipped the lotion into the wash bowl. Adding some water from a jug on the washstand, she began to splash her face.

A tap on the door was followed by Blossom's voice. 'I have some hot water for you here, Miss Angela.'

'Yes, come in, Blossom.'

Blossom opened the door and at the sight of her mistress's face asked, 'Are you unwell, Miss Angela?'

'I'm fine, Blossom. I forgot to take my parasol out with me when I was walking yesterday.'

The girl thought privately that the rash looked nothing like sunburn, but it was not her place to say. She topped up the jug on the washstand with hot water from the bucket in her hand.

'Can I get you anything else, Miss Angela? Shall I call for Miss Meredith?'

'No, that won't be necessary. I will be down to breakfast shortly.'

Blossom nodded and left, closing the door behind her. She didn't like the look of that rash. Her cousin, Alice, had had a sudden rash like that and had dropped down dead a few hours later!

After gently patting her skin dry, Angela removed her linen nightgown, took a square of jasmine-scented soap from a dish and began to wash herself. She never liked to look upon her pale, thin frame, but reluctantly she glanced over her body and was relieved to see there was no sign of the rash elsewhere. When she had finished washing, had dressed and had tied up her hair in that severe manner of which her mother disapproved, she examined her face in the mirror once more. The rosewater had had little or no effect: her cheeks were still marked with the rash which she could not deny looked quite ugly. However, as vanity was not a fault she possessed, and she did not want to alter her plans for the day, she decided that she would later rely upon the advice of Mr Hardwick.

At breakfast, she tried to reassure Hannah that she was not at all unwell, but she had noticed the servants glancing repeatedly at her face and with a feeling of self-consciousness, she left the house wearing a dark-veiled bonnet. She decided to walk the route from Piccadilly to St George's, which would take her a little more than half an hour. The weather was pleasant for strolling and she was curious to see how the work on the Blackfriars Bridge was coming along. The old bridge had become unsafe and was now under repair.

In his shop on the corner of Coventry Street, Mr Elias Hardwick was making up a mixture of olive oil and arnica, an excellent ointment for bruises. On his shelves could be found a cure for toothache made from cloves; nettle tea, an effective aid to digestion, and bottles of mustard-seed oil for chilblains. He had come from a long line of traders who had sold herbs and spices on their stalls, and who possessed knowledge of homely remedies, passed down through the generations. But Elias Hardwick had distinguished himself by being not only the first in the family to own a shop but also the first to have a licence from the Society of Apothecaries, of which he was very proud.

The door opened and Mr Hardwick looked up to see a woman in a veiled bonnet entering.

'May I help you, madam?'

Angela approached the counter and drew back her veil, and Mr Hardwick immediately observed the reason for her visit.

'As you can see, sir, I am afflicted with an unpleasant change in my complexion. If you could supply me with an ointment which might help me, I would be most grateful.'

Mr Hardwick put down his pestle and mortar, and wiped his hands on his apron. Pushing back the spectacles on his nose, he observed the burning red patches which marked Angela's cheeks, and that now appeared to be developing on her chin also.

'May I see your tongue, miss?'

It appeared to be of normal size and colour.

'You do not have any sign of fever?'

'No, sir.'

'May I ask if you are feeling at all unwell, or marked with the rash elsewhere?'

'No, I feel fine, sir.'

'No soreness in your throat at all?'

'No.'

'How about your digestion?'

'I am eating and am physically well in all respects.'

Mr Hardwick was struggling to find a cause. Perhaps if the

condition was not physical, the lady was troubled in some other way. He had realized when she had drawn back her veil that she was younger than her manner and dress had first indicated.

'Do you mind if I ask if you have recently travelled overseas? Or have been in receipt of any distressing news or circumstances?'

His question had been motivated by the sight of the dark-veiled bonnet.

Angela called to mind the unsettling events of recent months.

'I have not travelled abroad recently but, of late, I have had some difficulty sleeping.'

Mr Hardwick nodded. 'I see. Then I can tell you that I have known such skin afflictions to come about if a person of sensitive disposition is unsettled in some way. If I make up a poultice of comfrey and plantain, I think that will help, miss. The plantain will help to reduce the redness over the next few days. May I also suggest that you try to stay out of extreme temperatures?'

Angela nodded and took a seat at Mr Hardwick's invitation, while he withdrew to a back room to make up the poultice. At the sound of the shop door opening and aware of the presence of a gentleman, Angela drew her veil over her face again.

'I won't keep you a moment, I ...'

Mr Hardwick poked his head out of the back room to address his customer, and as he did, his face lit up at the sight of a young man with intelligent blue eyes.

'Why, it's the young Mr Wheatstone! What a pleasure to see you, sir. What brings you to London?'

Charles Wheatstone removed his buff-coloured leather gloves, crossed the floor and held out a hand of greeting to Elias Hardwick.

'I've come to pay a visit to my brother, William. He has rooms above my uncle's music shop in the Strand, and I wanted to show him a design improvement that I have in mind for the bellows and reed pan of the concertina. But I particularly wanted to search you out while I am here, as I have a piece of laboratory apparatus which I think you will find most interesting.'

Mr Hardwick nodded with enthusiasm. He felt pleased that a scholar like Charles Wheatstone recognized him as a man who was also educated and thought proudly of his licence from the Society of Apothecaries. It was good to see him again. Mr Wheatstone's uncle had been a loyal customer for many years, and had often been into the shop, accompanied by his young relative. Hardwick had watched with great interest the bright young boy grow up into an accomplished man of science.

Angela had been quietly observing the animated interchange between the two gentlemen and wondered whether Mr Wheatstone might recognize her. This was an awkward predicament. Should she acknowledge their former association? Or feign ignorance of his acquaintance and spare him the embarrassment at her affliction?

'If I can just finish assisting the young lady here, I will be with you shortly,' Mr Hardwick said cheerfully, the company of Mr Wheatstone always being a stimulating diversion.

As the apothecary withdrew to his back room again, Charles Wheatstone turned, politely raised his hat to the young woman in the dark-veiled bonnet, and began to casually pace the floor.

He cleared his throat. 'Please excuse my ... er, intrusion, miss.'

His manner had changed from the easy informality he had shared with Mr Hardwick, becoming stiff and awkward. He could never relax in female company.

'There is no intrusion, sir. In fact, I believe that we have been introduced before,' Angela said hesitantly. 'My father is Sir Francis Burdett of Foremarke Hall. We met some time ago at a ball.'

Wheatstone called to mind the unaffected young heiress who had listened to talk of his work with such absorption.

'Ah, yes, Miss Angela. How pleasant to ... to see you once more. I hope that you are ... keeping well?'

Wheatstone immediately realized that his words were ill-chosen in light of her presence at Mr Hardwick's shop.

The colour in his cheeks rose and he stammered, 'That is, I mean to say, I ... I trust that your family is well?'

'Yes, thank you kindly, Mr Wheatstone. And how are your inventions coming along? I was most interested to read in the newspaper of your recent lectures at King's College on the subject of sound.'

Charles Wheatstone pushed his hand through his fine, blond

hair, smiling shyly in acknowledgement of his achievements. At Angela's gentle prompting he began to gain confidence, expounding at great length with enthusiasm upon the topic of mechanical vibrations and sound waves, until Mr Hardwick reappeared at his counter with the remedies he had prepared.

Taking Hardwick's discreet cough as a hint, Wheatstone excused himself from Miss Angela's presence while the administration of the remedies was discussed.

'Ah, yes, if you could excuse me, Miss Angela, while I take a breath of fresh air for a moment?' And Wheatstone stepped outside.

'As I suggested, miss,' Mr Hardwick began, 'if you apply the poultice day and night, you should find some relief. I have also made up a preparation which will aid your sleep and ease any worries which might be weighing upon your mind.'

'Thank you, Mr Hardwick, I was sure you would be able to assist me.'

'You are most kind, Miss...?'

'Miss Burdett-Coutts. I believe you know my secretary, Miss Meredith, who comes here from time to time?'

Elias Hardwick immediately acknowledged the distinction of his veiled customer with a bow of his head.

'Oh, I fear that I have not afforded you proper courtesy, Miss Burdett-Coutts. I did not realize your identity at all. Please forgive me,' he offered.

Angela waved her hand dismissively.

'Think nothing of it, Mr Hardwick. Miss Meredith has often spoken highly of your remedies and I had no wish to trouble my physician for such a slight matter.'

Mr Hardwick bowed his head again.

'If I can be of further assistance, then please let me know.'

Angela bid him goodbye and exchanged a brief goodbye to Charles Wheatstone, who was standing outside the door.

'Quite a remarkable young lady, without the least hint of pretension,' Mr Hardwick commented with wonder as Wheatstone re-entered the shop. 'And walking about town without a chaperone. What do you make of that?'

Wheatstone looked after Miss Angela with an air of wistfulness.

Never had another woman shown such attentive interest in his work.

'Yes, Mr Hardwick, she is an unusual specimen. I … I will grant you that.'

'And now to matters of science, my young fellow. So what is it that you have to show me?'

And as the gentlemen examined the piece of equipment that Wheatstone had designed for the purpose of combustion and sterilization, the veiled figure of Angela Burdett-Coutts headed in the direction of the Magdalen Hospital, St George's Fields.

CHAPTER TWELVE

ACROSS THE MIRY fields, here and there dotted with farm buildings and grazing cattle, the building – known as the Magdalen Hospital – stood alone as if other properties feared corruption might seep into their bricks, should they come too close. South of the Thames, the marshy, low-lying landscape of St George's Fields had never been an encouraging prospect for builders. Here, for the price of £300, two charitable gentlemen had purchased the six acres of land on which the building now stood.

Walking with no mind to the mud splattering her shoes, a figure wearing a dark-veiled bonnet headed in the direction of the hospital. Approaching, she inspected the unremarkable appearance of the institution; its entrance flanked either side by four large sash windows. She rang the bell and waited a moment, feeling anxious. She knew so little of the lives which had been led by the women living there.

The visitor was greeted at the door by the matron.

'Good morning. Miss Burdett-Coutts?'

Angela nodded in response.

'We've been expecting you. I'm afraid that Reverend Dodd is engaged with writing his sermon for our Sunday service at the moment, but he has asked that we interrupt him in his study when we have finished viewing the wards.'

The matron tried to disguise her attempts to peer through the veil which obscured the visitor's face as she invited her to step in.

'Thank you, Matron. Please excuse my appearance. I am feeling somewhat unwell today but I did not wish to cancel my visit. Please, carry on and lead the way.'

The matron nodded and indicated the direction in which they would begin their tour. Hanging in the hallway above a large oak sideboard, Angela noticed an oil painting of Mary Magdalen, her eyes directed heavenward. Beneath it on a gilt plaque, the text read:

Wherefore her sins, which are many, are forgiven.

Angela reflected that the women living here must surely be objects for compassion. Following the matron along a corridor, she then observed the portraits of Jonas Hanway and Robert Dingley, their costume and attitude from an earlier age. Mr Hanway appeared to raise an eyebrow of enquiry at her presence. Mr Dingley, seated in his velvet coat and breeches, wore an expression of welcome.

'Those two gentlemen are our founders, Mr Hanway and Mr Dingley,' the matron acknowledged as she passed. 'Sadly, neither is still with us. But there have been many others who have continued the good work that they started.'

'May I ask how many women you have with you at present?' Angela enquired.

'A little over a hundred, although we have room for another forty,' she replied. 'Some stay barely a night before returning to their former associates, and others are with us for a year.'

They came to a large laundry room, busy with activity. There were figures stooped over the deep sinks which lined the room; these women were winding mangles and mopping water from the floor, hanging wet clothes on a line and taking dry clothes down to be ironed. There appeared to be little conversation between the women, and the matron explained that this was discouraged in case the topic turned to unseemly subjects.

'Most of our girls work here in the laundry. It helps to give them a worthy occupation and provides an income for the hospital.'

Carrying on along the corridor and turning left, they came to a room where groups of women sat at needlework and mending. Dressed identically in a stark uniform, one of their number read from a Bible.

'What happens to their own clothes, may I ask?' Angela asked curiously. 'Are they returned to the girls when they leave?'

The matron looked uncomfortable at the question.

'Their *own* clothes? Why, they are not usually fit for the life that the women hope to lead once they leave here. If the material has any wear in it and is a suitable colour, then the clothes are unpicked and made into something more fitting. In other cases they are sold to the old-clothes man who calls each week.'

'I see,' Angela replied.

She followed the matron down a flight of steps and they shortly came to the kitchen. The shelves were lined with copper saucepans and Angela observed the industry of those who chopped herbs, rolled out pastry and turned meat on a spit before a range.

'We teach the girls cooking and housekeeping with a view to them finding a position in a small house,' the matron explained.

It briefly occurred to Angela that perhaps she could offer a position at Stratton House to one of these women, but what a stir such an occurrence might cause to Mrs Mills. Leaving the kitchen, the two women continued across the basement floor and the matron stopped, gesturing towards the room at which they had arrived.

'This is the probationary ward for our new arrivals.'

She opened the door, which gave way to a room lit by a low fire. At the matron's invitation, Angela stepped inside and by degrees her eyes took in the stark surroundings: six beds and a dark-wood standing closet.

The matron gestured towards a tin bath hanging from a nail on the wall.

'After bathing, the women are seen by a doctor to receive any necessary medical treatment. And then we give them each a uniform.'

She opened the door of the standing closet where skirts and blouses made of stiff cloth were folded in neat piles, next to white cotton aprons and undergarments. Angela noticed the lingering smell of carbolic soap.

'Sometimes we are visited by undesirables, former associates of our girls who try to lure them back into their former life. But once they have been on this ward for a few weeks and demonstrated their commitment to stay, then we move them onto our intermediate ward. We—'

The matron was interrupted by the appearance of a girl standing in the doorway, dressed in the uniform of a penitent. Angela estimated that she could not have been more than fifteen years.

'O'Connor? Shouldn't you be working in the laundry?'

'My apron got wet, Matron. I've come back for another.'

'Hurry up, then.'

The girl passed the visitor without acknowledgement. Angela observed that although the girl's face was a young one, it bore no expression of anticipation; no indication of hope; no vestige of sadness, submission, anger or fear. It was a countenance without life.

In the light of the fire, Angela could also see that the girl's face bore a crude scar which travelled across her eye and down her cheek. The girl took a clean apron from the closet and if she had any thought or care as to the identity of the woman in the dark-veiled bonnet, she did not show it.

Angela found herself compelled to address her.

'Please excuse my intrusion in your room, my dear. Matron was just showing me around the hospital.'

The girl turned her expressionless face to the visitor, her one eye disappearing beneath a ragged eyelid, and shrugged her shoulders.

'Ain't just my room, miss.'

'Thank you, Mary-Ann.' The matron hurried her along, embarrassed by the girl's injury.

The young girl nodded and left the room, closing the door behind her. There was a moment's silence.

'She's very young.' Angela's voice was a whisper.

'Yes. We have many her age and some younger,' the matron shared. 'She was disfigured by the man who earns a living from her in Spitalfields. When he found that she had come here, he broke in and took a knife to her. Thankfully our steward, Mr Thomas, apprehended the man before he could do further harm. We now have two men on duty through the night. None of our girls venture outside these walls until we have found them a position of employment or a safe place for them to go.'

Angela hardly heard the matron's words. She was shocked. She had had some idea that such a dark world existed, but she had not imagined the brutality of its violence or that it claimed the innocence of those so young. Continuing with her inspection of the building and the yards outside, she was lost in her own reflections.

Returning to the reception hall, the two women were greeted by a gentleman of mature years dressed in waistcoat and breeches, his greying hair brushed forwards around his temples. A corner of his shirt hung from beneath his waistcoat and Angela noticed that his hands were ink-stained. He attempted to clean them with a handkerchief.

'I seem to have got myself in rather a mess.' He smiled, pushing his handkerchief back into his trousers pocket.

Matron made the introduction to the Reverend Dodd and the gentleman made a small bow.

'At your service, ma'am. Please excuse my delay in meeting with you. I hope that you have found our institute in good order?'

There was no answer from the veiled woman, who seemed quite distracted. He put his head on one side and enquired, 'Are you all right, my dear?'

She turned towards him, blinking.

'I'm sorry, sir. Did you say something?'

He nodded with understanding.

'Ah, yes. It must be owned that meeting some of our young women can be very difficult, can it not, my dear?'

'Yes, sir.' Angela's voice seemed to come from somewhere else, her heart brimming with emotion.

'That is why we need to continue our work with as much support as we can encourage.'

'Yes, yes, of course.' She tried to take a hold of herself. 'The work you are doing here is without equal, sir.'

She thanked the matron and indicated to Reverend Dodd that she would be happy to arrange a regular subscription to the hospital. The heiress followed the gentleman into his study and with sober reflection she pondered, how was it that providence had placed her at the time of her birth in a bedchamber at Foremarke Hall, instead of filthy, melancholy lodgings in Spitalfields? She wondered what accident of fate had designated her daughter of a baronet, and not the instrument of a man without morals. She was shamed by the rash upon her face and yet, she had no need to hide a ragged scar across her eyelid or a soiled reputation.

Signing her name upon a promissory note, Angela acknowledged that she had no power to alter the occurrence of the past, but with a fortune at her disposal she could influence the path of the future and she intended to do precisely that.

CHAPTER THIRTEEN

5 December 18—

*Last night I had the recurring dream that I was a child, cold and aban-
doned in a crib. I reached out, again and again for my mother, but she
would not turn her face to me or take me into her arms. In turn the scene
changed, and I found that I had become a man, following my wife through
the streets of London, calling after her over and over, but she would not
turn around, no matter how I called her.*

*Although my legs were heavy like lead and I could not lift them in
order to run or catch her up, it seemed remarkable when a lightness came
upon me and I began to fly, drawing closer to her.*

*When I set down on the ground before her and saw her face, I found
that the figure was not my wife's but yours, my angel.*

*Promise me now that whenever I reach out for you, you will take me in
your arms. Whenever I call, you will answer me and that you will never
turn your face from me or send me away....*

He put down his pen at the side of his journal and began to cry.

SITTING AT HIS desk, Richard Dunn pinched at his eyes with a
finger and thumb. The night before he had worked until the light of
his candle had given out, finalizing his case for the defence in preparation for the last day of a trial. He was well aware that Judge Gray
had limited patience and would not allow witnesses to elaborate at
length. He needed to present his summary of the defendant's good
character as persuasively as possible. As Dunn moved aside, a

litter of parchment scrolls tumbled to the floor, three large volumes entitled, *Reports of Cases Argued and Determined in the High Court of Chancery*. A barrister relied upon his books. They were the practical tools of his art, the asset of his trade; and these three volumes – their contents now mostly absorbed and mastered – had been inscribed and given to Dunn by his tutor, Mr Thomas Bosanquet, of Lincoln's Inn.

Dunn had been excessively busy of late and there had not been much time for anything else beyond his work. This was not a concern which troubled him as he was not a man who found pleasure in the company of others. Time and effort was involved in coming to know his fellow men, only to find that inevitably he would be disappointed.

Standing up, Dunn arched his back and walked to the window. At the sight of the dark-haired figure at the window opposite, Dunn knew immediately that it was his angel and he pressed his face to the glass, a rush of adrenalin flooding through his body.

'I am here, my love,' he whispered, his fingers searching for the swatch of velvet ribbon in his trouser pocket. 'Watching you, just as I promised I would.'

He had never seen his angel wearing the dress which he had sent her, but he hoped that she had been pleased with it. The months passed and each morning he had taken out his journal and in that thin, tall hand with little spacing, he would jot down conversations that he imagined they would have when they were finally together. At other times he wrote about places that he planned they would visit. In the fanciful world of his journal he found all the companionship he could ever need.

On Fridays he left his journal blank. On Fridays he did nothing of import. Friday was the day that his wife had left him, and each Friday thereafter was anathema to him.

He reflected that, in his long career, he had often come across women who were living the most terrible lives, among thieves and murderers, acting as their accomplices; and all because they believed themselves to be in love. His wife had been about Miss Angela's age when she had deserted him. Dunn had never been able to find out where she had gone, or with whom, but he was confident that she had fallen under the influence of an unscrupulous rogue. Yes, it was certain: he must protect his angel from the fate which had befallen his wife.

That morning he had risen at seven, and taken his breakfast at eight. Belle, who usually brought up his tray, had noticed as Dunn opened the door to her that he looked tired, his eyes darkly ringed. He had indicated with an irritable movement of his fingers that the serving girl should put the tray on the side table by his bed. Thinking that he meant the desk, Belle had hesitated, wondering where she should place the tray when there were so many papers scattered across it. She had also noticed his journal, which had lay open at a page on which were drawn a series of head-and-shoulder sketches of a young woman.

The girl had turned her head on one side to admire them, curious as to what connection the woman might have to a man who seemed to have no one. As Dunn observed her doing so, he had flown at her in a rage.

'On the side table, there, girl! Never mind looking at what doesn't concern you!'

Belle hurried across the room, putting down the tray, and with his temper subsiding, Dunn's attitude altered a little.

'Forgive me. I did not mean to fly at you just then. I did not get much sleep last night and I am rather tetchy.'

She had never been able to decide just what sort of a man he was. She had brought up his meals most days, ever since he had taken residence at the coffee house. There were times when he resided out of town if his work took him elsewhere, but he appeared to be a man without home or family, and spent all his time in London in these less than adequate rooms. Mostly he was quiet and never ventured upon small talk with her.

Once he had surprised her when he had asked if she had any ambitions beyond being a maid. She had laughed, and said that she had never yearned for something that was sure to be out of her reach. He had responded sadly that she was fortunate not to be tortured so.

'Perhaps you are working too hard, sir, and are in need of a change,' she suggested.

He had smiled to himself and nodded. 'My angel does not know it yet, but I am planning such a change very soon.'

'Your angel, sir?'

But he did not answer her, instead seating himself at this table and engrossing himself in his journal once more.

Leaving the Gloucester Coffee House Hotel, Dunn walked in the direction of the Sessions House in Newgate Street. He thought about the client he was representing today who might face the death penalty if he could not convince the jury that the act of murder had been an unintentional one. Dunn thought how typical it was that a woman should be at the cause of it all: a woman who had left her husband just as his wife had left him. Generally, it made little difference whether he was for the prosecution or the defence, but he felt a strong personal attachment to this case and he determined that he must work to find the accused innocent.

For him, every case was motivated by the desire to persuade others for sake of the sheer power of persuasion itself. He liked his work; there was a great satisfaction in being able to hold the fate of another human being in his hand and simply through the use of words, take their life in one direction or another. It was that which brought him the greatest satisfaction.

Coming to the doors of the Sessions House, he pushed them open and walked across the black and white tiled floor, his papers beneath his arm, nodding at Joseph Lloyd, the counsel for the prosecution, as he passed him. The woman at the centre of the case, Hannah Jennings, had stood accused of stealing from Dunn's client, William Grogan. Her own trial had already taken place and the woman had been found guilty and sentenced to transportation. Dunn had not yet decided whether to call her as a witness or not. Only she knew the truth of what had happened on 20 November, and yet her own indictment would surely set the jury against her as an unreliable witness.

The courtroom was full. Judge Gray had adjourned the day before as William Grogan, the accused, had been cross-examined. The jury had been left believing that Grogan had committed murder in a rage of jealousy. As the court settled down, Dunn stood up, invited by the judge to address the accused.

'Thank you, my lord.'

'Mr Grogan, you stand here today, accused of committing the murder of Mr Tobias Southall on the 20th of November 1839. At the centre of this crime is the woman, Hannah Jennings, whom we know has been found guilty of theft from your premises. Can you tell us, Mr Grogan, how you first came to meet Hannah Jennings?'

'Yes, sir. On the 7th of November, Mrs Jennings took short-term lodgings with me in Jermyn Street, identifying herself as a married woman whose husband had left her. She said that she was looking for temporary work as a seamstress so that she could earn enough money to travel to her family in Scotland. I let the attic room to her, which is a quiet room at the back of the property and well furnished.'

'And what impression did she give you regarding her feelings over her altered domestic circumstances?'

'She seemed much distressed by her situation and would often come out to talk to me in my workshop at the back of the house, sometimes weeping into her handkerchief with despair over whether her husband would return to her.'

'You work as an upholsterer in your workshop; that's right isn't it, Mr Grogan?'

The dark-haired gentleman in the brown corduroy waistcoat and breeches nodded.

'Yes, sir.'

'And when Mrs Jennings came out to you, weeping over her domestic situation, did you ever imagine that her story might be false?'

'Not for a moment, sir. I thought her face one full of innocence, her manner gentle and sincere. I wondered what sort of scoundrel could abandon such an angel.'

'And did you have any difficulty in receiving payment of rent from Mrs Jennings?' Dunn asked, his voice measured and steady.

'Not at first, sir. She paid her rent on time, both the first and second weeks.'

'Thereby undoubtedly reinforcing your belief that she was of a trustworthy character? So, can you tell us what happened on the 20th of November during the third week of her stay?'

'Yes, she came to me while I was working in my workshop,'

crying as she had done before, but this time with even greater distress. She said that she could not pay the rent for that week because she had been robbed of her purse while she had been at the market, and had no further means to pay me. I asked if anyone had given chase to the robber, but she said that she had fainted. And that although someone in the crowd attended to her, when she came round she could not get a true account of what had followed.'

'And can you tell the jury what occurred next, Mr Grogan?'

'Yes, I promised that I would go to the police station to see if they had received word of the incident.'

'And how did Mrs Jennings respond to this?'

'She seemed convinced that I would be wasting my time, and began crying again that she had nothing to offer me in payment for the rent. I reassured her that I would seek out the police anyway and I put on my coat and went into town.'

'And it was then that something happened to change your opinion about Mrs Jennings, wasn't it? Can you tell us about that?'

'Yes, sir. I did not tell the lady what I purposed to do, but I had in my pocket a brooch which had belonged to my late mother. I planned to take it to the pawnbrokers and raise some money to give to Mrs Jennings. As she did not have the money to pay her lodgings or make her way to her family, I saw this as a way of offering her a loan which might be of help to her.'

'And did you expect anything in compensation from Mrs Jennings for this act, as has already been suggested by my learned friend, Mr Lloyd, during yesterday's proceedings?'

'Not at all, sir.' His manner was earnest. 'I could see that she was a victim of a series of unfortunate events and it was my intention to help her where I could, as I would help anyone in that position, man or woman.'

Dunn turned to the jury. 'Indeed. Mr Grogan is well known among the congregation at St James's for his kindness and benevolence. A man who often makes generous donations. A man who ...'

The judge eyed Dunn with sternness, ready to warn him not to lead the jury, but he hesitated in doing so a little longer than he might for any other man. There was something about Dunn which often made him feel ill at ease, yet he could never put an exact name to the reason for it. Dunn curtailed his appeal and turned back to the defendant in the dock.

'So, Mr Grogan, you had every confidence in Mrs Jennings that this loan would be repaid at some later date?'

'Yes, sir. As I told you, her face was full of innocence.'

'So what happened to change your opinion about Mrs Jennings when you reached the pawnbrokers?'

'Well, as I entered the shop on the corner of Drury Lane, I noticed in the display cabinet some items which looked very familiar to me: a blue teapot, a small looking-glass with a gilded frame, and a set of fire-irons. They were all items which I recognized as belonging to the second attic room from my house.'

'And of course, you asked the shop-owner from whose hand these items had been deposited. What did he tell you?'

'When I had inspected these items to make sure they were my own, the shop-owner described Mrs Jennings as the woman who had deposited them, earlier that very morning.'

'And was the shop-owner able to tell you anything more of this woman, Mr Grogan?'

'Yes, he told me that he knew her to be a woman who had left her husband and was now in lodgings with a fellow in Abermarle Street. She often came into his shop with items to deposit.'

'A woman who had left her husband?' Dunn's voice was tinged with contempt. 'So not only was she a thief, but also a woman of low morals?'

The judge gave Dunn a precautionary eye once more.

'Yes, sir,' Grogan continued, 'although it did not seem that it could be conceived so from her appearance.'

'Gentlemen of the jury, you have heard all the facts. Mr Grogan has identified that his property was taken without his consent and deposited into the hand of Mr Rowe, the pawnbroker. Mr Rowe yesterday identified in court Mrs Jennings as the woman who did so.'

Dunn turned again to Grogan in the dock.

'And how did you feel on discovering that you had been made a fool of?'

'I was very angry. I returned to my house with the intention of ordering her to leave. As I opened the front door, and went up the stairs to confront the lady, I heard laughter coming from the attic room, the laughter of a man and woman.'

'And who did you find in the company of Mrs Jennings when you reached the attic bedroom?'

'I believed it to be the man with whom she had been keeping company since leaving her husband.'

'That would be Tobias Southall, the deceased?'

Mr Grogan nodded, a look of grief crossing his face.

'Can you tell the jury what happened next?'

Grogan spoke with some difficulty.

'Yes, Mrs Jennings and her … her visitor appeared to have been drinking, and they continued to laugh at me when I ordered him to leave.' Grogan swallowed hard. 'I asked her about the items which were missing from the room. The man got up from the bed and began to push me, calling me a fool. Then Mrs Jennings seemed upset, her aspect changed and she jumped to her feet, telling her companion to leave me alone. He …'

Grogan's voice faltered and he closed his eyes for a moment as if he saw it all again. He swallowed again and attempted to continue.

'He turned on her and hit her violently with the back of his hand.' Grogan's face became pale with the recollection of the sound of that jaw breaking.

'And then he lifted his hand to hit her again.'

'What took place next, Mr Grogan, are the actions which would have been taken by any self-respecting gentleman, isn't that so?'

Grogan did not appear to hear the question. He was back in the attic room at Jermyn Street, reliving the horror.

'I did not pause to think for a moment. I just wanted to prevent him from striking her again. I leapt at him and we struggled, rolling across the floor until we found ourselves at the top of the stairs. All the time she was standing over us, her mouth bleeding, shouting at us to stop. We got to our feet and without realizing the danger I pushed the man forcefully, only to send him hurtling down the stairs. When I reached him, there was no sign of life.'

He shook his head. 'I just wanted him to stop hitting her. It was an accident, a terrible accident. I never meant for him to die.'

Dunn turned to the jury. 'You have heard it for yourselves, gentlemen. What happened was an unintentional accident.'

As Dunn sat down, the counsel for the prosecution stood up.

'Mr Grogan, isn't it true that you found Mrs Jennings to be an attractive young woman?'

Grogan was still wiping angrily at his eyes. 'I … I considered her to be fair of face, as those of you here who have seen her have witnessed for yourselves.'

'You are unmarried, are you not?'

'Yes, sir, although I don't see what …'

'And her position as a woman who had been abandoned rendered her very vulnerable, wouldn't you agree?'

'Yes, but …'

'She would likely have been very grateful to any man who had not only overlooked a debt that she had little hope of paying, but who was also about to make her a loan of a significant sum of money.'

'Yes. But as you know, her story was not …'

'Just answer the question, Mr Grogan; is it likely or not that she would have been grateful for the actions of a man who overlooked her debt?'

'Yes, sir.'

'But when you discovered her entertaining a male visitor in her room, you realized that you had been taken for a fool and were angry, were you not?'

'Anyone would have been angry.'

'Yes, but we are not talking about anyone, Mr Grogan, we are talking about you. You were angry and humiliated; and in your temper you pushed down the stairs the man whom you recognized as a rival for the affections of Mrs Jennings.'

'No!'

'You hoped that if you said nothing more about the items she stole from you that she might cover your own act of violence, isn't that so?'

'No! No!'

'But she clearly identified you in court as the man who murdered Tobias Southall. The man who …'

Dunn stood up.

'My lord, he is bullying the witness.'

William Grogan began to shout angrily, thumping his fist on the dock, his custodial chains rattling. 'It's not true! It's not true!'

Lloyd turned to address the jury.

'I think we can all see that this is a man whose façade of gentle Christian benevolence hides a brutal and savage temper.'

As Mr Lloyd sat down with a look of satisfaction on his face, Dunn rose to his feet and spoke for the last time.

'Gentlemen of the jury. You see before you an innocent man who took pity on a woman whom he believed to be honest. He pitied what he thought to be her destitution which subsequently turned out to be a sham, and he pitied another man's violence against her. His acts of pity have brought upon him the most terrible of consequences for which he is rightly angry. I hope that you will now pity him and find him *not* guilty of murder.'

As Dunn took his seat again, he threw a look of disdain in Lloyd's direction. He planned to win, as he always planned to win. He hated losing. Losing a case; losing his wife; losing sight of his angel. The jury had adjourned to consider their verdict. Behind closed doors they deliberated among themselves: some shaking their heads, remonstrating with one another. Eventually they returned to the court, and the foreman announced to the judge that they had made their decision.

Dunn stared straight ahead of him, bringing to his mind an image of his angel on which he focused with determination.

Judge Gray asked, 'What say you, gentlemen? How do you find the defendant? On the count of murder, is he guilty or not guilty?'

'We find him not guilty, my lord.'

The courtroom came to life with the clamour of objection.

A slow smile spread across Dunn's face. The woman who had abandoned her husband was facing transportation. The man whose only aim had been to aid and protect her had been exonerated. Justice had been done: there had been no loss.

CHAPTER FOURTEEN

NOT FAR FROM Charing Cross, behind a smart black façade, stood the shop Wheatstone and Co. Founded more than fifty years before on a quiet corner of Pall Mall, the family business had moved first to 24 Charles Street and then to Jermyn Street, before settling in its current prestigious spot at 436 The Strand. Inscribed in gold on the window were the words: *Musical Instrument Makers, Music Seller, Engraver and Publisher*; and inside a handsome display of woodwind instruments. William Wheatstone oversaw the running of the busy workshop in the yard at the back of the store, and his brother Charles, an inventor, made improvements to the pitch and acoustics of the goods they sold. But the instrument for which Wheatstone and Co. were most renowned was the English concertina.

In 1829, while King George was still on the throne, a patent had been issued to Charles Wheatstone, inventor, to manufacture 'A Certain Improvement in the Construction of Wind Instruments' and its licence with the royal seal was stored with care in the shop safe at 436 The Strand. The document, which was ten pages long and complete with extensive diagrams, would routinely be retrieved from the safe by an enthusiastic Charles and explained in great detail to anyone who had made the mistake of expressing the slightest interest in the design and construction of wind instruments.

That morning in the garret attic room above the shop, Charles Wheatstone, his fair head bent over his desk, was deep in concentrated thought. The glimmer of the sun through the window fell upon the shelves lining the snug upper room which held a jumble of apparatus: lengths of copper wire, rubber tubing, test tubes, dismantled clocks, and an assortment of wood and ironmongery.

Wheatstone wrote rapidly upon the pages of a notebook, dipping his pen every so often into the inkwell before continuing. Set to one side of the desk were two identical wooden cubes. Putting down his pen he pushed back his wire spectacles, reached for the cubes and held them up in front of him, first closing one eye and then the other. He moved the cubes away and then closer again.

'Yes, it is a fact!'

He put the cubes down upon his desk, picked up his pen and began inscribing his notes once more.

... the projection of two obviously dissimilar pictures on the two retinae when a single object is viewed must therefore be regarded as a new fact in the theory of vision ...

He put down his pen and moved his notebook to one side. He reached across his desk, drawing towards him the strangest-looking apparatus, and as he did so, the appliance toppled to one side as if it was about to fall over.

Wheatstone steadied it with his hands and let out a whistle of relief. Two small mirrors were set, at an angle facing away from each other, on a wooden stand. Reflected in these were hand-drawn images – one to the right and another to the left – seemingly the same but, when viewed through the mirror, seen by the eye in three dimensions. Wheatstone held the apparatus in front of him and peered intently, allowing his vision to settle and thus seeing both images as one.

'An illusion of depth and dimension! Would you believe it?'

A knock at the door interrupted him and placing his invention on the desk, he turned to see his brother William, red-faced and a little out of breath.

'I have been calling you from the bottom of the stairs, Charles. Did you not hear me? You have visitors.'

'I must confess I did not, brother. But see here, my stereographic equipment is complete, and I—'

William gestured impatiently towards the narrow staircase behind him.

'Charles, you know that I'm the first to congratulate you on your inventions but I am running the shop single-handedly. Am I now expected to entertain your women friends too?'

'Women friends?' There was anxiety in his voice. 'But I am not expecting anyone. In fact, I don't believe that I … I have any women friends to speak of.' His face had turned pink.

William sighed. 'Miss Coutts and her companion, Miss Meredith. I believe that was how they introduced themselves. Now will you please attend to them and let me proceed? Some of us have real work to do.' He turned abruptly and his footsteps disappeared down the staircase.

Charles Wheatstone stood up, pulled his waistcoat down and straightened his cravat. Whatever could the young lady and her companion want with him? He had not seen her since the time they had met in Mr Hardwick's shop. Was it proper for a single lady to call upon him without an invitation? Perhaps he had given her some indication that he wished her to do so, but he did not believe he had. Oh dear, this matter of social protocol was a trial to him.

There had never been a significant woman in his life other than his mother, who had died when he had been a small boy. His life had been distinguished by men: his grandfather and father, his uncle Charles, and William. He had rarely thought about the subject of women. His mind turned mainly upon the subjects of waves and oscillations of the atmosphere, musical vibrations and many other wonders of the universe. From what he had heard, women took up a lot of one's time, which he had incidentally discovered could be measured in microseconds. No, as surprising as it had been to find a female mind such as Miss Angela's that was keen to demonstrate an interest in his work, science was far more fathomable to him than the opposite sex.

Wheatstone made his way down the narrow staircase, which opened out onto a small landing and led to two bedrooms, and a sitting room which was entered by means of a set of heavy brocade curtains. The two ladies were seated near the fireplace above which hung a painting of Wheatstone's father.

'Good day to you, ah … ladies. What a pleasant surprise.'

Wheatstone held out his hand.

Miss Coutts and Miss Meredith stood up. He took their hands in turn and made a brief bow.

Taking their seats again, Angela began, 'Please excuse our unannounced call, Mr Wheatstone, but I was visiting the bank, which as you know is in this same road, and I wished to call upon you to discuss a matter of business.'

What business could a lady possibly have with him, Wheatstone wondered.

'Tea!' he exclaimed, almost making the ladies jump at the announcement. Tea was always good in unexpected situations.

'Yes, tea is what is needed.'

He was muttering to himself now. 'I'm afraid, ladies, that my brother and I only have Mrs Ross, our housekeeper, to help us. We had not anticipated guests, and she is out in town at this precise moment, visiting her sister.'

He gave a little laugh of embarrassment and then felt embarrassed that he had done so. Oh, why was he so ill at ease in women's company?

'As you saw, my brother is occupied in the ... the ... ah, shop, but no matter. Please make yourselves at home and I will return with the tea shortly.'

He backed out of the room and in his absence, Miss Angela and Hannah Meredith, having looked at each other with some mirth, surveyed the sitting room, which was comfortably furnished; if not in need of some housekeeping. On the side table several books were piled up, among them Sir Isaac Newton's *Mathematical Principles of Natural Philosophy* and Aristotle's *Physics*. Another table held a collection of dismantled instruments, including the reed pan from a concertina, a pile of unwashed crockery and several days' newspapers.

'*Bachelors!*' Hannah mouthed to Miss Angela, raising her eyebrows.

Wheatstone returned shortly with a tray of tea, brought up from the kitchen at the back of the shop.

'Ah, here we are. I managed to find some of Mrs Ross's shortbread. If I can just ...' He looked about the room, wondering where he was going to put the tray when the tables were taken up with clutter.

'Allow me, Mr Wheatstone.' Hannah stood up and took the tray from him, enabling Wheatstone to gather up his books and place them on top of a bureau.

'Ah, thank you, thank you, Miss … ah, Miss … Meredith.'

Hannah indicated that she would be happy to take over and soon set about pouring out the tea, and offering the shortbread.

Miss Angela took a sip of her tea and nodded towards the portrait above the fireplace. 'That is a handsome painting you have there, Mr Wheatstone. It is your father, I presume?'

'Yes, yes, it is, Miss Angela. He opened the shop with my uncle Charles as a very young man, and was quite a fine musician you know. He instructed Princess Charlotte on the flute.' Wheatstone felt a little more at ease now that they had tea.

'And you have a talent for music too, Mr Wheatstone?'

'Alas, not for playing as my father did, Miss Angela, but for inventions, yes, I hope.'

Angela then explained her reason for calling. 'Well, that is the very purpose of my visit today, sir. To discuss with you the matter of your inventions.'

Wheatstone frowned. 'I'm sorry, I don't understand at all. My inventions?'

'Yes. I would like to invest a sum of money in the development of your scientific ideas.'

At the mention of money, and from the mouth of a woman too, Charles Wheatstone almost choked on his tea.

'My word, Miss Angela, what a suggestion!'

She raised her eyebrows and without a hint of a smile said, 'I can assure you, Mr Wheatstone, I am completely serious. I have followed the development of your work very carefully in the news-papers, and I believe that there is much you could do to advance the field of science in this country. Besides, you came to my aid once and I have not forgotten it. I'd like to repay your kindness.'

'Well, I … I confess, Miss Angela, that I am very flattered that you should consider me worthy of your kind opinion, but as for … well, as for offering me capital …'

'I am offering you a business proposition, Mr Wheatstone. Just because I am a woman, my suggestion should not seem more preposterous merely because it did not come from a man.'

'I did not mean to imply—'

She interrupted him sharply.

'I have a vested interest in the fortunes of our country, Mr Wheatstone, and I believe that your development of the telegraphic system, along with many of your yet-untried ideas, could revolutionize the way we live. I don't imagine that you earn a great deal from your post at the college, so I would like to offer you a subsidy to your wage to aid you in your endeavours. You could employ someone to help your brother. Another assistant for the shop? Or someone to make your tea, perhaps?' Miss Angela had a small smile on her face now.

In a daze, Wheatstone brushed crumbs of shortbread from his trousers, trying to make sense of this unexpected proposal.

'Are you interested, Mr Wheatstone, or not?'

Wheatstone slowly lifted his head. 'Miss Angela, I don't know what to say. It is a most generous invitation. Thank you.'

'You are most welcome, sir. I will ask Mr Marjoribanks to make the necessary arrangements for the transferral of payments.'

The elation he felt reminded him of the time when he had learned that he had been awarded the patent by the King for his 'Certain Improvement in the Construction of Wind Instruments.' And an excellent idea formed in his mind. He jumped to his feet and calling over his shoulder, headed through the set of curtains to make his way downstairs.

'Ladies, please help yourselves to more tea. I have in mind to show you a fascinating document that will be of the greatest interest to you.'

CHAPTER FIFTEEN

THE SIXTH DUKE of Devonshire inhaled with satisfaction the heavy scent of orange blossom which permeated his conservatory.

'Do you know, Francis,' the duke addressed the baronet who was strolling at his side, 'Paxton is going to need eight boilers to heat the new conservatory he is building me on the west lawn. The whole construction will be a feat of engineering when it is done.'

'That is most impressive, sir.' Sir Francis inclined his silver head.

'It is indeed.'

The duke's chest swelled. He was very proud of his gardens at Chatsworth House, which were fast becoming the talk of the country.

'He has based the architecture of the roof on the design structure of a giant leaf, you know. The man's an utter genius.'

Sir Francis nodded in agreement. The young Joseph Paxton was certainly making a name for himself as one of the finest landscape gardeners in the country.

'At this rate, I shall be the first to grow a specimen of the *Victoria Regia* in England.' A smile played about his lips. 'That will disgruntle the Duke of Northumberland, I'll be bound. He has been trying for almost two years without success, you know.'

Sir Francis had little passion for gardening. He could not appreciate the rivalry which existed between the two dukes in their race to breed this exotic species of water lily. In his mind flowers were for women. His interests centred more on science, astronomy and developments in industry. He did, however, share a common interest in politics and books with his Derbyshire neighbour and always enjoyed the generous hospitality of the bachelor duke whenever invited to his home.

'I am hoping that I can entice the Queen to return to Chatsworth and see the flower in full bloom when it is achieved, you know.'

'I'm sure Her Majesty would be keen to see it, Your Grace.'

The duke opened the conservatory door. The two men stepped outside and began to stroll in the gardens.

Headed in their direction, the figure of a woman approached with an air of confidence in the sway of her body. At the sight of her Sir Francis became uneasy.

'Lady Oxford!' The duke welcomed his neighbour. 'Have you come to pay me a visit?'

Her eyes were on Sir Francis, who grew increasingly uncomfortable at her presence.

'Not exactly, Your Grace. But you did say that I was welcome to take a walk in your gardens anytime, and so I have taken you up on your offer. But I see you already have a visitor.' She nodded and acknowledged the baronet. 'Sir Francis.'

The baronet nodded stiffly. 'Jane. You are well, I trust?'

'Yes, indeed.' She smiled her beguiling smile. 'But you have not replied to any of my letters, Francis. I was beginning to think that you have been trying to avoid me again.'

The duke sensed that there was private business afoot and decided to take his leave, making an excuse to look for his gardener.

'I will return shortly. Please feel free to enjoy the gardens.'

Sir Francis watched his friend leave with disquiet. He did not want to be alone with this woman. He had been making amends with Sophia of late. She had not been well, and he did not want any stray rumours to reach her ears and distress her again.

'I have told you before, Jane. We have nothing more to say to one another.'

'On the contrary, there is much for us to say.' She fell into step at his side. 'There is talk of both the present and the past. We were once very much in love. Don't you remember?'

Sir Francis did not dare to catch her eye.

'I choose not to remember. Those days are long gone and there is nothing left of them that remains.'

'Such feelings never die, Francis. If you look deep enough into your heart you will find, as I do, that they burn still.'

There was such appeal in her voice, and he wrestled with himself, willing himself to remember her ability to ensnare a man. He felt the flicker of a memory, the shadow of her body in the fire-light. He pushed it from his mind.

'There is nothing of those feelings that remain,' he lied.

'But there are our daughters. They are what remain of our love.'

I believe that we had reached an agreement, already. I have made a settlement on both Elizabeth and Charlotte and to that end, I believe my duty is done.'

'Your duty as a father is to meet your daughters and declare them as your own. Surely you owe them that much.'

She tried to take his arm in a persuasive manner, her beautiful face seeking out his own, but he stilled her hand.

'No, Jane. Elizabeth is married now and settled, and in time Charlotte will also make good. They view Edward as their father and always have. A meeting will only serve to upset them. I cannot see what is to be gained by it after all these years.'

She hesitated a moment, before saying, 'Aside from coming to know them, there are, of course, always additional expenses.'

Sir Francis turned on her. 'Damn it, Jane! Is there no end to your soliciting?'

'But you're a man of great fortune, Francis. And at least one of your daughters finds herself in a very favourable position. It seems very unfair that your other children should not equally prosper.'

He took her arm firmly. 'I'm warning you, Jane. If you seek to make trouble with my family, you will live to regret it. If Clara and Joanna were to know of this affair, a new hat or a pair of kid gloves would help them forget their consternation in a moment, but Angela would lose her regard for me completely and nothing would ever be the same between us again. I couldn't bear that.'

There was fire in Lady Oxford's eyes.

'I do not think you are in a position to make such threats. And if you think—'

The duke called out their names as he returned across the lawns, waving a large wallet.

'See here! You must see the preliminary drawings that Paxton has made of the fountains. They will be spectacular.'

Sir Francis was relieved at the sight of him.

'Lady Oxford was just leaving, Your Grace.'

'Ah, 'tis a pity. The company of a beautiful woman is always a pleasure to me.' He sighed.

'I shall return, Your Grace. Sir Francis need have no worries on that matter.' She made a small bow. 'Gentlemen.' And took her leave.

As she disappeared, Sir Francis said in a low voice, 'That woman always makes me uneasy. She leaves a wake of trouble behind her wherever she goes, and I wonder what sport she might make with me.'

The duke grunted. 'I have learned, sir, never to try to understand the workings of the female mind. 'Tis to be avoided at all costs.'

The two men passed the Temple of Flora, the goddess provocatively posed with her one arm outstretched as if beckoning them to a rendezvous. The duke nodded in the statue's direction and said, 'We are utterly in their hands, are we not, Francis? They bewitch and beguile us, making complete fools of us all.'

Sir Francis was aware of the duke's own history. It was well-known among aristocratic circles. As a young man he had been deeply in love with the capricious Lady Caroline Lamb, only to find that she was rudely snatched away from him by Lord Byron.

'I hope, Your Grace, that in these later years I can devote myself entirely to my wife's forgiveness. She has had to endure my own foolishness for too long, I am sorry to say.'

''Tis a noble ambition, sir, and I commend you for it.'

'I know her well of old, Your Grace. Her history has not been forgotten in England and she is still not readily received in the salons of other women.'

The duke placed his hand on Sir Francis's shoulder. 'The woman is still a beauty, there is no doubt about it. But with any luck she will leave you well alone and set her intentions upon keeping an ageing bachelor like me amused instead. Then we will both be satisfied, my friend,' he laughed.

CHAPTER SIXTEEN

17 May 18—

It is almost two in the morning, and I cannot sleep. I am sitting on the end of the bed, distracted by torturous thoughts about you, my angel. I wish that I could see through the threads and fibres of your drapes, and look upon your heavenly form, rising and falling with each breath that you take. I go to the window again, but all is dark within your house. The gas lamps on the street are burning low.

Oh, how I am tempted to conceal myself in the shadows they cast and find my way to your door. Perhaps there is a window left open, or a latch undone. If only I could stow away in your bedroom, hide myself in the armoire, then no longer would I be blighted to watch you from a distance.

Through the gap in the door I would watch and, when I was sure you were sleeping, I would steal from my hiding-place and stand at your bedside. I would place my face above yours and feel you breathing, silent and unaware. And the breath from my lips would merge with yours, and you would not know that I had been there; you would never know....

He put down his pen and walked to the window. Looking at Angela's study, his heart beat wildly and his brain was in turmoil.

BLOSSOM LOOKED SUSPICIOUSLY at the laundry soaking in the tub and nodded to Mary, who was winding a delicate lace collar around a glass jar to dry.

'Do you think them clothes are all right?'

'Which clothes?' asked Mary, a tongue poking from the corner of her mouth as she concentrated on her task.

'Them clothes of the mistress's.'

'Why, what's wrong with them?' Mary frowned.

'Well, that rash on her face, it ain't gone away. And I'm afraid that it might be … you know … catching. I picked them clothes up with a long stick afore dropping them into the tub.'

Mary set the glass jar on the windowsill so that the warmth of the sun would dry the lace, and she walked across the room to peer inside the tub. She wrinkled her round, snub nose in disgust and whispered, 'Just think of all them women she's been a-mixing with at that hospital. You'd think that she could find charitable work that was a bit more – well – respectable, wouldn't you?'

Blossom nodded. 'Mr Kilburn told Mrs Mills that he thinks the mistress should go out riding more frequently, the fresh air would do her complexion good and she'd meet gentlefolk that were more of her kind.'

Mary perched herself on the edge of the laundry-room table and then wriggled her ample frame onto it, her thick calves dangling over the end.

'Yes, and Mrs Mills said that Miss Meredith ought to encourage her to accept more invitations to supper, instead of letting her sit at that desk for hours on—'

The door to the laundry room opened and Mrs Mills entered, glancing sharply from one girl to the other.

'If you girls have got nothing better to do than stand in here gossiping, I'll find you something to occupy yourselves with. Blossom, there's the beds to make and Mary, there's the breakfast table to clear away. Now off you go, the both of you.'

'Yes, Mrs Mills.'

'Sorry, Mrs Mills.'

The housekeeper circled the tub, and cast a look of derision at the clothes soaking within it.

The black-veiled bonnet was placed to one side on the desk at which Angela was sitting. There had been some improvement in the rash which had marked her face. There were times when her cheeks were simply flushed but she was still conscious of it. Mr Evans had brought in herbs from the garden and urged Mrs Bishop to add burdock root to the mistress's soup. He reckoned it would get rid of any bad blood in Miss Angela's system. Conscious that her mistress was sensitive to the subject of the rash, even if she spoke of it dismissively, Hannah Meredith made no mention of it. But she had noticed that Angela continued to wear her veiled bonnet whenever she went out.

They had been to the Magdalen Hospital several times together since Angela's first visit. In addition to financial aid, she had donated lengths of fabric for the girl's uniforms, twenty pairs of leather boots and a dozen prayer books. Moreover, upon learning that many of the girls could not read, she had determined to set up an instruction programme to teach them.

Watching as usual, Dunn stood at the window opposite, observing his angel at her desk. His own room echoed with the silent emptiness of his life. His sleep the night before had been inhabited with strange dreams and voices. He tried to recall what had been in his mind before retiring to bed, and reached for his journal to read the words that he had written.

If only I could stow away in your bedroom, hide myself in the armoire, then no longer would I be blighted to watch you from a distance....

He glanced at his angel again through the window and a flood of frustration at his loneliness rushed through him. With a cry he cleared the table of his papers, crockery and candlestick; and flung the journal into the fireplace, setting sparks tumbling onto the carpet. The book began to glow and catch alight. Realizing what he had done, Dunn immediately regretted his actions and dashed his hand into the heat to retrieve it.

Snatching at the book, the flames caught at his wrist and began to tear at his sleeve. Violently shaking his hand and shouting with pain he dropped the journal and fell to the floor upon his arm, smothering the fire as he did so. He lay there for a moment, his heart pounding, and then sat up, clasping his hand to his chest. His breath sharp through his teeth, he got up and crossed the room to the washstand. He eased his arm out of the blackened sleeve of his coat, swearing with pain at the injury. As his coat fell to the floor, he lowered his hand into the bowl of water on the stand, feeling temporary relief.

He closed his eyes. 'Damn it! Damn it! Damn it!'

After a few minutes, Dunn removed his hand from the bowl and tore at the rags of his shirtsleeve with his teeth, making a strip of the material. He pulled it free from its stitches at the armhole with his good hand and then bound up his injury. He cursed with pain again and took another jacket from the back of a chair at his bedside. He noticed inconsequently that a button was missing from the sleeve. Returning to the window, he rested his forehead on the cold glass, staring into the room across the road. Rocking his head from side to side, his eyes fixed on the object of his desire, his shoulders began to shake and he let out a series of low sobs. He wanted her more than anything he had ever known, but he could not bear the thought that he might be rejected once more.

Angela, at her desk, shook her head at the contents of the letter in her hand.

'Hannah, Mr Marjoribanks won't hear of my suggestion to raise the bank clerks' salaries. He says that I have no right to intervene in the matter. Then what is the purpose of my position on the board, if my vote and opinion counts for nothing? This is not the first time he has disregarded my views.'

'Why don't you write to your father, and ask for his advice?' Hannah offered.

'I am not a child, Hannah, that I need his advice. That would only serve to reinforce Marjoribanks's opinion that I have no mind of my own. No, I propose to show him that my views will not be easily dismissed. I'm going to take legal action. I will instruct a solicitor to find me a brief and argue the case of my grandfather's will. I plan to establish that Grandpapa's intention was that my role would not be merely a nominal one.'

Hannah privately thought that her mistress might be better served seeking some advice before putting herself at odds with the board of Coutts and Co., and she crossed the room to the window to fetch her mistress some water from the carafe on the sideboard, hoping to calm her temper. As she poured the water into a glass, her hand was stilled at the sight of a figure at the window in a hotel room opposite. A man with his face pressed against the glass.

Dunn saw the woman looking up at him and drew back quickly

behind the curtain, conscious he had been observed.

'How very strange.'

'What is it, Hannah?'

'It seemed as if someone was watching the house from the rooms above the coffee house opposite.'

Hannah's eyes scrutinized the space where the figure had stood, but she could now see only the blackness of the room beyond.

Angela, still engrossed in her paperwork, waved her hand dismissively.

'It's probably one of those impertinent newspapermen spying on me with a view to manufacturing more fictitious nonsense about my marital intentions. According to *The Times* last Wednesday, having declined a proposal from both a Scottish duke and Prince Louis Napoleon, I am now about to become the fourth wife of the Emperor of China, don't you know.'

Angela dotted the end of the sentence that she had written, and returning her pen to the inkwell on her desk, she reached for her black bonnet, which she pulled on, tying the ribbon beneath her chin.

'Hannah, if you wish to accompany me, I'm going to the bank this morning and I will seek out Marjoribanks and warn him of my intentions. I do not mean to be put off in my purpose. Our clerks hold a position of great trust and responsibility, and should be rewarded for their integrity.' Angela crossed the room and pulled the bell sash to call for Mrs Mills. 'I am well aware that the Birmingham bank is poaching experienced clerks from our competitors, taking staff, business and customers with them.'

The door opened and Mrs Mills enquired how she could be of assistance.

'If you could ask John to ready the carriage to take me to the bank, please, Mrs Mills?'

Mrs Mills nodded and withdrew.

'After all, Hannah,' Angela continued, 'if we ensure that the clerks at Coutts and Co. are valued, we gain their loyalty. Of course, if it was the suggestion of a man, my proposal would be taken up immediately. But from the mouth of a woman it is nothing but a foolish fancy.'

At Miss Angela's enquiry if she would be accompanying her into town, Hannah replied that she had some letters to post and would be grateful to share the use of the carriage. Leaving Stratton House, Hannah Meredith glanced up at the rooms above the coffee house again but there was no sign of the figure she had seen earlier, and she dismissed further thought of the matter. The two ladies stepped into the carriage and the driver closed the door after them.

Upstairs, in Miss Angela's bedroom, Blossom opened the door of the cedar cupboard, the clean laundry across her arm. A linen collar slipped from her grasp and fell to the ground. Bending down to retrieve it, her eye was caught by the glint of an object on the closet floor. She knelt down, picked up the small object and then stood up again to examine what she had found. Her face formed a frown at the sight of a gilt button from the sleeve of a gentleman's jacket. She shrugged her shoulders and dropped it into her apron pocket.

CHAPTER SEVENTEEN

AN INVITATION TO the Princess Lieven's ball was a great honour. Anyone who mattered in society was always present; and that evening, seated on the perimeter of the ballroom, Lady Sophia Burdett, her hair a feat of architecture, was instructing her daughter on matters of social ambition.

'Watch and learn, Angela. The princess uses her intelligence, charisma and social skills to charm the most important men of the political world, all to the end of furthering her husband's career. She is, of course, by far the stronger character in the marriage. Her husband would be nothing without her.'

'And what exactly is it that I am to learn, Mama? How to further the initiatives of a man, whilst seeking nothing for myself?'

'Not at all! A woman is mistress over her own home, in which great satisfaction can be found. You must command your staff as if you are the leader of an army, my dear, and then there will be no mistake as to who is in charge.'

Angela, who had already refused several invitations to dance, replied, 'There is much more that I want from life than that, Mama. My charity work is—'

A gentleman approached and made a small bow. 'I apologize for the interruption, Lady Sophia, but I came to introduce myself. Perhaps you might remember me?'

Sophia took in the aristocratic appearance of the figure before her.

'I'm afraid not, sir.'

'Mr Brooke, madam. My father was an old friend of Sir Francis, and I believe some years ago that I took your daughters out riding when they were much younger?'

He acknowledged Angela with a polite smile.

'The young Mr James!' Sophia recalled. 'Yes, there has been talk of your return about town, sir. But my daughter, Angela, was but a small girl when you were last in England as a schoolboy. Well, I must confess, Mr Brooke, that you have grown to be the most handsome of men.'

Mr Brooke accepted the compliment with a small bow.

'You are most kind, Lady Sophia. I'm afraid that I caused my father a great deal of trouble when I ran away from my school all those years ago. As a consequence, he sent me to India to finish my education and I have since joined the army.'

'Yes, and the word is, Mr Brooke, that you are becoming quite a hero out in Borneo.'

'You are very generous, Lady Sophia, thank you. And your other daughters – are they quite well too?'

'They have had a stream of dancing partners throughout the evening, Mr Brooke, and I have hardly seen them all night.'

He looked at Angela and then at her mother.

'If she'd care to, I wondered if I might ask your daughter, Miss Angela, to dance?'

Before Angela had a moment to think of a reason to refuse him, her mother accepted without haste on her behalf.

'Two childhood friends reunited again. What a happy coincidence! Angela wouldn't dream of refusing you, sir.'

As her daughter reluctantly took to the floor with Mr Brooke, Sophia looked on with pleasure, wondering if her husband would be pleased at the match. Mr Brooke came from a good family, his mother being the daughter of a peer, and his father an eminent judge. She scanned the glittering ballroom lit with mirrors. Her husband had been gone from her side for some time, and her eyes flitted from figure to figure in search of him. In the far corner of the room, she observed Sir Francis engaged in conversation with a woman and two young counterparts, who appeared to be her daughters.

'This is not the time or the place, Jane!' Sir Francis whispered sharply.

'But if you will not receive our company at home, then where else should such an introduction be made?'

'Most certainly not in a public place! Why do you persist in hounding me?'

The baronet had been most unsettled at the sight of Lady Oxford the moment he had arrived at the ball, and did his utmost to excuse himself each time she had approached him; but she had been relentless in her course. Sir Francis turned to leave her, but Lady Oxford continued in his wake.

Sophia took in the scene and was filled with bitterness at the sight of the woman who had caused her so much unhappiness. Francis had shown renewed warmth of late, but she had not been able to shake off her anxieties of former years.

As Angela resumed her seat at her mother's side, she observed her mother wince with pain in her side.

'Mama? Are you unwell?'

'A little indigestion, my dear,' Sophia replied dismissively.

'Allow me to fetch you some cordial, madam,' Mr Brooke offered, and disappeared in the direction of the refreshments.

'Don't mind me, my dear. I am only thinking that I wish to see you settled and happy, and Mr Brooke is such a fine man. They say that his military assistance is being sought by the Sultan of Brunei, and the rumour is that he has returned to England for the season to find himself a wife. I thought that we might invite him to Foremarke and give a ball in his honour before he returns.'

Sensing the direction in which her mother's intentions were heading, Angela objected, 'Mr Brooke is at least ten years my senior, Mama, and if he has not found himself a wife by now then there must be something wrong with him.'

'On the contrary, he has pursued his military career with a passion and was injured for a time. He simply has not had chance to focus on matters of a personal nature, but now—'

'The man is probably in search of a fortune to finance his military ambitions,' Angela interrupted heatedly.

'Not at all, my dear. He has a substantial inheritance of his own and would be a most eligible catch.'

'Thank you, Mama, but I have no desire for a marriage to be engineered. When I meet the man with whom I choose to fall in love, I wish it to be an unexpected surprise.'

Her mother protested, 'But, Angela, these things cannot be left to chance. Marriage is a matter of great importance and must be managed very carefully if it is not to be a disaster. As I said, I only wish to see you settled and happy.'

'I am happy, Mama, and it will take the most remarkable of men to make me any happier than I am already. Arrange a ball if it pleases you, but I cannot promise to fall in love with your Mr Brooke.'

As Mr Brooke returned with the cordial, Angela's thoughts turned to someone else who had been occupying a great deal of her attention. She smiled to herself, and brought to mind the features of a fair-haired scientist of whom she was becoming most fond.

Lady Oxford, who had followed Sir Francis outside, caught him by the arm.

'I am warning you, Francis, if you do not do as I ask one day, there will be great pain for those you love.'

'And I am warning you, Jane, that if that were to ever occur in my lifetime, I will ruin your husband, strip him of his fortune, and you will be out on the streets, where you deserve to be.'

She saw the anger in his eyes and retreated. If there was anything left of the man he was before, she knew he would be good to his word. Without further communication she left. There would be another time.

CHAPTER EIGHTEEN

5 July 18—

A man has been calling upon my angel at Stratton House and I have been watching him closely. There have been many suitors since she first took up residence, but she has never encouraged any of them. Her virtue is unequalled and I have watched them leave one by one. But this one persists and his weekly calls increase. How I despise him as I watch him smoothing down his fair hair and straightening his cravat as he stands on her doorstep, waiting to be let in.

The dog is just another opportunist seeking to seduce her into marrying him and to take her from me. I must find a way to warn her, for he is certain to break her heart....

'ALLOW ME TO introduce you to Mr Charles Dickens.' Miss Angela gestured to the gentleman who was seated in her sitting room.

'Mr Dickens, Mr Charles Wheatstone.'

The young man with the brown curls stood up and took the hand of the fair-haired scientist who had just entered the room, shaking it enthusiastically.

'Mr Wheatstone, I can't tell you what an honour this is, sir. I am a great admirer of your work and have read a great deal in the newspaper about your research.'

The hesitant Wheatstone was alarmed by the manner in which his hand had been taken, and quite overwhelmed by the rapid speech and animation of the young man, who was wearing the brightest red waistcoat he had ever seen. He was not expecting to find anyone else at Stratton House and was unsure whether it was resentment he felt towards this interloper or anxiety at his own inadequacy in social situations.

'How providential that I should have in my own house at the same time England's most promising young writer and most promising young scientist.' Angela was delighted. 'Would you believe, Mr Wheatstone, that I chanced upon Mr Dickens in the bank?'

She turned her head anxiously towards the brown-haired gentleman. 'I hope you won't mind me telling Mr Wheatstone that you have just opened an account at Coutts and Co., Mr Dickens?'

Dickens shook his head. 'Not at all, Miss Coutts.'

'Yes, I had just come out of a meeting with the partners, when Mr Marjoribanks informed me of the news. Mr Dickens was just about to leave the building when I invited him to come and take tea here with me and Miss Meredith.'

She moved to the table by the window and picked up a copy of the periodical, *Bentley's Miscellany*.

'I have been reading *Oliver Twist* for some months now, and I have to confess that its storyline has captured my attention entirely. Have you read it, Mr Wheatstone?'

'No, Miss Angela, I … I am afraid that my time is taken up altogether with my research, but I have heard that it captures the plight of a young waif in the most touching manner.'

'Not just touching, Mr Wheatstone. It is a painful portrayal of the truth. And Mr Dickens has not shied away from exposing the hypocrisy of those with sufficient wealth and power to do something about the appalling conditions that such children have to face.'

Wheatstone nodded with what he hoped was sympathetic effect, but he had to confess that he had little time to take note of what was going on in the world around him. He had tried to understand the human condition without success. Those fascinating elements – carbon, oxygen and hydrogen – followed reactions which could be anticipated, even controlled. Yet the motives and passions of the average man were something which Wheatstone had observed could never be entirely predicted.

He had wanted to share with Miss Angela his concerns that Sir William Fothergill-Cooke had come to him lately, asking for advice about his own experiments with telegraphy. Wheatstone had supported the younger scientist, only to find that Cooke now wished to claim himself an equal share in the patent of the system that Wheatstone had invented. But now, instead of a sympathetic ear, he found Miss Angela taken up with the romantic tales of a dandy in a red waistcoat. Wheatstone took a sip at the tea which had been offered him by Miss Coutts and sulked as Dickens continued to hold centre stage.

Dunn focused a set of opera glasses on the windows of Stratton House, moving them quickly from one room to the other. With frustration he threw them onto a nearby table; he could see nothing. Not only had that fair-haired mongrel come to the door, but another was already there before him. He had to find a way to advise his angel that she was in peril.

He sat down at his desk, took a piece of paper and dipping his pen quickly in the inkwell, scribbled a few words which he blotted and then rolled up into a small scroll. He tied it with a piece of string taken from the desk drawer and then put it into an inner pocket of his jacket. Retrieving his cane, hat and cloak from a stand in the corner of the room, he headed down the staircase. A servant girl passed him but Dunn heard nothing of her greeting; she noticed that his lips were moving wordlessly, his eyebrows knitted together with intent.

Dunn stepped out of the coffee house onto the busy Piccadilly thoroughfare and crossed the muddy track of a road without care for an approaching cab. Even at the sound of the horse's whinny and the angry shouts of the driver, he seemed to have no awareness of their existence. Coming immediately to Stratton House, he began to walk its circumference with a purposeful manner; his heart thumped in his chest. He had no way of knowing in which room Angela could be found. He looked up at the numerous sash windows above him, some with iron balconies, others with stone balustrades, and he knew that it would be pointless to try to climb.

Arriving at the back of the house, Dunn looked about him and spying a young boy loitering on the street corner, he beckoned him.

The boy approached and Dunn held out a coin, instructing him to bring a cab immediately to that spot. He advised that there would be another payment when he returned with the carriage. The boy ran off and Dunn turned his attention to the house again, pressing his face and gloved fingertips against one of the windows. The shadows and shapes within were obscure and motionless. He could see nothing.

'Where are you?' he breathed. 'Where *are* you?'

Perspiring heavily, he moved to another window and then another, pressing his face against each one and then moving on again. He stopped for a moment and peered with intent as he thought he noticed something. Swiftly a shadow appeared and moved slowly towards Dunn at the window. He started momentarily.

This is your chance now, man, take it! Take it!

Raising his cane as if it were a dagger he smashed it into the window, shattering the glass. He withdrew the scroll from his pocket and posted it through the broken window and screamed, 'Tell her to take heed! Do you hear me? Tell her to take heed!'

A carriage appeared around the corner of the street with the boy running at its side. Dunn signalled to it, threw the boy the promised coin and jumped in, indicating the driver to move on with a bang on the roof.

At the sound of shattering glass, Wheatstone spilt some of his tea.

'Hello! What's going on?' asked Dickens, seemingly unperturbed.

Angela remained calm. 'Perhaps one of the maids has met an end with the tea tray. I have the clumsiest of maids, Mr Dickens, you know. No amount of money can secure me one without two left feet.'

The door opened and Hannah appeared with a look of concern on her face.

'I think that you should call a police constable, Miss Angela. There has been a disturbance in the next room.'

'A disturbance? Well, what kind of a disturbance, Hannah?'

Dickens took to his feet. 'I will go and call the constable myself personally, Miss Coutts. I am very familiar with the comings and goings of the police as I often sit in at the law courts. After all, you never know where the next idea for a novel is going to come from.' He grinned.

Wheatstone would not have been at all surprised if Dickens had winked at her. He was vulgar, uncouth and all too familiar with the opposite sex. Had the man no shame?

Angela excused herself and she followed Hannah into the room with the broken window, leaving Wheatstone at a loss as to something useful to do. Observing the shattered glass, she enquired with some growing concern, 'Has there been an attempt at a break-in, Hannah?'

'Of sorts, Miss Angela, yes.'

'Well, either there has or there hasn't.'

'I believe that broken window was just a means of getting your attention rather than a bid to enter the building.'

'But who on earth would want to attract my attention in this manner?'

Miss Meredith held out the scroll which she had picked up from among the glass on the floor. She had taken the liberty of untying it. Angela took it from her and as she opened it, she immediately felt a chill at the sight of the strokes of the pen, which were tall and thin, the letters written with little spacing between them.

Take heed, for he will break your heart in two....

'What is the message intended to mean?'

Her heart began to race; the image of a dog chasing a man flickered before her eyes. She could hear his rasping breath, she could see his hand clubbing the dog's skull again, and again....

'Miss Angela? Miss Angela?' The governess saw that her mistress had turned pale.

She held out the paper to her companion.

'I think that we both recognize this hand. I believe we should ...'

The door opened and Dickens entered with a police constable at his side.

'Good day, miss. I'm told that you have had a little disturbance here this afternoon.' The constable's eyes went immediately to the shattered window. 'Has anything been taken, miss?'

'It's Miss *Burdett-Coutts*,' Hannah said curtly, by way of an introduction.

'Ah, much obliged, ma'am.' The constable nodded. 'Has anything been taken, Miss Burdett-Coutts?'

'No, Constable, but my secretary, Miss Meredith, believes that there was some other motive, a ... a romantic motive.' With some embarrassment, she held out the scroll of paper and the constable took it.

When he read it out loud, Miss Angela coloured.

'It is a foolish gesture, Constable. I think that we are undoubtedly wasting your time. Nothing has been taken, and no real attempt has been made to get into the building. I am sorry we have brought you here on a pointless errand.'

The constable's face was stern and he shook his head.

'No, Miss Burdett-Coutts, you are mistaken. This is a serious matter. Did you not read about the intruder who was recently discovered in Buckingham Palace? He has made several successful attempts, and has eluded the police each time he has been happened upon. On one occasion he had about his person a very intimate piece of the Queen's apparel.'

The constable could not say in a lady's company that the criminal had put an item of Her Majesty's underwear inside his own britches, but he thought that certainly indicated the depravity of such an individual.

'No, we must take this matter very seriously. I would like to recommend that you leave the house. Go to the coast for a few days.'

Angela took in his words for a few moments and then found that her fear turned to anger.

'Constable, am I to be driven from my own home because some madman believes that he can dictate with whom I might decide to fall in love?'

Dickens had been listening and observing the events with the greatest absorption and wondering whether he could work such an adventure into a new story. The young heiress haunted by a mysterious prowler. He took a sidewards glance at Hannah Meredith, who seemed to read his thoughts and glared at him. He decided that any such prowler would have to have nerves of steel to get past her.

'I am merely doing my job, miss. And that is my advice to you,' the constable counselled.

Dickens offered a suggestion. 'Could you not ask a member of your night patrol to walk his evening route this way for a few weeks, Constable? And if one of your day officers might kindly do the same, I think that might bring a satisfactory conclusion to the matter.'

Hannah fixed Mr Dickens with a glare. 'Mr Dickens, I think that Miss Angela's father might have something to say about the matter of her staying put in London and ...'

Angela interrupted. 'Under no circumstances is my father to be made aware of this incident. I believe that Mr Dickens's idea is an excellent one and if you think that you can manage it without too much inconvenience, Constable, I shall be very grateful.'

'Yes, miss, if those are your wishes.' The constable nodded and made his exit. Miss Meredith followed, after giving Mr Dickens another frightful glare.

'I don't think that any intruder would survive that withering look!' Dickens said under his breath, raising a humorous eyebrow at Miss Angela.

She laughed, and said, 'I think that you are right, Mr Dickens.'

As they left the room she gave a nervous glance over her shoulder at the shattered window. She did not want to admit that she was terrified, and instead tried to focus her attention on her forgotten visitor.

'I think that we had better go and rescue Mr Wheatstone. The poor man has had quite a shock.'

CHAPTER NINETEEN

DUNN OPENED HIS eyes slowly. His desk – a jumble of books and papers – was turned on its side. He frowned, lifted his head from the arm of the sofa, and realized as the room righted itself that he had been asleep. He rubbed at his hair, trying to remember what day it was and what had happened before he fell asleep. He could only recall the hazy images and dull voices of a dream that had made no sense. He had dreamt of his mother, his wife, of words written on a page which he could not read. It had been months since he had last been in court. He had been escorted from the Sessions House when he had stumbled over his words, unable to coherently delineate the soundness of his case. The weeks which had followed seemed to be filled with indistinct memories.

At the sound of a soft tapping which came from across the room, Dunn knitted his eyebrows. He turned his head to listen and the tapping came again. Holding onto the arm of the chair, he took to his feet uncertainly and crossing the room, he tripped over a tray of dirty dishes on the floor. Beneath his breath he cursed at the stupidity of the servant girl who had not cleared up.

'Who's there?'

No answer came, and he shivered as a breeze lifted the curtain at his window.

The tapping continued and he pulled at the door, opening it violently. The corridor was empty.

'Belle!' he shouted.

He looked up and down the corridor and shouted again, 'Girl!

Come do your job, there are dishes here!'

A door along the hall opened and a face appeared, frowned at Dunn's outburst and quickly withdrew again. Dunn turned back into his own room, mumbling to himself. He glanced at the curtain which was billowing softly at the opened window and by degrees, his scowl was replaced with a smile.

'Ah, was it you, my seraph, tapping at my door while I was sleeping?' He shook his head and laughed gently. 'Yes, I see it now, you are playing with me. Setting my hopes alight that I might be in your presence.'

He walked towards the sash window and drew it up further.

'Are you hiding, my love, hmm? Or perhaps you have flown out of the window back to your palace.'

Evening was falling and at the sight of a man's figure leaving Stratton House in the dusk, Dunn became anxious.

'Everybody wants something from you, my innocent one, but it is only me who is without selfish motive. I wish only to protect you.'

He looked at the light which burned low in a downstairs room of the house. If only he could find the courage then he would tell her in person how he felt. Tell her how she enchanted him and how the desire that he had for her was driving him insane, but he had been rejected before. He could not bear it again.

At the sound of tapping on the door he turned from the window. If Belle was making sport with him he would knock her head off her shoulders.

'Damn you, girl!' He crossed the room, clenching his fist. 'If you ...'

He pulled the door open and, with his words faltering, took a sharp intake of breath at the sight of the woman who stood before him.

'Hello, my dear,' she said.

He stepped back into the room, shaking his head. 'How ... how did you know I was here?'

The woman entered Dunn's room and stood before him, smiling gently.

'I have always known you were here. I see you watching from

your window each day.'

'You have seen me?' There was disbelief in his voice.

'Yes, of course I have seen you.'

He shook his head in wonder and began to circle her, taking in the sight of her from head to foot. She was dressed in a dark-olive muslin gown, edged with velvet ribbon.

'You are wearing the dress I sent you,' he remarked.

'Yes.'

The dark-haired woman lifted her slender hands to her throat and ran them down her chest and abdomen and spread them out into the folds of her skirt.

'It is the most beautiful gown I have ever had. And knowing that each detail was chosen by you means that it is not something simply commonplace, but it is something extraordinary.'

Dunn's pulse began to race at her words.

'Do you know why I sent it to you?'

He was circling her again.

'Yes, I believe that I do, but I came to hear the words from your own mouth.'

He stood behind her, placed his hands on her shoulders and whispered in her ear, 'I wanted you to know that the day you left London, I did not leave off guarding you. I found out where you had gone and I followed you.'

He inhaled deeply, taking in the scent of her hair and closing his eyes.

'Even when you were seated on the lawn talking with your mama, I was watching over you. And when I learned of your most personal and particular taste, I wanted to show you that I had listened to every detail, and paid attention to it so that you might judge if any other man alive would honour and serve you as I do.'

The woman turned around and found her face close to his.

'I know that there is not another. If you say the word I will marry you, my love.'

She reached behind her neck, undoing the clasp of a silver locket, and removing it from her neck, she held it out to him.

'I give you this as a sign that we will be together soon. Keep it with you always and it will serve to bind us together.'

He held out his hand, which was trembling. Taking the locket, he knelt down and nestled his head against her abdomen.

'Oh, my angel, my angel, I will never leave you. Never! If you fail to walk I will carry you. If you have no breath I will revive you. Whatever becomes of you and wherever you go, night and day, I will never let you go.'

He felt her fingers in his hair and he clasped her tight to him.

Belle, carrying a candlestick in her hand, walked along the corridor. She heard the sound of laughter, and drawing further along the hallway, she realized that it was not the sound of mirth but the sound of crying. She came to the room occupied by the man with the darkly circled eyes. His door was open and she stopped, troubled at what she saw: a man on his knees, his hands clasped about his arms, his eyes focused on nothing, his voice addressing no one.

BOOK TWO

CHAPTER ONE

Two years later

THE LOUNGE AT Thompson and Fearon's gin palace in Holborn was populated with gentlemen, the low hum of their voices frequently punctuated with laughter; the fabric of their well-cut frock coats trapping the smell of cigar smoke, alcohol and cooked meat. Some were seated on bar stools, their faces reflected in the gilded mirror which ran the length of the mahogany bar. Others sat at tables, their empty plates pushed aside while they conversed and drank wine with their companions. Thompson and Fearon's was not the watering place of dockers or river workers: the gentlemen illuminated in the sparkle of the gas lamps were most likely to be older men with a profession, or young men who could afford to deliberate endlessly over their intended profession to the disapproval of their affluent fathers. If they were married, they were married to women who would never consider asking where their husbands spent the evening; and those who were bachelors happily did not answer to their mothers.

A few streets away, John Bettesworth-Trevanion meandered along the lanes of Holborn with the destination of Thompson and Fearon's specifically in mind. His wife, Susan, was staying with her parents in Derbyshire. It was so much cheaper that she did so, eating and sleeping at the expense of her father, Sir Francis, rather than drawing upon the frequently strained pocket of her husband. It was not that Trevanion had always been short of funds. Not at all;

his own father was a man of property and Trevanion himself had been well schooled. But that unfortunate bit of business which had caused his expulsion from his commission in the army had cut him off from his father's assistance, and most likely from his inheritance too, unless his father could be prevailed upon to change his mind.

Seated in an upstairs room of the gin palace was Henry Seymour, a friend from Trevanion's schooldays, who was – by the most lucky of coincidences – an excellent whist player, and had for some time been in profitable partnership with Trevanion, parting scores of gullible young men from the contents of their ample wallets. The partnership worked like this: Trevanion, dressed in his finest frock coat and cravat, engaged a couple of likely-looking fellows in conversation in the fashionable gin palaces of London, while Seymour sat in a room upstairs marking the highest trump cards with his thumbnail. There was great risk attached, of course. Serious consequences of a physical nature were inevitable if one was caught cheating by the wrong player, but the opponents of Seymour and Trevanion were chosen with a practised eye.

Overlooking that these were, after all, sham games, the success which he achieved at the side of Henry Seymour created in Trevanion's mind the fanciful belief that he actually was in fact the most superior of card players. And so it was that as often as Trevanion filled his pocket with another man's guineas, he was apt to lose it just as quickly the following day. Henry Seymour, on the other hand, did not have Trevanion's instinctive nose for discerning exactly the right prey for the evening's game, and so it was that with such mutual dependence their partnership continued to flourish.

As he drew closer to Thompson and Fearon's, Trevanion reflected that a few years ago he had believed that all of his money troubles were over for good. His wife's grandfather had been on his deathbed, and the entire family were in expectation of their share of his fortune. He had anticipated that his mother-in-law, as the only daughter, would naturally receive the largest share but as the old banker had been mightily fond of his grandchildren, Trevanion had been confident that Susan was about to become a very wealthy woman. Thankfully the law, in its wisdom, decreed that both a woman and her wealth were the property of her husband entirely and therefore it followed that Trevanion had believed that he had been about to become a wealthy man.

No one could have anticipated that his homely-faced sister-in-law, Miss Angela Burdett, should become the major beneficiary named in the will. It was an outrage. And how quick she had been to remove herself from the family home in Derbyshire to that mansion in Stratton Street, London, and luxuriate shamelessly in her grandfather's wealth. Trevanion had at least hoped for some sign of chagrin on her part in the shape of a pecuniary gesture to those who had been flagrantly short-changed. But instead, with the typical hysteria of a woman, she had turned her attention to works of charity. There were enough do-gooders in this world, without a woman who had been little more than a girl taking such foolish ideas into her head.

The dazzling lamps behind the frosted windows of the gin palace came into view as Trevanion turned the corner of the street. he felt a little flutter of nerves in his stomach, which he attributed instead to hunger. After all, were not he and Seymour an unbeatable partnership? He would settle himself with a chop first. Seymour would undoubtedly amuse himself with one of the garishly dressed barmaids while he was waiting. Seymour had to understand: Trevanion was a master at his art, and finding exactly the right pair of clowns to fleece was not a matter to be rushed.

As there were number enough drinking establishments in the city for the wily duo to conduct their business without attracting a name for themselves, there was little chance of Trevanion being recognized as anything other than a man in search of an evening's relaxation and as he entered the gin palace, he invited only the most cursory of glances. He approached the bar and was greeted by a man, an apron folded around his generous waist. Running the back of his hand along his gingery whiskers, he asked what his customer might care to take.

'I'll have a couple of pork chops and a glass of ale,' answered Trevanion.

While the man with the ginger whiskers pulled a glass of ale from a polished pump on the bar, Trevanion took a moment to scan the room for prospective dupes. The sound of youthful laughter coming from a corner of the room caused him to direct his eyes to three companions gathered around a table, on which another round of drinks were being deposited by a barmaid.

'I'll wager you a guinea to guess her name!' called one of the trio as the barmaid put their drinks in front of them.

'Bertha!' shouted out his companion. 'The most beautiful, bewitching barmaid, Bertha!' And he slapped down a shilling on the table.

His associates burst into gusts of laughter, one leaning back on his chair and running his hand through his mop of curls, and the other loosening his bright, silk cravat as if to ease the passage of his humour.

'Daisy!' One of them banged his tankard of ale on the table, its contents partly sloshing over the rim. 'The devilishly, depraved, Daisy!' he hooted, and threw a shilling from his own pocket onto the table.

'She looks …' the one with the mop of curls choked back a laugh, 'more like …' choking again, 'a … a Winifred to me. Winifred the … ah … the … the wondrously wicked waitress.' He broke into hysterics at his own cleverness and threw in a shilling of his own.

Trevanion smiled to himself. He could relax and enjoy his chops and ale at leisure, for here were three of the likeliest sitting ducks that he had ever seen in his crooked career. The more they drank, the more careless they would become with their money, and the more brandy flowing through their veins, the more reckless they would become when seated at a card table.

Upstairs, Henry Seymour was beginning to wonder what was taking Trevanion so long. He had only drunk soda water so far this evening and was desperate for a glass of ale but when he had a game in mind, he had to keep his wits very much about him. There were a number of ploys which he and Trevanion used and this evening, Seymour was about to transform himself into Count Nicholas of Mecklenburg-Strelitz, cousin to Prince Albrecht of Prussia. He had practised adopting an air of regal arrogance which he imagined a Prussian aristocrat might possess. He attempted a few staccato phrases in what he hoped sounded like a Prussian count who spoke some English with difficulty. And of course, for anyone who knows anything about Count Nicholas of Mecklenburg-Strelitz, it was obvious that he had contracted polio as a child and consequently walked in the manner of a cripple.

Trevanion had finished his dinner and had approached the table of the trio of jokers, and introduced himself with the accent of an eminent member of the house of Mecklenburg-Strelitz, making a small bow.

He lowered his voice. 'Gentlemen, may I introduce myself to you. I am Freidrich von Hovenberg, diplomat, in the service of the royal family of Prussia.'

The trio of young men had been stopped in their laughter, and the young man with the bright silk cravat looked up at Trevanion, his mouth slightly open in wonder.

'Forgive me for the intrusion, but I could not help noticing that you enjoy a little wager, yes?' He glanced in the direction of the barmaid who had been the subject of their humour a while earlier and the trio nodded with amusement.

'There was due this evening a card game with two of my associates in the diplomatic corps. Sadly, the gentlemen were involved in a carriage accident earlier this afternoon, and we are now short by two players. If I can interest two of you gentlemen, you would be assisting me with a great favour,' he continued.

Trevanion put his hand in his pocket and retrieved two gold sovereigns which he put down on the table.

'A little gift as … how you say … an incentive?'

The three young men looked on with disbelief at the large sum of money.

Trevanion lowered his voice further. 'My employer is from a noble background, and will be most disappointed if I am unable to indulge his pleasure. He has no interest in money, and rarely wins, but he enjoys the diversion.'

A moment's hesitation was followed by a sudden burst of activity as the curly-haired youth and the young man with the bright silk cravat reached out and slapped their palms down on the coins in a greedy manner.

'Hah! Bad luck, Mildmay!' they laughed at their associate. 'You will have the pleasure of watching, so it seems.'

Trevanion, in the guise of Friedrich von Hovenberg, made another bow, and then indicated that they should follow him to the salon upstairs.

'The count is staying at the Hotel Continental in Regent Street, but he enjoys the amusements offered here in your little English side streets.'

The two young gentlemen, who by now had introduced themselves as Rupert Hogg and Alfred Redmayne, raised an eyebrow in awe and mouthed the words 'a *count*', to one another as they ascended the stairs.

The upper salon of Thompson and Fearon's was as brightly illuminated as the room below but here the large space was divided by a dark-wood screen. On one side of the room was a stage for entertainment and on the other side chaises where, as the evening unfolded, ladies took up their station, draping their arms about the necks of men who loosened their waistcoats and braces, and drank whisky.

Seated at a card table, Henry Seymour smoked a cigar, a single gaslight illuminating his head. Trevanion and his new companions approached; Henry pushed back his chair and stood up immediately, almost momentarily forgetting his childhood disability and his aristocratic arrogance. He composed himself, remembered both, and with a scowl limped forwards, addressing Trevanion angrily.

'Where *haf* you been?'

Mildmay, Hogg and Redmayne looked at the man before them, dressed in an open-necked frilled shirt, and pair of grey trousers tucked into long boots, and had every reason to believe that he was indeed a count.

'Von Hovenberg! You keep me waiting too long. And where are Rudy and Rajewski?'

Trevanion bowed sharply. 'There has been an accident, sir. They are both injured. But by great fortune I have here two excellent gentlemen, who will join us in a game of whist, and this is their friend.'

Trevanion turned and motioned to a passing young woman with highly rouged cheeks that she should bring them a bottle of brandy. Henry Seymour looked suspiciously at Mildmay and extended his jaw threateningly; he did not want an observer at the table who might chance to notice his underhand dealings. With a swaggering gait he rolled towards Mildmay and menacingly put his face close to the young man's.

'Since when did Count Nicholas Mecklenburg-Strelitz need someone to watch him play cards, eh? Send him away!'

He circled Mildmay slowly with an ugly and unmistakable limp.

'The girls will entertain him, the *trink* will entertain him, but the count will *not* entertain him. Send him away! Send him away!'

Trevanion clicked his heels together, made a small bow, and then turned to Mildmay.

'Forgive his manners,' he whispered. 'Another time, perhaps?'

At that moment, the young woman returned with a tray of glasses and a bottle of brandy, setting them down on the table. Intrigued by her, Mildmay watched her disappear again behind the dark-wood screen, indicated with abstraction that the game was of no matter to him, and headed off to pursue her trail.

Trevanion gestured towards the table. 'Shall we?'

The four men took a seat. Trevanion poured four large glasses of brandy which Hogg and Redmayne, who were already rather drunk, eyed keenly. With frequent swigs at their own glasses yet not actually drinking anything, Seymour and Trevanion were well practised in the art of keeping their wits about them. Seated to left of Henry Seymour, Hogg was offered the cards, which he shuffled, and then passed to Redmayne, who cut them. Redmayne passed the deck back to Seymour, who began to deal. He threw the two young gentlemen a doubtful look.

'Count Nicholas hopes that you have more than gilt buttons to play with, *ja*? Rudy and Rajewski are wealthy men. They do not waste the count's time.'

'Do not fear, sir, the two gentlemen are here to win, and have the means to do so, yes?' Trevanion turned to Hogg and Redmayne and discreetly rubbed the side of his nose with his finger.

'Yes.' They both laughed a little nervously.

'What have they to offer the count then?' Seymour enquired.

'I have twenty shillings in my pocket,' offered Hogg.

'And I have a guinea,' Redmayne said.

Seymour got up from the table and made as if he was going to walk away. He snorted, 'Bah! The count is not here to play for mere shillings!'

Trevanion interjected earnestly, 'And the gentlemen have a gold sovereign each, is that not so, gentlemen?'

'Yes.' They both laughed again, their confidence rising a little.

'And what if the game becomes interesting and they wish to play for more than a few shillings, a guinea and two gold sovereigns?' Seymour asked with contempt in his voice. 'Don't they know that the count is a very rich man? Have they come here to insult him?'

'Not at all, sir, my father has an auctioneer house. Hoggs in Long Acre. I can sign a cheque in his name without fear.'

Emboldened, Redmayne proposed, 'And my mother has a collection of the finest jewellery ever to grace the London season.'

'And you expect the count to believe that?' he mocked.

'It is plain to see, Count. They are men of means and men of honour. Is that not so, gentlemen?' Trevanion appealed, thinking to himself that if he made no further success as a trickster, then the Regency Theatre would dearly love to employ him.

'Very well, then,' said Seymour and sat down again.

The two young men placed ten shillings each on the table, and Seymour and Trevanion did the same. Seymour turned over a card and placed it on the table: the six of spades.

'The suit is spades then, gentlemen.'

Redmayne took a mouthful of brandy and then followed with the five of spades. Trevanion played the five of hearts, Seymour could not follow suit and threw in the eight of clubs, and Hogg took his turn playing the three of hearts. The cards were played again, Seymour groused and grumbled in the guise of the disgruntled count, and Trevanion cursed at his own bad luck, until the play returned finally to Hogg, who laughed out loud and threw down the three of spades.

'Ha! My win, I believe, gentlemen.' He reached for his winnings on the table and drew them towards him.

'The luck of a beginner,' Seymour observed.

Hogg drained his glass and Trevanion was quick to refill it. Hogg winked at Redmayne and put in another ten shillings, the other players put in their stakes and another round was played. Now it was Redmayne's triumph as he threw in a trump card. Hogg slapped him on the back and topped up his companion's glass.

'I drink to your success, my friend!'

'It seems it is not the Count's night,' Seymour complained bitterly again; but everything was going exactly to plan.

The hands on the clock moved on. The upper salon, by degrees, grew more alive with the business of night. The stakes were raised, Redmayne and Hogg seemed unbeatable. Trevanion announced that he was about to withdraw. Seymour tempted him with the promise of more money but then lost again, and got up and limped around the table, grasping his hair. Redmayne grinned at Hogg, Trevanion called for another bottle of brandy and some water. Another round began: the Count threw in more money, saying his luck had never been so bad, and called for the stakes to be raised again. Hogg lit a cigar. This time, Trevanion put in four gold sovereigns. Redmayne took two large gulps of brandy and thumped his fist down on the table.

'Show the table four *sovereignsh*, Hogg, my man.'

Hogg pushed his sovereigns across the table. '*Ish* my lucky night, Redders, old *schap*.'

Two more rounds were played with Hogg and Redmayne winning again. Backs were slapped, the drinks were poured, cigar smoke swirled in the gaslight and with every penny on the table, Seymour and Trevanion rolled out their plan.

The count stamped his foot on the ground and growled, 'Here is my family signet ring.' He threw it on the table. 'And I will write a cheque for one hundred guineas; what are you prepared to stake, gentlemen?'

There was a moment's silence, the two young men looked at one another, and then Hogg gave a shout.

'A cheque for the same!' He reached for the pen which Trevanion had brought to the table, and scratched out a promissory note.

'My mother's *shjewellery....*' Redmayne belched, using the pen to scribble down his parents' address and pushing it to the centre of the table.

The barmaid, who had been the object of the young men's humour earlier in the evening, appeared from behind the dark-wood screen. Hogg drained his glass with a gulp, started to laugh and called out to her.

'Ah! *Ish* the devilishly depraved Daishy. Come and fill up my glass!'

He was laughing hysterically now and Redmayne was hysterical too. Seymour dealt the cards, slipping in an ace of hearts to the bottom of the deck which he finally dealt to himself. The round circled the table for the third time, Trevanion and Redmayne threw in their cards and shook their heads anxiously in turn. Finally, Hogg threw down the two of hearts. He leapt up from his seat and gave a great whoop.

'Redmayne, my man, we are *risch! Risch* beyond our *dreamsh*. Ha-hah!' He lay across the table and began kissing the coins, the signet ring, the pieces of paper, going from one to the other, and laughing again.

'The count has not finished,' Seymour said quietly.

Hogg was not listening, and kept his head bowed, continuing to kiss his winnings. Seymour raised his voice, heavy with inflected accent.

'I *said*, the count has not finished!' Seymour was holding his final card, and casting it with precision, it landed among the curls on Hoggs's head. Hogg kept his head very still, and Redmayne, who by now was looking very ill, reached for the card and slowly turned it over.

'Oh, God!' he moaned. 'It's an ace, Hogg. It's an ace.'

Hogg lifted his head from the table and Redmayne, who saw the room spinning before his eyes, bent over double and vomited on the floor. Seymour, observing the desperate state of his opponents, said with satisfaction, 'The money means nothing, gentlemen, but the count could never bear to be parted from the signet ring of the house of Mecklenburg-Strelitz.'

Well after midnight, Trevanion lolled contentedly in a maroon-coloured velvet chair, his one leg thrown casually across the arm.

From his mouth hung a cigar, on which he chewed and dragged alternately, and in his pocket a goodly sum of coins and two chits of paper. The evening had been a success beyond anything he had imagined and he allowed himself to indulge in a glass of whisky now. Seated opposite was Henry Seymour, who smiled at Trevanion and raised his own glass.

'To our future, *Count*,' Trevanion grinned.

'To the future *von Hovenberg*,' Seymour smiled, and in his mind he retraced the plan he had yet to carry out: to play the ultimate trump card against the man lolling opposite him in the maroon-coloured velvet chair.

CHAPTER TWO

TREVANION TOOK A handkerchief from his pocket, dabbing at his forehead. He stood before the mahogany desk of Edmund Marjoribanks in the offices of Coutts bank. A large fire roared in the grate, but it was not the heat which was troubling the unrepentant gambler. With some trace of embarrassment he explained his current position to the grey-haired banker.

'While I was sleeping that night, Seymour took everything from me. The winnings, the promissory notes, my own jewellery and some jewellery of Susan's which I had given him to look after.'

Marjoribanks was not moved with sympathy. 'And did it not occur to you that you were … ah … placing yourself in entirely the situation that you have now found yourself in, hmm?'

Trevanion felt a trace of irritation; of course he had not foreseen the situation. Had he suspected for a moment what Seymour had been planning, he'd have turned the tables on his companion and taken the upper hand himself.

'Seymour was an old and trusted friend, sir. I had no reason to mistrust him. Now everything I had is gone and I find that I am in a desperate position, which if my wife or Sir Francis should discover, I am ruined.'

'And you … ah, hoped that your sister-in-law might bail you out in some manner, I'll be bound?'

'Now see here, Marjoribanks, I know that you have never held me in high opinion but Seymour's efforts to ruin me could bring a stain upon the family name too, you know, and of course that is of great concern to me.'

Marjoribanks gave a snort. 'Trevanion, since the day that you stood next to Susan in church, you have never cared for anyone or anything except for those oily whiskers of yours or how much is in your silk-lined pockets. I ought to expose you entirely to the wrath of Sir Francis and be done with it but I am aware that he is worried about Lady Sophia's health at the moment. The stress would do him no good.'

'Well, those are my sentiments exactly, sir.'

Marjoribanks shook his head. 'I will make an application on your behalf to Miss Coutts for a monthly allowance, Trevanion, and if it does not quite meet your wife's expectations then you will have to find a way to explain the need for economy to her. Economy, sir!'

'A monthly allowance!' Trevanion's face burned with anger. 'But that is of no use to me.'

Realizing that he had no bargaining power he moderated his temper, and appealed. 'It is capital I am asking for. An amount that I might invest and … and realize further gain from. You are a man of business, Mr Marjoribanks; you understand.'

'I understand, Trevanion, that any such capital is only likely to be invested in a card came, and then I will find you here again in precisely the same predicament you are in right now.'

Trevanion thought of the little blonde-haired girl who was sitting in a carriage, waiting for him two streets away. He recalled that he had made promises to her which were fast becoming unreliable. It was capital he needed in order to make a clean break. An allowance would tie him fast to this family and he wanted to be free.

The door opened and a woman's voice offered reassurances to an unseen figure. 'I know that Mr Marjoribanks is not expecting me, but I can see myself in, thank you.…'

As she entered the room, Angela Burdett-Coutts's face fell at the sight of her brother-in-law.

'Oh, Trevanion. What a surprise. I don't believe we were expecting you in London.'

Trevanion's brain was already several steps ahead and he immediately saw his sister-in-law's presence as an advantage; women were his speciality. He turned his blue eyes upon her, adopting an air of the pathetic.

'Angela, sister, you could not have arrived at a sadder moment.'

Her heart stilled at his words.

'I hope that there is not bad news from home?'

She looked at Marjoribanks with concern in her face. Her father had last written that her mother had been under the weather, but that it was nothing more than dyspepsia.

'I think that you could say that it is very *close* to home, Miss Angela. I believe that I have some bad news for you, sister,' Trevanion said.

Angela looked from her brother-in-law to Marjoribanks, hoping that the older man would enlighten her as quickly as possible.

Trevanion continued in a plaintive manner, 'I have been robbed, sister, robbed by someone whom I considered to be an enduring friend.'

He began to pace the patterned burgundy carpet.

'It is bad enough that I have been betrayed by a companion that I trusted, but the fact that he has taken everything from me will surely finish Susan. And what shame my circumstances might bring to your father, and your poor mother already unwell. It is a bad position, sister, and I find myself appealing entirely to your own spirit of kindness to relieve me of this situation.'

Marjoribanks stood up and offered his chair to Miss Angela, but she declined, sensing that Trevanion had duplicity as his motive. She intended to be on her guard. Marjoribanks took his seat again.

'Your brother-in-law has not told you the setting for this sorry situation, Miss Angela. And you should know it all so we can decide how I should manage it.'

In the early months of Miss Angela's good fortune, Marjoribanks would have spared her the embarrassment of touching upon the subject of gaming tables, but he had found that time spent in her new circumstances had equipped the young woman to be entirely unafraid of a man's world.

The rueful expression on Trevanion's face turned to a scowl.

'Sir, you cannot expect a young lady to be party to such a conversation!'

Angela nodded with understanding.

'Ah, I see. So am I to believe that this incident came about as a result of the art of speculation?'

Trevanion's laugh was a sleazy one.

'Well, upon my word, sister, how life has educated you.'

'Mr Trevanion, I'll thank you to remember that you are in the presence of a lady, and to remember your ... ah, manners, sir,' Marjoribanks warned.

Trevanion bowed his head with mock graciousness.

'But of course, I apologize for my vulgarity, sister.'

Angela pulled at her left glove finger by finger and briskly removed it, followed by the right one.

'Mr Marjoribanks, please will you draft me a cheque for a thousand pounds to sign?'

Trevanion's face was a picture of delight.

'Why, sister. This is exactly the kind of generosity that one might expect from someone with such a reputation for charity.'

'Ah, no. You misunderstand me, Trevanion. This is not charity, this is business. I am building a school in Spitalfields where I intend women and children to learn practical skills. Anyone who is willing to work will be educated and found useful employment. And if the poor are willing to work for their living, then I can expect no less from you.'

A look of scorn crossed his face and he leaned across the desk, appealing to Marjoribanks. 'Surely she doesn't expect me to attend this school for paupers? Has she lost her mind?'

'On the contrary, brother, I plan to minimize the costs of the building project so that my wealth is used advantageously. There are many more projects that I would like to patronize and I don't intend to employ my money in a wasteful manner. My proposal is that I will engage you in the post of a surveyor. You seem to have a liking for numbers so you will advise me on the procurement of building materials, oversee the financing of the project and issue me with detailed progress reports at every stage. In return for this, a set monthly allowance will be released from the account to be paid directly to your creditors. The bank will be instructed that a capital of one thousand pounds cannot be touched, and if you disappear the account will be closed immediately.'

Marjoribanks glanced up at a portrait of Thomas Coutts hanging on the wall, and acknowledged that he had been absolutely right in entrusting his legacy to this shrewd young woman.

'You are expecting me to work?'

'I am indeed, brother, I don't believe it will do you much harm.'

Trevanion opened his mouth, but nothing intelligible came from it.

'Well, Trevanion?' Marjoribanks dipped a pen in the inkwell upon his desk.

Trevanion turned away from his sister-in-law, a black look upon his face. He folded his arms defensively and without saying a word, gave a brusque nod of his head.

CHAPTER THREE

Mr Charles Wheatstone stood alone in the conservatory at the back of Stratton House, his hands behind his back, staring out at the gardens. The hothouse opening out onto the garden had become one of Wheatstone's favourite rooms, a place where he and Miss Angela had spent many hours examining the different shrubs and flowers, talking of her charitable work and his hopes for future patents. Beads of perspiration had begun to form on his top lip. Wheatstone had not realized that he would be so nervous.

A slim figure came into view, walking briskly across the lawns towards the house. She was carrying a bunch of long-stemmed lilies and her face was full of contentment. Looking up to the conservatory, Angela caught sight of her visitor and anticipation rose in her stomach. It had been some weeks since she had last seen Wheatstone and she was sure that it was his waistcoated figure she could see through the conservatory doors. Her smile became a laugh as she drew closer and she raised a hand and waved at him.

His brother, William, had teased him that he was soon to become one of the richest men in England when the heiress proposed to him. Wheatstone was alarmed at the suggestion and had rejected the idea as preposterous; he and Miss Angela were nothing more than friends. But on his last visit, he had suddenly noticed how her eyes sought his as if she was trying to read his thoughts and he realized that his brother's prophecy was not so far from ridiculous after all.

He watched as Angela's brisk walk turned into a gentle run.

She had been desperate to see him. She pushed open the door and noticed that Mr Kilburn had oiled the hinges and he had left a sticky residue on the handle.

'Oh, how careless!' she remarked to herself, and then wondered where to lay down her flowers and how to wipe her hands. 'Charles, I had no idea that you were coming. Look at me, I am a mess, and not at all fit to receive you.'

'On the contrary, you look … very well, Miss Angela.'

She had found that the sun on her face seemed to help the rash which afflicted her still, and softened the harsh redness to a kinder shade.

He took out his handkerchief and offered it to her.

She laid down the flowers on a small ironwork table and took the handkerchief from him, opening it out and wiping her hands on it.

'As usual, you are my true companion and have come to my rescue in an instant.'

He shifted uncomfortably. 'I … I wish it were true, but …'

Her face changed to one of concern and she ceased wiping her hands asking, 'Is something wrong, Charles? Are you upset with me in some way? I would hate to think …'

'No, not at all. It is I who must seek *your* forgiveness.'

She sat down on the bench next to a large potted fern by the conservatory door, and indicated that Wheatstone should join her.

She held out the handkerchief to him in return.

'Come now, my dearest friend, I am only disappointed that you have taken so long to visit. And you have not answered the last two letters which I sent you. But I know that you have been absorbed in your most recent experiments. Will you believe me when I say that you are completely forgiven?'

Wheatstone declined her invitation to sit and knew that he must make a start on what he had to say, or he would lose courage altogether.

'I'm afraid that this is not a social visit, as such, Miss Angela. I …'

She laughed nervously. 'Why, Charles, you look so serious. You have taken the time and trouble to come across town, now surely you can find it in your heart to stay. Please come and take a seat and I will call for some refreshment. It is neglectful of Hannah to have left you waiting for me.'

'No, I asked that she … I mean, I didn't mind waiting.'

The easy conversation that had long been established between them had changed in a moment and she looked at him, trying to make sense of the reason behind it.

'Charles? Are you sure nothing is the matter?'

His eyes met hers very briefly and then he lowered his head, shaking it.

'Please, Miss Angela, allow me to … to say what I have been rehearsing for some days.'

'But of course, please go ahead.' Her smile was uncertain.

'Thank you.' He clasped and unclasped his hands and began to pace the tiled floor of the conservatory.

'You may not realize it, but I had known little feminine company before my friendship with you, Miss Angela, and I never longed for it or … or sought it. But you listened so intently to talk of my work and encouraged me whenever I expressed self-doubt that I began to believe that you viewed me, not merely as a scientist, but … but in the light of a dear personal friend.'

She interjected, 'Why, yes, that is precisely my view, Charles, you know it….'

He held up his hand, 'Please, Miss Angela, allow me to finish before you speak.'

She nodded apologetically.

'The capital you are investing in my inventions is surely changing my life and the regular visits which I make to your home have benefited me in a way that you … you cannot imagine. I could hardly speak, ma'am, before I enjoyed your company and now I can converse with greater ease than I ever thought possible. And the satisfaction this has brought me caused me to entertain the belief that perhaps I … I might be in love with you.'

At these words Angela stood up and held out her hands to him. 'Oh, is it possible? I had begun to believe, but …'

He indicated that she should resume her seat. 'Please remain seated, Miss Angela, I have not finished.'

147

She obeyed him immediately, her eyes full of hope.

'I have a cousin, a distant cousin named Emma, who recently came to the shop to purchase a flute. I … I had never met her before and it was my brother William who served her. He spent a great deal of time demonstrating the range of octaves available. He's always very helpful to the customers like that, you know.'

Angela gave a small smile, encouraging Wheatstone in his story, which seemed to have no bearing on the fact that he had just stated he believed that he might be in love with her.

'My cousin purchased the flute and then she asked my brother about me.' He swallowed. 'I suppose that she had read something of my work and she wondered if she might meet me too. We are family, after all.'

He seemed to offer this as mitigation for something, and Angela began to wonder why he thought this sentiment might be deserving of reproach.

'Well, of course,' she agreed.

'She stayed for tea and I … William and I … we entertained her. William played the concertina for her, and she asked me about my inventions and I showed her the patent for the "Certain Improvement in the Construction of Wind Instruments."'

'Well, my dear Wheatstone. How pleasant that you should find so much in common with a newly discovered relative. But I do not see the reason for the sadness in your eyes. Has something happened to the young lady?'

Wheatstone was searching for words, words which would explain the difficulty of the position he found himself in. If it had been an electrical circuit that he had had to complete, the connections would have been without fault. If it had been the reed pan of a concertina he was constructing, the music flowing from it would have been a thing of beauty, but the science of words had never come easily to Mr Wheatstone and instead what he said next was clumsy, and entirely without consideration for a woman's vanity.

'I believe, Miss Angela, that I have found in Emma the … the meaning of completeness. I realize now that what I thought was love for you, was mere glory in your praise of me. I know that now. And then when William said that you might ask me to marry you, it did not seem right to allow you to believe …'

Angela's face flushed red with emotion. 'Charles, I …'

'I have asked Emma to be my wife and I have come to tell you that I will not be visiting you again. Please believe me when I say that … that the friendship we have shared has been very important to me. You have shown faith in my work, and the patronage you have given me has been more than generous.'

Angela turned her head away. She was trying to hide the tears which had sprung up in her eyes.

'But to allow you to continue to sponsor me and to cultivate the belief that I might …'

She interrupted him angrily, 'You can have no fear that I was trying to buy myself a husband, Mr Wheatstone!'

He was startled by her anger.

'Of course not, Miss Angela. I never thought that for one moment.'

'And it's quite ridiculous that you should cease your visits just because …' her tone had become clipped '… because you are engaged.'

Rising, she walked across the conservatory, still in possession of Wheatstone's handkerchief, her fingers folded about it tightly.

'Well, I am very grateful that you have made your feelings plain, sir, and I wish you and your cousin every happiness.'

At these words Wheatstone walked towards her, turned her around and fell down on one knee, taking hold of her hand.

'You are one of the kindest and most generous people that I know, Miss Angela, and … and what we shared between us in the way of friendship, I will never forget.'

She could hardly bear to look at him and she whispered, 'I suppose that it was too much to hope that you might ask to marry me because you loved me, Charles. I know that I am no great beauty but I hoped that the understanding we had in common was more than a meeting of minds.'

He opened his mouth to speak again; she pulled her hand from his.

'Please get up, Charles … Mr Wheatstone. You are making fools of us both.'

He nodded and stood up again. 'I'm so sorry. Truly I am.'

She was in possession of herself now and if there were any tears left in her eyes they sprung from anger, anger at her own foolishness as a woman.

Turning her back on him she said, 'I began my sponsorship of you, Mr Wheatstone, as a business venture and as an investment in the future of our country. I intend to continue that sponsorship and I will suggest that the bank asks to see progress reports on your work from time to time, to ensure that my money is not being wasted.'

'I really couldn't,' Wheatstone protested.

'I have already invested a small sum in your work, sir. Am I to see nothing for my investment? If I were to pull out now, then my capital so far would have been wasted.'

'As you wish, Miss Angela.' He nodded assent.

She reached for the bell sash to summon Hannah to show him to the door.

'I am grateful to you for so many things,' he offered.

'And I am grateful too,' she replied, a slight sharpness in her voice. 'I have learned a very valuable lesson, Mr Wheatstone. Never to confuse business with sentiment!'

The door opened. 'You called, Miss Angela?'

'Yes, Hannah, if you could show Mr Wheatstone out, please?'

He made a small bow with his head.

Angela realized that she was still holding his handkerchief. She held it out to him and taking it, their hands touched very briefly. With a polite nod he left her.

Crossing the room to the flowers scattered on the table, she collected them and asked that a jug of water be brought to her. Hannah assented and leaving the room, she inwardly acknowledged that she would shortly be writing to her intended, Dr Brown, to postpone the wedding again

CHAPTER FOUR

LEAVING GRAY'S INN Lane behind him, Dr William Brown made his way cautiously along a squalid alleyway. Lined with tottering tenements, their jagged faces leaned cheek by jowl as if seeking support from their neighbour. The doctor had been called for by a man seeking aid for his wife, and approaching the end of the lane, Dr Brown reached for his handkerchief. The day was airless: a sickening smell hung in the air and he knew it at once as the smell of fever. Passing beneath a low archway where the plaster was crumbling, he also found that a sewer had burst and its contents pooled in the yard. The doctor aimed his foot with care as he crossed the footpath.

Looking at the staggered dwellings, he knew they harboured several families each within their damp walls. The sound of a window being opened in an upper garret caused him to look up. A girl with a crying child on her hip nodded to him. Doctor Brown approached the front door and knocked. A few moments later and the same girl opened it. He estimated that she must have been about twelve years of age. Her feet were bare and the thin cotton gown which she wore would have offered her little warmth. He noticed inside the house that other children of differing sizes were sitting on the floor in semi-darkness.

Keeping his nose and mouth covered, the doctor entered and immediately saw his patient in a low bed in the corner of the room.

'How long has she been this way?' he asked.

'Since yesterday, sir. She tried to get up to see to see to my father's breakfast and to the children but she was too weak.'

He crossed the room and observed that the woman's hands were bluish and she was perspiring heavily. Taking her arm, he found her pulse to be weak.

The doctor turned to the girl and asked in a low voice, 'Are there many of you living here?'

'There's 'leven of us in all, sir. My father and older brothers are at work, and the lodger, Mrs Bishop, has gone to the pump to fetch water with her two children.'

'Can your mother not be moved upstairs where the air is fresher?'

'No, sir. The stairs ain't sure enough for her to be carried up them. And the roof is lettin' in the rain.'

'I see. Then if we cannot separate your mother from the rest of the family, is there no one with whom you could stay until she recovers? The clerk at the parish workhouse informs me that your mother's case is the fourth in as many days in this area.'

'There ain't nowhere else we can go. If you please, sir, won't you let her be taken to the hospital?'

'If it was my decision, miss, I would agree immediately, but we have no beds free at present and there are many more like your mother, I'm afraid.'

The girl's face fell.

'I'm sorry that I can do no more, miss. I have some camphor which you must administer in half-hourly doses. Give her plenty to drink and keep her cool. Once the fever breaks, she will start to regain her strength.'

They were empty words and he knew it. The disease would pass rapidly into its last stages and the woman would likely be dead by the morning. Only the girl's youth and strength might save her from following the same route as her mother.

As the doctor was leaving he turned to add, 'Keep the windows open and try to get the children outdoors as much as possible while she is ill.'

The girl nodded and thanked him.

'I will call again in a few days.'

*

At the sound of a knock on his door, Dr William Brown lifted his head away from the microscope on his desk.

The door opened and a maid entered.

'There's a lady to see you, Dr Brown, a Miss Meredith.'

'Miss Meredith?' He took his watch from the pocket of his waistcoat and examined the time. 'I was not expecting a visitor but the intrusion is a welcome one.'

He had been absorbed in thoughts of the recent cases of cholera in the parish and wished that he knew how the condition occurred. The diseases of poverty were well known to him and he was anxious to learn more about halting their spread. It was a mystery that men of science had yet to solve.

He stood up, tightened his white cotton cravat and took from the back of his chair his brown wool jacket, which he always removed when he was working.

'Do we have sugar for the tea?'

'I'm afraid not, sir. I bought poultry instead as you instructed.'

'Ah, that is a pity. Never mind, show her into the parlour, Kate, will you?'

Dr William Brown was a plain and simple man, whose moral conscience dictated that the basic comforts and conveniences afforded the rich, such as clean water and good food, and well-ventilated housing, should be the rights of the working classes too. He offered his services as a doctor without charge at the London Fever Hospital but made an adequate living as a medical man to some of the hospital's wealthy patrons. His lodgings at the hospital were modest and found no conflict with his principles.

Some time had passed since he had last seen Hannah, although they corresponded regularly. Their friendship had begun some years before when he had been attending Sir Francis Burdett at his London home. He admired the determined young governess and had been pleased to note that she appeared to admire him too. The months that they had been engaged had now turned into years, but his admiration for her had not changed.

As Dr Brown entered the room, Hannah, seated at the table, turned her head and smiled. His appearance was that of a man who had little interest in fashion but in his eyes was a kindness and compassion which no one of tender heart could fail to notice. She stood up and he immediately kissed her cheek.

'Hannah, you should have told me to expect you. I would have been able to receive you with better hospitality.'

She noticed that a button was hanging by a thread from his tweed waistcoat.

'William, you're not taking care of yourself at all!' she said with dismay, twisting the thread around the button and breaking it off sharply.

'That is why I need a wife to take care of me.' He smiled, raising an eyebrow in mischief, trying to take hold of her by the waist. She caught his hand and gave him a warning look.

'The maid, William!'

He laughed and, taking a wooden chair from the table, he sat down opposite her.

'You look well, Hannah,' he continued, 'And I can tell you that your visit is a welcome diversion. There's been an increase in the number of cholera cases admitted these past few days, all from the same area of the city. I've been working late into the night.' He leaned forward, eager to hear what she had to say. 'Come, tell me of your news so that I might know that there is life and light outside this place. How is Miss Angela?'

Hannah's smile faded.

'She works very hard. There is always some new cause she wishes to devote herself to.'

'But surely she must understand that you wish to be married?'

Hannah shrugged. 'I think that she has forgotten about our engagement. She used to speak regularly of a time when she would let me go, but now she speaks as if I will be at her side when she is an old maid.'

'Then you must remind her, Hannah, you have every right to a life of your own.'

'But I can't help worrying about her. Remember when I wrote and told you about the disturbing incident of the break-in some time ago? She insisted that her father was never told of it because she feared he would demand her return to Derbyshire. Since then there have been more letters, obscene letters which appear to come from a madman, and there is a gentleman who has begun to appear before her often when she goes about town. He swears that she gave him a silver locket and promised to marry him. She is rarely able to walk far from the steps of her carriage without looking over her shoulder.'

'I hope that *you* are not in any danger.'

'I don't believe he even knows I am at her side. His obsession is with Miss Angela entirely.'

'How terrible for her. How in God's name does she cope?'

'She copes remarkably well. There are times when I am in awe of her.'

'You have been such a devoted companion to her, Hannah, no one could ever question that. But if she will not allow her father to offer her protection, then you must not take this burden of care upon yourself.'

'I cannot help it, William, I have known her since she was a girl and to leave her vulnerable goes against my sense of duty towards her.'

'Is there no sign that she might accept a sensible offer of marriage?'

'I hoped that there might be. There was a time when she became very fond of Mr Charles Wheatstone.'

'The scientist?'

'Yes, I think I wrote and told you of his visits.'

'And you thought that he might propose?'

'I thought that it was very likely. They seemed to be so much of one mind. But it seems that he fell in love with someone else and although she tried to hide her disappointment, I can tell that Miss Angela is broken-hearted.'

'Is there no one else whom she might accept?'

'Oh, she has had many offers since the day she first inherited. As you know, the newspapers never leave off speculating who may be the next to propose to her. But the men she keeps company with are either married, or old enough to be her father. It's as if she surrounds herself purposely with men she cannot fall in love with and her energies are focused more than ever on her charitable goals. I don't think that she will ever marry now.'

'And so you intend to give up your own hopes of marriage and devote yourself entirely to Miss Angela, is that it?'

'William,' she appealed, 'you must understand. I am not thinking just of *my* future but of yours too. You have waited patiently for too long. I cannot ask you to wait any longer.'

'Then do not ask it,' he said. 'Let me do it willingly.'

'But if Miss Angela does not marry, you will be waiting indefinitely when there is a chance that you might meet someone else.'

'I have no desire to be married to anyone else, Hannah. Our engagement is a promise that I do not intend to go back on, unless of course you wish to break it.'

She stood up and went to him immediately, taking up his hands in hers.

'If you do not wish it, then nor do I.'

The door opened and as the maid entered with a tray of tea, the lovers broke apart and resumed their seats.

'Thank you, Kate, we can serve ourselves.' The girl nodded and retired.

While the doctor poured the tea, Hannah reached inside her purse and withdrew a letter.

'I almost forgot to tell you, Miss Angela has written to you. I have no idea what is contained in the letter.'

'A letter for me?' the doctor queried.

He opened the letter and read it through.

'Miss Angela would like me to consider offering my services to the school she built in Spitalfields. She is offering me a small monthly wage as a retainer for my services.'

He folded the letter in half and lifted his eyes to Hannah.

'Perhaps this is Miss Angela's way of indicating that we should marry soon, after all. Think of it, Hannah: with this extra money I can afford to leave these lodgings and move closer to you in Piccadilly.' He took her hands. 'Let us set a date now. I will accept Miss Angela's offer and begin looking for accommodation immediately. You can continue to work just as you do; you will not have to choose.'

At the realization that this man was not like any other she had known, nor would ever be likely to encounter again, she nodded.

Her life could be something more than it was now and the thought filled her with happiness.

'Very well. We will set the date for a month's time and Miss Angela must agree.'

CHAPTER FIVE

THE GLASS AND the silverware shimmered in the candle-lit dining room of Stratton House. Seated at the top of the table, Angela Burdett-Coutts, dressed in an ivory silk gown, looked like the woman of influence she had now become. The soft lighting was kind to her complexion, her gestures were graceful but emphatic, and the confidence that she exuded as a woman of property gave her an appearance which could be considered not displeasing to the eye.

Sitting to her left were Mr Charles Dickens and his wife, Catherine, whose bracelet had just dropped into her soup. She was attempting to rescue it surreptitiously with a fork.

'For heaven's sake! Leave it, Catherine,' her husband whispered sharply. 'I will have a quiet word with the footman and ask that it be retrieved later.'

His pretty plump wife complied demurely.

To Miss Angela's right sat the politician Lord Ashley and his lovely wife, Lady Emily Cowper. It had been in the act of examining the exotic plait of Lady Emily's hair that Mrs Dickens had spilt her soup, and lost her bracelet trying to dab the splash from her dress.

The purpose of the intimate dinner was to bring together those who had recently assisted Miss Angela in acts of philanthropy. Her current occupation was with the matter of the pitiful housing in the labyrinth of lanes around Westminster, a place where she had ambitions to improve not just the buildings, but to offer hope of gainful employment to the residents there. Against the counsel of Marjoribanks, she had asked a constable to accompany her there so she could see the truth for herself. She had shaken her head in disbelief at the mounds of ashes and refuse, among which were houses, shored up with blackened beams, sinking into the water-logged ground.

Sitting at the foot of the table, Hannah Meredith was reluctant and resentful. She felt out of place and had no wish to be a part of this soirée. Her mind was elsewhere on matters more personal: thoughts of marriage to Doctor Brown. The weeks had passed since she had last seen William, and in each of the letters she had sent she had reassured him that she would speak upon the matter shortly and give him a date for their wedding, but so far both the circumstances and the courage had failed her.

Earlier that evening she had protested to Miss Angela that she did not feel well enough to come down to the dinner, as she had a headache. Miss Angela knew well that Hannah found her social position a difficult one but insisted that she was more than fit to dine with Lord Ashley. At the same time – in the dressing room of his home in Devonshire Terrace – Mr Dickens had also found himself in need of reassurance: what kind of trousers should one wear in the company of a peer of the realm?

Dabbing asparagus soup from his mouth, Lord Ashley turned to Miss Angela and said, 'So I asked Dr McMichael whether he believed that any curative process was actually going on in the lunatic asylums of London, as my own inspection found that they seem to be a place simply for dying and nothing more.'

'And could he give you an affirmative answer?'

'Ma'am, he could say nothing in their favour at all. The patients held in such places sleep naked on a bed of straw, are chained up like animals, and they are only washed clean of their bodily waste every two days in water which is nothing short of freezing.'

'My dear!' Lady Emily protested. 'Perhaps Mrs Dickens does not wish to hear of such things.'

Miss Angela frowned and she interjected snappishly, 'As women, we cannot hope to be enlightened if we remain insensible to such matters.'

Mrs Dickens, who had been anxiously watching the disappearance of her favourite bracelet at the hands of a footman, nodded abstractly and said, 'Quite so.'

'So what do you propose, Lord Ashley?' Miss Angela persisted. 'Will parliament accept your findings and improve these conditions?'

'Well, I have had to concede that there have been some improvements under the earlier County Asylums Act but still too few of these places have a resident physician. And it is heartbreaking to see children of unstable mind removed from the workhouse, only to be placed in these hell-holes instead.'

Lord Ashley turned to Mr Dickens and asked, 'I'd be interested to know what you think, Dickens. I have read your books, and you write about the plight of our little ones with such feeling.'

Mr Dickens, who had worked as a boy of twelve in a blacking factory when his own father had ignobly found himself in debt, had indeed written from his heart; a heart which still raged against those shameful circumstances and which had made him the man of success that he was now.

'Sir, the act which you introduced into the Commons to restrict the working hours of children to no more than ten per day was a great aid to improving a child's chance of education. I further believe that the availability of ragged schools will help to lift many of them out of poverty.'

The butler served the lobster.

'Mr Dickens has been a great aid in a number of my charitable projects,' Angela said with gratitude, 'and I have him in mind to assist me with some of my other fledging ideas.'

Dickens inclined his head. 'Indeed? Then I am greatly honoured, Miss Angela.'

'Yes,' continued the hostess, 'after one of my recent visits to the Magdalen Hospital, I have in mind a proposal which I hope will offer better prospects to fallen women.'

At the mention of her husband's potential involvement with women of the street, Mrs Dickens was greatly alarmed. Her husband was a handsome man, whose fame had caused him to be mobbed in the most improper manner during his recent reading tour of America. She didn't like the thought of his entanglement in something which sounded so unsavoury.

But Mr Dickens rarely paid heed to his wife's opinion and so Catherine nodded and simply said, 'Quite so.'

Miss Angela continued, 'I also hope to utilize the skills of Dr Brown, who has recently accepted my offer to work at the school in Spitalfields.'

'Yes, I remember you introduced him to me when you invited me to see the school myself,' Dickens replied. 'What a fine man! A principled man!'

'The lobster is really excellent, Miss Angela, my compliments to your cook!' Lady Emily remarked.

The guests continued to enthuse among themselves over the food, but at the mention of Dr Brown's name, Hannah, who had contributed very little to the conversation, turned her attention upon her mistress.

'Do you think that Dr Brown will have the time to manage any other duties?' she asked in a low voice. 'I believe that he now has other plans of ... of a personal nature.'

'Really excellent!' Lord Ashley agreed, shaking his knife in appreciation of the dish before him. He turned to his wife and said, 'You must ask for the recipe, my dear.'

'What other plans?' Miss Angela replied to Miss Meredith beneath the buzz of gossip.

Hannah had found her courage now and began. 'Your offer of work at Spitalfields has enabled Dr Brown to move closer to Piccadilly and we—'

'Well! That is an excellent plan. I shall have him closer at hand to put him to good use.' Angela smiled at the guests sat around her table, who were engrossed in eating and general chatter.

In response to a gesture from Miss Angela, the butler moved from the sideboard and began serving the wine.

The colour in Hannah's neck rose. 'If I may say so, Miss Angela, the doctor is not your personal property. To be used for whatever fanciful purposes you might wish to turn your attention upon to amuse you!'

Mrs Dickens turned to address Lady Emily. 'Madam, I have

been secretly admiring your hair. I'm afraid my own maid is a little out of date in matters of style.'

Angela lowered her voice to a whisper and fixed a warning look upon her companion. 'Hannah ...'

'How kind of you, Mrs Dickens.' Lady Emily patted her hair.

Miss Meredith had now lost all sense of propriety and continued in a low sharp voice, 'The doctor has moved to Piccadilly with the intention that we set a date for our wedding, not to convenience you or suit your own particular plans!'

Angela smiled affectedly, glancing about the table, trying to ensure that her guests had no hint of the discord.

'Ah, Hannah, what a wit you are. And so you shall set a date for your wedding, but I need you to accompany me to Brighton next month. I think a spell at the Royal Albion Hotel would be good for both of us. And after that ...'

The footman who stood behind Miss Angela's chair shifted his eyes to the butler and raised his eyebrows with alarm at the sight of Hannah's growing rage.

The butler caught his meaning, bent down to Hannah's ear and said gently, 'Miss Meredith, would you just care to come out into the hall a moment, I ...'

Hannah stood up, dropped her napkin upon the table and said quite firmly, 'I am afraid that it won't be possible for me to accompany you to Brighton or anywhere else, Miss Angela. The doctor and I intend to wed immediately and although I will continue my duties with your permission during the usual hours of the day, I intend to take up a life of my own outside of those duties.'

'Hannah, please!'

'And may I also say, that for someone who shows such charity to the neglected and forgotten, in your blind ambition for such matters you have become selfish towards those closest to you!'

She nodded her head in apology to the other guests. 'And now I really must be excused. Good evening, everyone.'

With her face burning, she turned and left the room, which had fallen silent.

'I can only apologize—' Miss Angela began.

'Come,' interjected Dickens cheerfully, 'let us not abandon our merrymaking. The food is exquisite and there is nothing in the world so irresistibly contagious as laughter and good humour.' He raised his glass. 'A toast to the marriages of fearfully obstinate companions.'

After a moment's hesitation, the guests laughed and raised their glasses.

'The marriage of fearfully obstinate companions!'

CHAPTER SIX

3 August 18—

> *Whatever months and years may pass,*
> *My fever for you remains …*

DUNN SWALLOWED A mouthful of mutton chop and, dabbing the gravy from his lips with a napkin, turned his eyes towards Belle, who was stoking the fire in the corner of the room. She sensed his eyes upon her and she turned to him with a small smile.

'I hope the meat is tender, sir?'

He nodded but did not speak, unsure as to what tone he should adopt to answer her. The meal was the first that he had enjoyed for some time seated at a table. He had a vague recollection of the girl feeding him while he was propped up in bed, her hand at the back of his head as he had tried to drink from a cup. Her hazy silhouette had been a constant in his dreams, and upon waking, wherever his eyes had fallen, she had been there. Of former times, his manner towards her had always been aloof but there had been a change in their relationship now. He knew that he owed her a debt of gratitude.

He could recall little about his illness. The doctor, called to his room by the girl, had diagnosed delirium brought on by pneumonia. It had been early March and although snow had come, Dunn had been circling Stratton House throughout the night, against a biting frost. There was a window which he knew always to be open and which he had often used to gain access to his angel to sit at her bedside, watching her through the night; but when he had last tried to use it, he had found it locked and was unable to force it, even in his anger.

The thought that there might be a man in her bed had incensed him. With the frost upon his fingers, he had struggled with the window once more in vain. If he could not reach her then he vowed he would act as a sentinel, pacing the outskirts of the house until sunrise came. In this manner he reasoned that he would be able to see who was coming and going. As morning dawned, he had seen the lamp alight in his angel's room and he stumbled home in the knowledge that she had awoken once more and was safe.

Belle had found him huddled by the fire in his room, gripping his arms and shivering. His was rocking back and forth, his lips moving rapidly, and he was talking to himself. His eyelids closing by degrees, he had turned to the girl and before slumping to the floor he had whispered, '*My angel.*'

In his delirium the room had swirled with shadows and voices, and Dunn had heard the doctor talk of an asylum. If it had not been for the girl insisting she would care for him, he would have been taken away; he was sure of it.

Swallowing down the last bite of his meal with a swig of ale, he looked at Belle again.

'Was I very ill?' he asked quietly.

She came to him immediately, picking up his empty plate and with her eyes lowered said, 'Sir, you frightened me very much, pulling on my sleeves and crying like a child.'

Dunn felt ashamed at the thought.

Belle did not tell him that she had sat at his side while the doctor had bled him and that she had tended to him with mustard poultices, checking on him frequently between her tasks at the coffee house. Although waiting upon him for some years, she had come to know very little of his life. Dunn paid his rent well in advance, and often left a generous gratuity in his room for service. From his books, the girl had concluded that he was a lawyer, but in the months before his illness she recalled that he had ceased to venture in the direction of the Sessions House entirely.

In the moments he had been asleep, she had found herself looking through his scant belongings for sign of a keepsake or a memento of someone he might call a beloved one. If he had ever paid a call then it was never returned, for no one ever came to ask for him. She had found his journal and dared to open it, frequently raising her eyes to check that he was not watching her. Finding a tendril of brown hair between the pages, her finger traced the words which she could read only with difficulty. The pages of Dunn's life were blank, but in this book another life was revealed and it seemed to be the life he believed himself to be living.

When he had been ill, he had looked into Belle's face in one of his moments of delirium and smiled – a smile of pure joy which changed his face completely, from a man with the darkest soul to a man of beauty – and she felt something stir in her heart. Never once in the years that she had known him had she seen an expression of happiness upon his face. In that brief moment, he had known for a certainty that here was someone who cared for him. It had been her privilege alone to nurse him: the man who was loved by no one.

Evening was falling and Dunn, seated at the table, reached for the newspaper the girl had put close at hand. Dated 14 June 184_. He turned the pages slowly, becoming absorbed. His eyes fell upon the society section.

Mr James Brooke, Rajah of Sarwak, has been awarded the Freedom of the City of London, appointed Governor and Commander-in-Chief of Labaun and Knight Commander of the Order of the Bath. The honours have been bestowed upon him in recognition of his ongoing support of the Sultan of Brunei. He will be entertained this evening at Apsley House at the pleasure of the Duke of Wellington and Miss Angela Burdett-Coutts in celebration of his new status.

A sketch of Mr Brooke in his uniform was accompanied by a sketch of Miss Burdett-Coutts and the septuagenarian duke. At the sight of it Dunn stood up, crushing the newspaper and hurling it onto the table.

'Predators!' he shouted.

The girl, who had left the room for a moment to take away the dishes, returned and saw her patient stumbling towards the coat stand.

'Sir, you cannot be thinking of going out?' She moved towards him, her hand outstretched.

He waved it away from him and reached for his coat, pulling it so hard that the coat stand fell over.

'Leave me be, Belle!'

'Sir, you have not long been on your feet. It will kill you if you go outside.'

'Get away from me! Don't you understand that she is in danger? I have to go to her.'

'Sir, there is no one in danger. Please, you are still not well … Richard, I beg you.'

At the sound of his Christian name, he was interrupted in his haste and he frowned. He could not recall the last time he had heard it from a woman's lips.

'Who gave you leave to know my name?' His eyes narrowed, he walked unsteadily towards her.

She backed away from him.

'I … I meant no harm, sir.'

'Then let me alone.' His voice was a whisper.

Bending down, he retrieved a walking cane which had fallen from the coat stand onto the floor. Momentarily he directed it at the girl, anxious that she was about to hinder him, but seeing fear in her eyes he lowered the cane and supported himself upon it from the room.

It was but a short walk along Piccadilly to reach the duke's residence from the coffee house, but Dunn was not yet strong enough to attempt it. He had quickly realized this by the time he reached the street, and instead he managed the short distance to a cab stop. He signalled a carriage and once seated, directed the driver to take him to Apsley House, the residence of the Duke of Wellington.

With the turn of the wheels, he wiped the spittle from the corners of his mouth with the back of his hand, murmuring to himself.

'Wellington, that grey-headed butcher! Thinks he can conquer a woman with his fantastic tales of heroism.'

He darted glances out of the window for signs in the gaslight that he was reaching his destination.

The direction in which he was headed was a fashionable drive for those who delighted in circling Hyde Park and crossing the Serpentine Bridge, but Dunn was in no mood for pleasure. The papers ran frequent reports of those who threw themselves into the river from that bridge and he understood why. He imagined sinking slowly, staring lifelessly into those murky depths, knowing that his last considerations would be *her* and how she had forsaken him.

Yes, perhaps he should end his pain, be damned with it all and ask the driver to take him to the lake. After all, was his own life not one of abandonment: a mother who had never shown him a moment's kindness, a wife who had left him, and now a woman who would not acknowledge that he even existed? Never once had she answered his letters, nor received him kindly when he had approached her in the street.

Nearing Apsley House, Dunn banged on the roof of the cab which drew up close to Hyde Park. He held on to the door frame as he climbed down uncertainly onto the pavement. The driver attempted to assist him but was refused, finding instead the fare pushed into his hand. The sound of Dunn's breath rasped in his ears. He rested upon the cane, walking with great effort towards the Palladian entrance of the house, which was surrounded by railings and lit with torches. At the sight of the footman opening the door to a guest, Dunn momentarily hung back until the door was closed.

Leaning upon his cane again he entered the front gate, cast his eyes around and made towards an oval window in the basement. He looked about him for a moment and then began to heave himself against the windowpane repeatedly, only stopping to catch his breath. The window eventually gave way and with care Dunn began to push himself through.

Lowering himself to the ground, he found himself in a gloomy passage where he took a moment to brush himself down. In the shadows and silence he could hear laughter coming from the rooms above. He walked towards the stairwell, reaching over to the balustrade for support. As he began his ascent with difficulty, he made an affirmation with each step.

'This time … you will not send me … away. I have the locket you gave me and … and,' he stopped to catch his breath, 'and now you must … fulfil your promise … my angel. You must!'

Dunn was almost at the top of the staircase, but hung back for a moment, observing the footmen walking back and forth with silver trays across the hallway. He followed their destination with his eyes and estimated the location of the dining room. At an opportune moment, he mounted the last of the steps and fixed his gaze on the room from which came the sound of good-humoured gossip.

'No one … will … come between us. I swear it!'

Step by step he leaned upon his stick and focused on the room ahead.

'Whoever dares … will regret it!'

Dunn reached the panelled doors of the dining room and he pushed them open with the force of his passion.

A large chandelier hung over the extended table which seated twelve. Not all of the guests took immediate note of the interloper, so engrossed were they in their gossip. Dunn's eyes fell upon his angel, who was seated only a matter of yards from him and dressed in a vivid-green evening gown. As her gaze was drawn in Dunn's direction, a cold flood of fear rushed through her. She broke off from her conversation with Rajah Brooke and the duke seated either side of her.

'I made a vow!' Dunn shouted, grinding his cane into the floor, partly in anger, partly for support. 'A vow that I would protect you!'

One by one the guests fell silent. Miss Angela reached for the duke's hand and clasped it.

He looked at her for explanation. 'Do you know this man?'

She was unsure how to respond, for although she had no knowledge of the man's name, he had become a familiar sight to her when she went out about town. He constantly attempted to speak with her as she left her house, calling after her in her carriage. One night she had awoken to find him sitting at her bedside, and had lain completely still with terror as he had cut a strand of hair from her temple before disappearing. She had told no one but instructed that each window thereafter had been nailed shut, and when he had been absent for some time, she hoped that at last he had ceased to follow her.

'I … I know his face, he has been a trouble to me for a long time but I know nothing of who he is.'

She felt the duke stir to his feet and she whispered sharply, 'No, sir, leave him. He may have a gun!'

Dunn shouted, 'I made an oath! And so did you when you gave me this.'

He reached in his pocket for the silver locket and believing he was about to draw a weapon, the Rajah jumped to his feet and shouted to a footman, bewildered by the disruption.

'Take him to the ground, man!'

Dunn launched himself at Miss Angela, and both the Rajah and the duke grasped him about the neck, the footman now coming to their aid.

Dunn attempted to free his head, and sought Miss Angela, gasping, 'You gave me this, you … you gave me this.'

His hand was outstretched but there was nothing in it.

'You said you would marry me!' he pleaded. 'And now instead you murder me! Murderess!' he screamed, struggling to free himself from the hold of the men.

'For God's sake, someone call a constable!' the duke shouted.

Two footmen came running into the room and with the aid of the third, dragged Dunn away, his arms flailing.

'I am not a stranger to you!' he shouted at Miss Angela. 'Tell them … tell them, I beg you, my … my angel. I am not a stranger.' He was sobbing now.

Angela's face was ashen as he was taken away.

'Oh, my dear,' the duke said, patting her shoulder.

She tried to compose herself, conscious that she had been the cause of a scene.

The Rajah poured a measure of brandy from a decanter and offered the glass to her.

'You were brave as a soldier, ma'am.'

Her hand shaking, she took a sip from the glass and handed it back to him.

'Thank you, Mr Brooke, you are most kind.'

'How the devil did the man know you were here?'

The duke was shaking his head: he was a man of military precision, and he did not like the idea that the enemy had caught him unprepared.

'Please, gentlemen, let us not discuss it now. You have guests, Duke, and I do not wish to occasion any further distress to them. Please take us through to the drawing room, and then entertain us with your picture gallery. I do not want the evening to be a catastrophe on my account.'

Mr Brooke inclined his head and gathered the guests together in a helpful manner, directing them to another room.

The duke took Miss Angela's arm.

'We must talk about this, young lady, and I will not be put off. I will heed your request for now but will return to this matter on another occasion. I believe your father should be told of this.'

CHAPTER SEVEN

Coutts and Co.
The Strand
London

16 August 184—

My dear Miss Coutts,

I am sorry to tell you that the solemn duty has fallen upon me, to inform you that in a matter of days, both your mother and your father have passed away.

I know what pain it will occasion you, knowing that this tragedy occurred when you were not at their side, but while you were out of town, your mother became unwell. Although the doctor was called, he could do nothing for her so your father insisted that I did not inform you until your return. Sadly, it seems that the loss of your own mother affected him deeply and this morning, he could not be roused from his sleep.

Your brother, Sir Robert, has been informed and called back to Foremarke to be with your sisters.

I await his instructions for the funeral arrangements but I must confess that I sense a lack of sympathy in his manner, and would seek your own gentle touch upon the proceedings.

I remain your humble servant,
Edward Marjoribanks Junior

*

THE SHORT JOURNEY from Foremarke Hall to the parish church took the carriage along a narrow country track. Gently rocked by the vehicle, her gloved hands folded in her lap, Angela Burdett-Coutts looked out on a world which had now declared her an orphan, and she was distracted in thought. Hannah noticed how the woman before her all at once had the appearance of a lost child: small and abandoned, torn and shaken. She reached into her purse and retrieved a small bottle which she offered to the woman dressed in black and seated opposite.

'Here. Take some of the tonic which William recommended.' She held out the bottle but Angela did not take it. 'My dear?'

Angela shrugged her shoulders.

'Of what use is it, Hannah? It will change nothing.'

'No, it will not change anything, but the doctor knows that you need to keep yourself nourished. Grief can be exhausting and you have eaten nothing again this morning.'

Hannah's voice became a backdrop to the scene which Angela looked out upon through the carriage window: a farmer moving his sheep to greener pastures, their feet splashing in the mud. The thought that her mother and father would not see the summer again took hold of her. Only days before, she had been in Brighton, walking on the beach, breathing in the salty air, the wind pulling gently at her hair. This shocking news had been unexpected.

Angela spoke very quietly. 'What is so hard to bear, Hannah, is that there was no warning at all. The holiday with you and William was such a pleasant trip to the coast and I was beginning to feel so much better than I had done for a while.'

The shadow of Dunn's figure came into her mind and Angela forcefully rejected it.

'I was thinking that I no longer had cause to look over my shoulder, and yet I realized that I should have been paying more attention to matters at home.'

She recalled the moment when she had heard the news. She had just returned to Stratton House and had been laughing as she'd undone the ribbon from under her chin, pulling the bonnet from her hair and remarking on how wonderful her trip had been. The black-edged envelope had severed that joy as soon as Mrs Mills, her face grave, had handed it to her mistress.

At the sight of it, Angela had found her thoughts drawn suddenly again in the direction of that madman, Dunn, and his frenzied letters. After the incident at Apsley House he had been arrested, brought before the Bow Street magistrates and held in Coldbath Fields Prison. There was no indication as to how long he might be held for, but Angela had taken the advice of her friends, who had counselled her to take a holiday and put this dreadful matter behind her.

She had been terrified to turn the envelope over and observe the handwriting for fear that it would be his. Hannah had looked with disapproval at Mrs Mills, whose determined expression indicated that on this occasion she was handling matters aright.

Seeing that the hand was not his, Angela had then prepared herself for what news the correspondence might bear. She held the letter in her hand, tears falling, anger rising. It was as if providence had chastened her for the size of her fortune and had now taken both of her parents in compensation.

'I begged the duke not to speak to Papa of that madman,' Angela reminded Hannah bitterly.

'I know, my dear, but the Duke of Wellington had his reasons. He knew for certain that once the newspapers caught hold of the story, your father would be bound to find out about Dunn and would be angry that he had not been told of his existence.'

'It was not the duke's decision to take! Since when has my life been directed by a man?'

'Angela, your father's death was not the fault of the duke any more than it was the fault of that maniac. He went out riding in a rainstorm after the death of your mother and caught a chill.'

Angela lowered her eyes to the ground.

'And you did not want to acknowledge it, but the doctor feared some time ago that your mother had cancer of the stomach. Her conditioned worsened suddenly, and when your father found that she had died in the night, it seems that the news affected him profoundly. The simple truth is that the effects of a chill took hold of him fatally. You cannot blame the duke for that,' Hannah concluded.

The carriage slowed and the horses stopped outside the ancient parish church, sinking tombstones at its entrance. A moment of silence passed between the two women before Hannah spoke again.

'Are you quite insistent at attending the ceremony?'

Angela drew the veil of her bonnet across her face. 'My brother has instructed my sisters to stay at home lest their emotions overcome them, but I have not allowed him to direct me so I will remain quite in possession of myself, Hannah, he need not fear.'

'I will remain at the back of the church and wait for you,' the governess advised.

As executor of the will, Edward Marjoribanks Junior, who had succeeded in his father's place, had attended to all the necessary arrangements but Angela had immediately seen to it that the servants at Foremarke had been reassured that they would be taken care of. If her brother was about to become heavy-handed in his dealings, she had every intention to see that not one of the workers at the estate was rendered without work or a home.

Stepping down from the carriage, Angela accepted the assistance of the driver and was followed by her companion.

The sound of a man's voice caused her to raise her head.

'You came then, sister?'

Her brother Robert made his approach, his face disapproving.

'Are you really willing to make a spectacle of yourself by being here? It is not at all necessary. Twenty minutes and the whole thing will be done.' He tapped his cane regimentally against his leg.

Addressing her brother quietly from behind her veil, she said, 'Any spectacle is being made by you, Robert. And it is rather an ugly one.'

His mouth was an arrogant pout which appeared to have been formed by drawing his lips against his upper teeth. His eyes moved briefly towards Hannah, who was standing remotely by the carriage, but he made no acknowledgement. He made a slight incline of his head in Hannah's direction, scorn in his voice.

'Why have you brought the governess?'

'Hannah. Her name is Hannah.'

'She should not be here. All of the servants are in mourning at the house.'

'Hannah is not a servant. She is my secretary, and since her marriage to Dr Brown, she continues to help me in my work. I don't think ...'

At the sight of the hearse approaching, Angela fell silent. Hannah moved towards her mistress, sensing her distress, but Angela indicated with a motion of her hand that she wished to remain unattended. She would not give her brother the satisfaction of seeing her weakness.

The stiff, military figure of Robert Burdett stood upright at the door to the church. He made a curt nod in the direction of his sister, indicating that she should fall into line at his side. She took no heed and lowered her head, instead merging by degrees with the black figures of ageing politicians and men of business who followed behind the coffin. In a moment she had disappeared among them, slight and spare, the desolate figure of a woman who appeared to belong to no one.

CHAPTER EIGHT

DICKENS CIRCLED THE desk in his study at Devonshire House, addressing Miss Burdett-Coutts, who was seated in an easy chair. He had a particular matter which he wanted to raise with her, but how was he to manoeuvre the conversation in order to bring it up? As an author, he had become the master at setting a dramatic scene, magnetizing an audience, and by means of emotive words, holding them captive completely. He had to find a way to similarly engage the woman sat before him.

He came to rest himself on the desk and – folding his arms with a casual air – suggested, 'What you need is something to absorb your attention, my dear Miss Angela, something to take your mind away from the sad events of recent times.'

Her eyes looking past him at the garden through the window, she inwardly remarked that she had in fact been thinking upon the same notion herself and had of late found that something in particular – or should she say *someone* in particular – had quite taken her mind away from all the things which usually preoccupied her. Lately that grey-haired gentleman had become a great comfort to her, almost like a father, allowing her to lean upon him emotionally in the way that she had allowed no other man to support her.

He was a man who had achieved considerable military success and had been decorated with a knighthood; a man who had forced the French to withdraw from Spain and Portugal; and when Napoleon had been removed from his throne, Field Marshal Arthur Wellesley had found himself created the Duke of Wellington.

Hannah had noticed the look of affection which had begun to shine in Miss Angela's eyes whenever that celebrated gentleman came to Stratton House, and that in his company she had begun to laugh again. When Hannah had been transcribing a letter of business for her mistress, she had noticed how the duke had taken it upon himself to correct Miss Angela's recommendations and rather than chide him for it, she had amiably deferred to his opinion. He had recently given her a portrait of which he was the subject, handsomely dressed in his regimental uniform; she had hung it above her desk. Hannah was not the only one to notice the appearance of the portrait, or to observe the change which had come over Miss Angela since its arrival.

Dickens had purposely invited her to Devonshire House to discuss an important matter with her away from the duke's influence, and he was mindful that the idea he wished to broach could just be as quickly quashed by the Iron Duke, whom she now seemed so keen to please. Personally he was finding the old man a damn nuisance. Whenever he chanced to call upon Miss Coutts, he either found her away at Apsley House, or not at home to him because she was dining with the duke. Surely she could not seriously consider the ageing adventurer as a suitor?

Refusing to be distracted by further thoughts of the Waterloo hero, Dickens knew that he had to appeal to Miss Angela on the basis of a woman's instinctive compassion. He was sure that the matter was one about which she would feel strongly enough to overrule any objection on the duke's part.

There was no need for Dickens to manufacture any excitement in his voice as he withdrew from the pocket of his vivid red waistcoat a green, cloth-covered book.

'Yes, what you need, Miss Angela, is a new cause that is unlike any other you have turned your attention upon.'

He pulled at the ribbons which held the journal shut and wagged the notebook at her saying, 'In here, are contained the details of all sorts of women – women desperately in need of your help.'

'Really, Mr Dickens, what have you been doing to chance upon such information?'

'Not chanced upon, Miss Angela, it has been a careful inquiry that I have been making. I have made several visits to the Coldbath Fields Prison in Clerkenwell to visit the governor there, a man very keen on moral reform.'

Angela frowned. 'My dear friend, you know that I am happy to assist through my various charitable programmes, but I cannot be expected to personally visit every woman in the Coldbath Fields Prison who is listed in your little casebook.'

Dickens stood up and began to circle his desk again, his excitement propelling him into motion.

'Ah, but what if those women could be found in a little home off Lime Grove, Shepherd's Bush? What if those women had been personally selected by the governor as being those not beyond hope of rehabilitation?'

Angela shook her head. 'You've lost me entirely, Dickens.'

'The prison does not merely hold those women as wicked by nature, but those who have become corrupt through starvation and poverty. Take the seamstresses, for example.' He prodded his desk for emphasis. 'During the early part of the London season, there are not enough hours in the day for them to make up dresses in the latest fashion. But when the season is over, so is the work, and many of the needlewomen fall into a low way of life simply to exist.'

Angela nodded thoughtfully.

'Or, in point of fact, domestic servants who have been seduced by their masters. Without a reference they have no chance of another post, and once more find themselves making a living on the streets.'

Angela nodded again and Dickens lightly struck the page of his notebook with the back of his hand.

'And see here, the case of two women held on bail for trying to commit suicide, merely to escape a way of life that they had become ashamed of.'

'And you say that these women can be found in a little home in Lime Grove?' Angela asked, with interest rising in her voice.

'Well, not exactly.' Dickens sensed her increased attentiveness and took his chance.

'What I actually said was, what *if* those women could be found in a little home in Lime Grove. You see, there is not such a home at the moment....' He cleared his throat nervously. 'But I have seen a house which could be used as such.'

Angela gave up her casual repose in the easy chair, turning her attention markedly upon him.

'What exactly is it that you are proposing, Dickens?'

He steeled his nerves.

'I'm asking if you might consider renting such a house, somewhere that such women of hope could reside as a small family, learn domestic skills that would enable them to emigrate, and start anew.'

The idea had taken its hold upon him for some months since he had begun visiting the prisons with a view to some research for his latest novel. At first, his attention had been taken by the debtors and then the hardened criminals; but next he had observed the surprising number of women inmates and found himself drawn into their world, longing to know their stories.

Intrigued, he had begun a casebook. Case number one had been Julia Mosley. At twenty-one she had come to London from Gloucestershire, seeking work after the death of her parents. In the streets of Devil's Acre, she had found herself drawn into a gang of pickpockets and had been caught and jailed. After six months, released back onto the streets, she knew of only one other occupation which would keep her out of the workhouse. Back in prison again, a fallen woman without any hope of a reference, her current sentence was almost up. She had told Dickens bitterly that death would be preferable to release. She was not in good spirits.

Case number two, Rosina Gale, was a former seamstress in the exact predicament which Dickens had outlined to Miss Coutts: a young woman with insufficient work to keep a roof above her head. Yes, if such women could learn skills which would give them a new life abroad and with a reference from the home, they could start again, he proposed.

'And am I to pay for them to emigrate too?' Angela's eyebrows were raised in astonishment.

Dickens pretended not to hear her, submitting another sorrowful case inscribed in his notebook.

'And see here, a woman of twenty-five who would have broken your heart, Miss Angela. On the streets since she was no more than fourteen, and in the employ of the most vicious of men. She had a terrible ragged scar across her eye and down her cheek and ...'

The image stirred a faint flicker of the familiar within Angela's memory and her curiosity was aroused. She leaned forwards with great interest.

'A scar, you say? Do you have knowledge of her whereabouts too?'

Dickens was pleased at the response. The appeal was going much better than he had hoped. He consulted his book, flicking through the pages.

'Ah, yes. Here we are, Mary-Ann O'Connor. She is still in the prison at Clerkenwell, but due for release shortly. The girl has been in prison many times before, and the houses of penitence would not take her in again as she had already been in the Magdalen Hospital but fell back into her old ways once more....'

Angela nodded slowly, the expressionless countenance of that young, adulterated girl coming back to haunt her; the memory of the felon who had taken his knife to her face.

She whispered softly to herself with recognition and quiet horror, '*He came back to take her away again.*'

'It was so pitiful, Miss Angela, it was like she was dead inside, I ...'

Angela took to her feet decisively. 'I'll do it, Dickens. Tell me exactly where this house is and I will instruct my solicitor to negotiate the price of a lease.'

Her resolve startled him for a moment. The time could not be better to strike a deal for all the necessary arrangements and his face flashed with light and motion.

He shook her hand with enthusiasm. 'I am in your debt, Miss Angela. You will not regret it. Of course, there will be builder's alterations to be made, furniture to be bought, fabrics for the girls' clothing, and a vegetable garden to be planted.'

She was still thinking about the girl with the scar, wondering if it was too late to help her and whether she really could be rescued by such a scheme.

'I will make one thousand pounds immediately available to you, to do with as you see fit, Dickens and—'

They were interrupted by a knock at the door and it was opened by Mrs Dickens, who entered with a boy of about nine at her side.

A look of irritation crossed Dickens's face. He did not want to be disturbed by trifling matters and his pretty, plump wife smiled apologetically.

'I'm sorry, my dear, but Charley here wished to bring our guest the cake that the children have made for her.'

Catherine nodded at Charley, indicating that he should step forward and Angela welcomed him warmly, ruffling his fair hair with her hand.

'What a dear boy you are. The confection looks delicious. You can tell your brothers and sisters that I am very grateful.'

He looked at his father for his approval, but Dickens was already busy at his desk again. He had sat down and begun flicking through his casebook, making rapid notes upon a fresh sheet of paper.

CHAPTER NINE

AT THE SIGHT of the fair-haired scientist in the newspaper, Angela's heart stilled. The sketch revealed him to be older than she remembered – his hair was receding now – but his expression still held that same look of apology. She had not seen Wheatstone again since the day that their friendship had ended, and she had not been able to forgive him for wounding her so deeply. It was only natural that he should have been flattered by the interest of an heiress but it had not been reason enough for marriage. She glanced away from the picture and reflected that perhaps she *had* been trying to buy herself a husband, after all. She should be grateful that Wheatstone had taken his time over the matter of love and had more noble motivations than money.

Angela had been true to her word and had continued to patronize his work, but all future dealings had been carried out through the bank and Mr Marjoribanks. Now, Wheatstone was a wealthy man in his own right and no longer had need of her patronage. The use of the telegraph was now in advanced use and Wheatstone had received a sum of £33,000 for the use of his invention. He had also been awarded the Royal Medal for his contribution to science. If her money had given him a point from which to launch himself, it was his own genius which had propelled him this far.

The noble figure of the Duke of Wellington reclined in a fireside chair, his legs stretched out before him, reading the newspaper in which Angela had caught sight of Wheatstone's news. He himself was absorbed by news of events in the Punjab: the sound of horse hoofs and gunfire echoed in his head and momentarily, he found himself transported back to the battlefield. How he yearned to be out there in India, in the thick of the action once more. His happiest years had been those in uniform.

On his feet he wore a pair of silk slippers, hand-made by his wife; the last present she had given to him before her death. Kitty had been gone more than fifteen years, and at her passing he had thought how strange it was that after a lifetime together, they had only understood one another at the end. As a man of honour he had kept the vow he made to her before leaving for war – if his prospects improved and her father's opinion of him should alter for the better he would return and marry her. Eight years later, he had not recognized the plain, portly woman who greeted him at the altar as the girl who had stolen his youthful heart. That disappointment had propelled his swift return to battle and the rest of their marriage had been conducted chiefly by letter. Kitty had been completely in awe of him, as was everyone, and he could not love her for it.

Now he had taken to leaving his slippers beneath the chair at Stratton House where he found himself quite at home. Angela, seated opposite, the papers for the purchase of the house in Lime Grove on her lap, had been telling him of her plans. The duke lowered his newspaper abruptly and looked up at her with his light-blue eyes.

'That's the third time you've sighed in the last half-hour.'

'I'm sorry, my dear. I was just thinking about the many paths one's life might take.'

'There's never anything to be gained by looking backwards, Angela.'

'I realize that, but there are some people for whom the path seems predestined, such as the women Dickens has identified for the Home for Fallen Women.'

The duke frowned and returned to his newspaper. 'You know my thoughts on that subject.'

'Yes, my dear Arthur, I do indeed.'

He shook his head vehemently. 'It's not to be countered, Angela. Such an idea is completely out of the question for you.'

'But I have already considered it, and made the funds available to Mr Dickens as we speak.'

'I might have known Dickens would be at the root of such an idea. I don't suppose he is putting a penny of his own money to such an ill-fated scheme.'

'He is a family man, my dear, as you know. His assets are bound up in his domestic life.'

The duke leaned forward, bewilderment on his face.

'Angela, have you lost your senses? Such a venture is bound for failure on every level. Your money will be wasted and those women will have lived off your kindness without any intention of change whatsoever.'

'Well, I disagree entirely. Dickens has made a careful study of the intended subjects, and the prison governor has marked them out as ideal candidates for rehabilitation.'

She referred to the papers, saying, 'The house is perfect. It will be nothing like the prisons or the houses of penitence. It will be a place that the women can call home. They will be like a family to one another.'

The duke was scornful.

'Such women are unruly, beyond change, Angela. And it is fool-hardy to believe otherwise.'

She turned her head from him sharply. 'That is such a narrow-minded view, and typical of your high-handed attitude, Arthur! They are not disobedient soldiers who should be flogged or shack-led in irons. They are daughters of misfortune, who have found themselves at the mercy of a cruel change of circumstances.'

Her face was flushed with anger and at the sight of it, the duke's own temper cooled, a smile playing about his lips. Not one of his men would have ever dared argue with him as she did.

'What are you smiling at?' she said crossly, her face turning back towards his.

Putting his newspaper to one side, he stood up, crossed the room to her side and kissed the top of her head.

'You will have your way, my dear. You usually do.'

CHAPTER TEN

A pamphlet by Mr Charles Dickens

I have been told by those that govern the prison that they see hope of virtuous inclinations within you still, and by means of such you can pass from this prison into a perfectly new life.

If you have ever hoped for a chance of escaping from your life of sadness, having a place to call home, peace of mind and the return of your self-respect, then I can offer you the certainty of all these blessings, if you will determine to prove yourself worthy of them.

You know the streets well and the cruel companions who cause you to practise the vice which marks you out from all other kinds of women. I appeal to you that you no longer need be hunted by the police, imprisoned over and over again or grow old in such a way of life.

I urge you to take this offer to begin life afresh....

Mr John Chesterton, governor of the Coldbath Fields prison, pondered with uncertainty at the words he had just read, folded the pamphlet, and placed it in the inner pocket of his jacket. Was it really possible? Could Dickens's idea really work? Experience had shown that such women could not change unless they committed themselves to the rest of their life within a convent. With uncustomary patience, Dickens had explained at length to Chesterton that Urania Cottage would not be run like the religious institutions which already existed to reform the fallen woman. On the contrary, from the moment that they stepped over the threshold the lives which they had formerly led would not be mentioned again.

They would not be expected to confess, pray and be penitent. Neither would it be necessary for them to embrace a life of religion. The reform was to be a practical one. An opportunity to learn skills which could offer them something which they had never had before: a chance of honourable employment.

O'Connor had been one of three women to whom the governor had shown the pamphlet issued to the prison by Dickens. Chesterton looked out of the window of his two-storeyed house, positioned where the grating sound of the prison treadmill could not be heard, and his gaze came to rest on his vegetable garden. He tried to imagine O'Connor working in such a garden, the warmth of the sun upon her face and the clean air of the countryside in her lungs.

Two days before, Chesterton had called her to his office and, seated at his desk, read out the offer of a new life which the pamphlet contained. If O'Connor had felt any emotion at the proposal, her face had not shown it. With her head hung low, it had briefly occurred to him that despite being held prisoner, she had no place that she might prefer to be or wish to escape to.

Chesterton had found himself strangely moved by the words which he read aloud to her. Despite his dour exterior, he was a man who recognized that his prisoners were slaves to crime not through choice, but through necessity. Seeing no sign of emotion in O'Connor's face, Chesterton had wondered if she had comprehended the offer which was being made to her.

'Do you understand, girl?' he had asked.

She gave no response; she had stopped trying to understand many years ago. To understand meant to be conscious of thought, to fathom out meaning in life. If she dared to be conscious of the life that she was living or aimed to make sense of it, then she could not hope to endure its vileness as she did. She found herself idly wondering what it would be like to lie with a man like Chesterton. She momentarily amused herself at how he might respond if she made such a proposition. Would he be outraged? Would he be tempted? What could this baggy-eyed, flint-faced gentleman know or understand of her stale and solitary life which neither appalled nor repulsed her? The governor leaned forwards and offered her the pamphlet, which was a meaningless gesture, for she had never been taught her letters.

'Mr Dickens and Miss Coutts are offering you a new beginning. A place in a home where you can learn to be useful and perhaps in time employ those skills abroad, where your past is unknown.'

She raised her head slowly, her eye disappearing beneath her ragged scar, emotion still absent from her face.

'There is no point. He will still find me.'

Mr Chesterton frowned for a moment, wondering of whom she spoke, and then he understood. She was thinking of that reptilian individual known as Bale, the man who earned his living by means of this poor creature.

He shook his head. 'On this occasion, I think not. Mr Dickens's home will not be generally known as a place for ...' he hesitated, trying to temper his words, '... women like you.'

Chesterton stood up from his desk and turning his back on her, went to the window, looking out on the grim prison courtyard.

'Besides, I have let it be known that you are not due for release for another month. Bale will not be back to claim you before then. If you accept this opportunity, I will ensure that you are gone before he has time to hear of it.'

O'Connor stared down at her boots, wondering if she should dare to allow the light of hope to enter her heart.

The clock struck nine. Chesterton turned from his recollection. It was time for him to begin his morning inspection of the prison. He took no time to check his appearance in the looking-glass. He had no wife to straighten his cravat or to take him to task for the smear of porridge on his lapel, for what woman of charm would welcome a proposal of a life within the grounds of a prison?

Putting on his hat and opening the front door, he headed out with the purpose of seeing the oakum house and to ensure that the prisoners were being usefully employed. He crossed the courtyard and passing a turnkey who was leaving his watch, the governor turned into a narrow stone passage between two cell blocks. He came to a heavy oak door studded with nails, and banged it with his fist.

The warden who unlocked it greeted him.

'Good morning, Mr Chesterton, sir.'

The governor nodded and began to walk among the rows of prisoners bent over lengths of old tarry rope, unravelling and picking the fibres. There had been no conscious intention in the governor's mind to look for O'Connor, and yet he found himself scanning the pathetic faces in sight of the ragged eye which marked her out in such a distinctive manner.

His attention fell briefly on a woman, scarred on her upper lip and eyebrows, her nose disjointed. He did not linger on her misshapen features and his gaze continued along the row of her grey, disconsolate companions. O'Connor was not among them. The hands of the woman he had glanced upon left her work for a moment and she sucked at a finger and thumb, raw from picking at the rope. Mindful that the governor was present and the eyes of the wardens upon her, she quickly returned to her task.

Her name was of no consequence. There was no one who cared to know it and conversation between the prisoners was forbidden. At the time of her apprehension, she had been of no settled abode and her crime: stealing a pair of boots, for which she had been sentenced to three months' hard labour. It was not a new occurrence. The year before, she had received six months for stealing and pawning items not her own. In fact, the woman with the scarred lip could not remember a year in the last ten when she had not paid a visit or two to the Coldbath Fields Prison. The only moment of brief acknowledgement that she had received that morning, in the stretch of meaningless hours ahead of her, was from the young woman who had shared her cell. The gaoler's keys rattling in the door, she realized that the time of that young woman's release had arrived.

With a pitiful bundle of belongings clutched to her side, the girl with the ragged eye gave a brief nod of farewell to the woman with the scarred upper lip who had slept on a straw mattress at her side. Mary-Ann O'Connor had decided to take her chance.

CHAPTER ELEVEN

DUNN SQUINTED. IT was difficult to see in the darkness of the cell. He sat hunched over a small desk and had tried to position himself where the light through the window fell upon the page. His hand was shaking and he cursed as the pen spotted his journal with ink. His trial was shortly approaching. He could not remember how long he had been in prison but he knew that he was being held unlawfully and that he could prove it, if only he could keep his thoughts together.

There were moments of lucid memory. He recalled the sensation of walking the streets of Piccadilly and his eyes watching a woman's form in a window, and the sound of his own panting breath and a serving girl's voice and the smell of coffee from the rooms below and the rumble of men's laughter. Then there were the nightmares which haunted him both in daylight and darkness: he tried to talk but no voice came out, he looked at the words on a page but they had no meaning. He awoke to find himself in his rooms at the coffee house and then awoke again, his eyes focusing on the paint flaking from the damp brick walls of his cell. He did not dare to think, for as soon as his thoughts began to form, another voice would run alongside each suggestion: echoing, chattering, screeching and yapping.

Dunn inhaled deeply, having caught the scent of jasmine soap and heard the rustling of a woman's skirt. He looked up and smiled.

'You see, my dear, you must tell them that there has been a terrible *misunderstanding and that we are to be wed, after all. They must not know what I have done. There, there, my dear, don't cry ... you know that Wellington could not be allowed to live. He couldn't be trusted and there was no other way to protect you.*

'I am relying on you to be my alibi....'

Dunn looked down at his journal. He opened his hands and saw that they were sticky with blood; he smiled, and then suddenly began to sob uncontrollably.

Strolling the length of the blue corridor at Walmer Castle, the Duke of Wellington and Angela Burdett-Coutts walked arm in arm. The rain had precluded their plans to take a turn in the gardens, and they talked of dinner the night before.

Clasping the duke's arm fondly, Angela remarked, 'It was kind of you to entertain Lord Ashley last night. He is such a great help to me in my work, and I was keen to hear news of his progress with the ragged schools.'

'Indeed, a place of education where those poor young ones can be schooled and learn a trade, can only be an influence for good,' Wellington acknowledged.

'Lord Ashley told me that there are now more than sixteen schools in the city and with Dickens's own recent donation, we can engage paid teachers as well as volunteers.'

'That is very good news, my dear.'

It pleased him when she was happy. He knew that she was troubled by the upcoming trial and had been trying to put it out of her head. He had hoped that a stay at his country residence would be a comfort to her, but thoughts of the trial were never far from her mind.

'Mr Humphreys has tried to prepare me that Dunn will try to prove that the magistrate's action to imprison him on the basis of unpaid bail cannot be upheld any longer. I am still anxious, Arthur, that he will shortly be released.'

'And Mr Humphreys also made it clear, that the man has frequent moments of delusion,' the duke countered, 'and that there is no guarantee he will represent himself in court with any sense on the day.'

Angela shook her head.

'If only I had kept the letters which he sent, the content of that alone would show what sort of a man he is. But I destroyed every one of them the moment I recognized his hand. How I wish I could now produce them in court.'

The duke's eyes held a look of tender concern.

'Try not to worry, my dear. We have the testimonies of the police who had to restrain him with great force at his arrest. They can testify to his violent conduct.'

Angela found herself consoled by his words.

'Now I know, Arthur, why your men felt so safe under your command. You have the innate ability to inspire courage in the face of an enemy.'

He laughed gently at her words.

They came to the Lantern Room with its glass ceiling and Angela stopped by the fireplace. The duke moved to the window, inspecting the skies to check if there was hope that the weather might improve. Angela ran her eyes over his figure, his hands clasped behind his back, and as the rain fell upon the glass like whispers she could not contain what unexpectedly sprang up in her heart.

'Arthur?'

He turned with an enquiring smile.

'Yes, my dear?'

'There is something that I have been meaning to ask you.'

'You know I will oblige you, if I can.'

'We are dear companions, are we not?'

'Indeed, you have been such a delight and comfort to me. And I am never more content than when I am in your company.'

'Then perhaps we should make our companionship a permanent arrangement?'

'Are you talking of marriage, Angela?'

Her eyes searched his face, trying to read his heart, but there was nothing she could be sure of.

'Do you know that there was a time when I almost hated you?' she said. 'I blamed you for the death of my father and yet I found myself drawn to you still. Without any conscious effort on your part you caused me to love you, Arthur. I have come to realize that I am only truly myself when I am with you.'

She moved to embrace him and he held her gently, stroking her hair.

'Angela, you are anxious about the trial. It is to be expected. Don't let us talk of marriage now. It is natural that you should seek a protector, and you know that I am happy to fulfil that role. But don't confuse the comfort you find in my protection with love.'

'So you don't feel as I do?'

'Yes, I feel as you do. I only ask that you wait until the trial is over, and you can be more certain of your feelings.'

She stood on her toes, so impressive was his frame, and briefly placed her lips upon his.

'My feelings will not change, Arthur, but I will wait until the trial is over to show you the truth of my words and the strength of my feelings for you.'

CHAPTER TWELVE

THE COURT WAS full. Journalists from the London newspapers had jostled for a front seat in the public gallery, eager to record every word, every look between the famous heiress and her provocative suitor. No one knew what Dunn would make as his defence and no one cared; the public gallery was greedy to hear extracts from the letters which Dunn had reputedly sent to Miss Coutts.

Dressed in a black and ivory striped gown, lace at her cuffs, the complainant entered the court with Mr Humphreys, her solicitor, at her side. Her hair was tied in a chignon, and the net veil of a small black hat covered the upper part of her face. She whispered something aside to Mr Humphreys, who nodded briefly.

The Duke of Wellington had returned to Apsley House and Angela was now beginning to regret that he had not accompanied her. She had argued that the sight of him in the court might agitate Dunn and cause a scene, but she was also conscious that the newspapers slavered at the rumours of a love affair between them. One salacious court case alone was disgrace enough.

Sitting on the opposite side of the court, Dunn fixed his eyes upon Miss Angela, his smile holding a hint of amusement. She did not dare to look at him. Beneath the net of her veil a rash burned once more upon her cheeks. Just knowing that he was in the same room brought back memories that she had tried to forget.

As the Lord Chief Justice Denman entered, the court rose. He took his seat on the high-backed chair overlooking the room, and Mr Coleridge, for the defendant, stood up to address the court.

'My lord, the prisoner, Richard Dunn, has made a writ of *Certiorari* in order to review the earlier decision of the magistrate's court. Having been detained in default of sureties for a period of two years, he now applies to this court for discharge.' He paused, speaking slowly and deliberately. 'If, in the opinion of this court, there is no threat or evidence warranting the quarter sessions and a full jury, the prisoner will be released.'

Mr Coleridge took his seat and Lord Denman nodded in response. 'Thank you, Mr Coleridge, for your summary. Although an appeal has been made by Mr Dunn, the court should not forget that it must also discern whether the complainant, Miss Coutts, was threatened as first presented – either in language or in conduct – and that if the defendant were to be released, then the complainant is assured to be free from further molestation.'

Lord Denman turned to Miss Angela.

'You have asserted, madam, that there has been a long episode of persecution and annoyance by Mr Dunn, including correspondence of a most indecent nature which has caused you distress and given cause for you to fear for your bodily safety.'

'That is correct, sir.'

Her voice was quiet.

'Could you please tell the court, Miss Coutts, when you first met Mr Dunn?'

She raised her voice slightly and responded, 'My lord, he has never been introduced to me and as far as I am aware, has no connection with anyone who might wish to make such an introduction.'

'But you do know him, Miss Coutts?' Lord Denman gestured towards Dunn with his hand.

She avoided looking at Dunn and said, 'I know him as the man who obtained a room above the Gloucester Coffee House Hotel opposite my house in Stratton Street with the purpose, I believe, of spying on me.'

'And have you proof of this?'

'If you were to ask the landlord of the establishment, he would verify that Mr Dunn has occupied a room there since shortly after I first moved to Piccadilly. From there he was able to observe all my movements.'

'But that is not evidence that the man wished to do you harm, I'm sure you'd agree, Miss Coutts?' Lord Denman observed.

'Sir, when the provocation first began some years ago he came to my father's house in Derbyshire with the intention of making mischief. He was disturbed by the dog and made his escape, killing the animal as he fled.'

'And you identified him on this occasion?'

'No, my lord, I did not see his face at the time, but I found a scrap of paper at the scene with his handwriting upon it.'

'Can I ask how you knew that the writing was Mr Dunn's?'

Miss Angela adjusted the lace at her cuffs and answered, 'I first received some correspondence of an unpleasant nature a year after I first moved into Stratton Street. The style of handwriting was quite singular. Thereafter, I always recognized it and was cautious of anything addressed to me in this hand.'

'Miss Coutts, I hope you can understand my difficulty when I say that it is not possible for me to see how you can be sure that the handwriting belonged to a man whom you claim never to have been introduced to or whose face you did not see. Can you produce any of the correspondence you say that you received so that the court may see the evidence, and compare the writing to that of Mr Dunn?'

The journalists in the public gallery leaned forwards eagerly.

Angela looked at Mr Humphreys to her left and then turned to her right, wishing that the duke was present to give her courage.

'I am afraid, sir, that I destroyed all of the correspondence which Mr Dunn sent. The content was so upsetting and I burned the letters immediately.'

The disappointment in the gallery was palpable.

'I see,' said Lord Denman. 'Miss Coutts, are you able to give the court any other proof of harassment on the part of Mr Dunn?' His voice was kindly and patient.

'Yes, sir, I can. There was an occasion when I was taking a moment to quietly worship at a church in Albemarle Street. I opened my eyes from prayer and was alarmed to find Mr Dunn present.'

Lord Denman shook his head apologetically. 'Unfortunately,

Miss Coutts, the church is a public place and a court cannot find a man guilty for being present in a place of worship.'

'But he was so insistent to be in my company. If it had not been for the chaplain taking a stand for my privacy—'

'Are there other occasions you can name?' Lord Denman asked.

'There are many, my lord. Three summers ago, I was riding in my carriage in the direction of Regent's Park for the purpose of walking there. As I was driving along Bond Street, I observed Mr Dunn on foot going in the opposite direction, and I recognized him as the man who had approached me in the street outside my house on numerous occasions before. I tried to hide my face but he had already seen me. I believe that he must have changed his direction and followed me to the park, as shortly thereafter he approached me and began insisting that I fulfil my promise to him.'

'And what was this promise?'

She tried to retain her dignity, holding her head high.

'That I should marry him.'

There were murmurs in the gallery.

'I'm sorry, Miss Coutts, I did not hear you. Could you repeat yourself for the purpose of the court?'

She stared beyond Lord Denman and repeated in a firm voice, 'Mr Dunn falsely believed that I had made a promise to marry him. But I can assure you that I have never made such a promise.'

'And can you tell the court what happened next?'

'Yes, sir. My driver observed the incident and immediately escorted me back to my carriage, asking Mr Dunn to leave me alone. The driver took me to the home of Mr and Mrs Thomas Alexander in nearby Hanover Terrace. But as Mr Dunn had been observing all of my movements for a long time, he must have guessed precisely where I was headed and arrived at Hanover Terrace not long after, knocking on the door. The police were called at Mr Alexander's request, but Mr Dunn took flight before they arrived.'

Lord Denman shook his head. 'Miss Coutts, I am truly sympathetic to your embarrassment at the unwelcome attentions of Mr Dunn. The magistrate was perfectly correct in applying bail, and then a jail sentence for non-payment of this surety to keep the peace. But as yet I have not been convinced that you were at any time in actual danger.'

She mustered courage, glancing sideways at the public gallery.

'There was a time when he entered my house and … and stood at my … bedside.'

An excited hum rippled through the gallery.

'I am not sure how he gained entrance, but I awoke to find him standing over me … and … and he took a cutting from my hair, believing me to be sleeping.'

The gallery gasped.

'If it was dark, can you be confident that the person you say you saw at your bedside is the man here in court today?'

'I am confident that it is the same man, my lord.'

'And why did you not cry out, Miss Coutts?'

'I feared for my life, sir, and thought that by remaining perfectly still I would be safer. I admit that he caused me no physical harm, but the incident rendered me fearful of what might happen next time.'

'And was there a next time?'

'I always ensured that the property was secured thereafter, my lord. But you are aware that he later came to the London home of the Duke of Wellington and disturbed me at a dinner party. He was apprehended and wrestled to the ground in a state of insanity while shouting violently.'

Lord Denman nodded. 'Of that, I acknowledge, there is absolute evidence. Thank you, Miss Coutts. You may now be seated.'

He turned to Dunn and asked that he stand.

'Mr Dunn, what have you to say to these charges?'

Dunn stood up.

He could sense the voices in his head jostling to take first place.

Don't worry, my angel, it will soon be over, and we will be together again.

In his hand, he clenched a tiny shard of glass which he had found in the prison yard. He allowed it to pierce his palm, the pain focusing his thoughts.

'I stand before you now, my lord, and propose that there is not one scrap of evidence to show that I entered the lady's house, visited the home of her father, or wrote letters of an obscene nature.'

Liar! Liar! Liar!

He squeezed tighter on the glass.

'And the lady herself acknowledges, my lord, that such evidence does not exist. I assert that Miss Coutts has proved false to a promise that she made to me, a promise that we would become engaged. And further to that, she offered to pay me £100,000 if I accepted.'

The court erupted in uproar. The journalists scribbled fervently on their notepads: the homely heiress who paid for a suitor. Lord Denman asked for order and Dunn continued.

'That is quite a proposal to make, my lord, as you can imagine. But I accepted it in good faith. I did not expect to be insulted with the suggestion that I had imagined such a proposal.'

Lord Denman queried, 'As a man of the law, Mr Dunn, did you not expect to have such an arrangement drawn up in writing?'

It is all in writing, every word that ever came from those enticing lips of hers....

He focused hard. 'My lord, the proposal may well have been a business arrangement, but even so it would have been indelicate of me to suggest such a thing to a lady who was about to become my wife.'

You had a wife ... but your wife left you.... Who did she leave you for? It was that assassin, Wellington!

Lord Denman, who was a man of great experience, appeared momentarily perplexed.

'You acknowledge that you broke into the home of the Duke of Wellington and harangued Miss Coutts?'

Yes, and I slit his throat!

'Yes, I did, my lord. I was angry at being ignored and being made a fool of. I regret my actions now. But at the time of my arrest, I stubbornly refused to make surety that I would cause no further nuisance to the lady as I held great resentment over the whole matter.'

'Are you ready to make that surety now, Mr Dunn?'

Dunn dug the piece of glass harder into his palm and felt the ooze of blood within it.

Concentrate, damn you!

'I am, my lord.'

'Very well. You may be seated, Mr Dunn.'

Dunn sat down and slid his bleeding, pulsating hand into the pocket of his breeches.

She will be yours very soon … you have done well.

Lord Denman addressed the gallery.

'Ladies and gentlemen of the court, we have heard the views of both the defendant and the complainant. Without evidence, it is not possible to say with certainty what took place between the two parties. I believe Miss Coutts to be a lady of honour, and it is not the place of this court to disbelieve what she has asserted. However, it may be that Mr Dunn has misunderstood Miss Coutts's intentions. There is no basis in law to detain him further and I am therefore bound to decide that the prisoner must be discharged.'

Angela gave a little cry of distress.

Lord Denman turned to Dunn and said, 'May I remind you, Mr Dunn, that you are now bound to keep your distance entirely from Miss Coutts, and if you are found in this court again having caused further annoyance, then you can be sure of a jail sentence. I declare the matter to be disposed of up to the present time. You are free to go.'

Dunn gave the chief justice a gracious nod as the judge left the court. Leaving his seat, he cast a glance at Miss Angela and smiled at the sight of her bowed head, and trembling shoulders.

Thank you, my angel. I knew that you would not let me down.

CHAPTER THIRTEEN

Devonshire Terrace
Devonshire Square
London

28 October 184—

My dear Miss Coutts,
    I called on Wednesday to talk over with you recent progress with the Home for Fallen Women, but your maid said you were indisposed. I chanced to find you at home again on Friday but I was once more informed that you were not at home to visitors.
    I hope that you are not keeping out of the way on account of my having offended you in some small matter? In everything I have tried to bestow my best exertions and reflection regarding this enterprise.
    You will be pleased to know that there are two more girls recently discharged from prison by Mr Chesterton, who were received on Saturday last. It was most encouraging that both remained resolute in their determination to come to the Home for Fallen Women, even though some of their old companions were waiting at the prison gate ready to bear them away.
    We now have eight girls in total, and I have taken great pains to find out their dispositions so that I might be able to give the matron some useful foreknowledge of their nature. What an extraordinary and mysterious study it is, but touching to the extreme.
    One girl, only seventeen, born of drunkards, ill-used from infancy up, shows signs of great promise. I hope we will improve them all by

education, affectionate kindness and trustfulness, and that they might come to be a cheerful family while they live together.

Perhaps you might pay a visit, for to see them now you will truly know what good you have done when they at last turn out well. I hope that if your health is ailing in any way you will let me know, that I might readily be of assistance or comfort.

I am most faithfully yours,
Charles Dickens

CHAPTER FOURTEEN

'WHERE ARE YOU? Where *are* you?'

Dunn ran his finger down the newspaper columns one after the other, turning each page with rapid succession. Frantic with madness he scrutinized every word, desperate to know where she dined, with whom she danced, and what gown she was wearing. But there was nothing.

He had sat daily at a table in Simpsons-in-the-Strand, her favourite restaurant, his eyes moving wildly from face to face in search of hers. He had sat weekly in the opera-house stalls, watching intently for her to occupy her usual box. He had threaded his way through the galleries of the Royal Academy, and paced the aisles of the arcade in Adelaide Street, pressing his face to the shop windows, but she was nowhere to be found. Angela Burdett-Coutts had disappeared from London society and there was not one word of her movements or whereabouts.

'Where are you? Damn you, woman. Where *are* you?'

Hannah Brown had been very contented in her married life and her husband, a forward-thinking man, saw no reason why his spouse should not continue in her role as a companion to Miss Angela. It was good that his wife was occupied during the long hours he kept at the fever hospital. The Browns' quarters at Stratton House, however, had been unoccupied since the end of May. With the emptying of drawers, closets, cabinets and larders, and the packing of baskets, boxes, trunks and carriages, Miss Angela had moved her entire household to Holly Lodge, a retreat in Highgate.

Although Dr William Brown was well versed in the diseases of consumption, cholera and smallpox, as personal physician to Miss Angela, he was at a loss to find a cure for the unsightly rash upon her cheeks and her frequent bouts of sleepwalking. He was not a doctor of the mind. Even so, his patron had insisted upon his attendance. With the passing of the trial, she had selected those closest to her to be her guardians and her companions at her hideaway. William hoped that in time, she would find the courage and the energy to fill her house with guests again; her solitude concerned him.

The doctor had been reluctant to leave his work at the London Fever Hospital but as the facilities had recently moved to larger premises in Islington, he was encouraged by Miss Angela that this was the ideal time for him to ease up and focus on his research with greater leisure. There was an airy attic room at the lodge which overlooked the views at Highgate and he would not be disturbed at his work, she had assured him.

With the move to the country, Hannah had found her duties as a secretary taken up again, informing a select group of Miss Angela's friends and associates that the lady was now residing at Holly Lodge. Hannah was under strict instructions, however, to inform that intimate group that the address was not to be common knowledge generally made known. Miss Angela's intention was for her life at Holly Lodge to be a private one.

Dr Brown had recommended that Miss Angela take a brisk walk daily across Hampstead Heath to aid both her sleep and her complexion, and Angela had acknowledged his advice. With the weather good that morning, she stood in front of the looking-glass in the sitting room, tying her bonnet.

As the door to the sitting room opened she turned, with the intention of scolding Hannah for the time she had taken to put on her walking boots. Her maid, however, entered with an announcement.

'I know that you are just about to go out, Miss Angela, but there are two ladies waiting to be received.'

'I was not expecting visitors today.'

There was a note of disquiet in her voice.

The maid held out a calling card to her mistress.

'The lady claims that she and her husband were friends of your father's, and that she and her daughter are calling with greetings from the Duke of Devonshire.'

Angela took the card and read it.

'Lady Jane Oxford?' She shook her head, puzzled. 'I scarcely know the name. My father never made mention of her. My mother maybe did so, in passing.'

She returned the card to the maid.

'I'm sure Mrs Brown made it clear to all my associates that my whereabouts was not to be made commonly known.'

'Do you wish me to tell her you are not at home, ma'am?'

Angela hesitated and then said, 'Please say that I am about to go out walking, but that her greetings from the duke are most welcome.'

The maid nodded and left the room.

A few moments later, she returned. 'I'm sorry, Miss Angela, but Lady Oxford is most insistent to see you. She says that the duke will be offended if she does not deliver his greeting in person.'

Angela sighed; Hannah was certainly taking her time.

'Very well, as I am waiting for Mrs Brown, you may tell the ladies I will see them *briefly*,' she agreed testily.

The maid showed Lady Oxford in, who glanced about the room, impressed by its size and grandeur.

Angela held out her hand and looked with interest at the older woman, whose face held reminiscence of great beauty. Lady Oxford in turn held out her own delicate, veined hand in response. She observed that the representations she had seen of her hostess had been too generous; the young woman had a poor complexion, in her opinion, and no figure at all.

'Miss Burdett, or should I say, Miss Coutts? Thank you for receiving us unannounced and I apologize for my insistent manner. I can assure you our visit will be brief.' She gestured to the younger woman at her side. 'May I introduce my daughter, Lady Charlotte Harley.'

The woman, of similar age to Angela, made a polite nod of her head. There was no warmth in the acknowledgement.

Angela gestured to the sofa. 'Please be seated, ladies. I understand, Lady Oxford, that your family were acquainted with my father?'

Lady Oxford, sitting down, began, 'Yes, It was very sad to hear of his passing. I would, of course, have sent a note of sympathy but I was out of the country at the time for the benefit of my husband's health.'

'I hope that your husband made a good recovery,' Angela offered.

'I am pleased to say that he did, and he continues to prosper well for his age.'

'And how did your husband know my father?'

'They knew one another in their younger days. My husband admired your father for his politics,' Lady Oxford replied.

Angela looked briefly at Lady Charlotte, who appeared to have no desire to contribute to the conversation, and turned her attention back to Lady Oxford.

'The last I saw of your father,' Lady Oxford continued, 'was at a ball given by Princess Lieven. I spoke with him personally and there was no hint at all that he was not in good health.'

'Indeed, his death was a shock to us all,' Angela replied.

There was a moment's silence, as Angela pondered on the purpose of Lady Oxford's visit.

'You have greetings from the Duke of Devonshire, I believe?' she said.

'Not exactly. I have to confess to another purpose for my visit,' Lady Oxford said in a direct manner. 'And although it is a matter of delicacy, I hope that you will allow me to speak plainly with your permission.'

'Oh, I hope that the duke is not in any sort of trouble?'

'No, it does not concern the duke, it is … a personal matter, a matter of family connection …'

Lady Oxford was distracted momentarily by the sound of cross words in the hall.

Angela apologized. 'I'm sorry, Lady Oxford, do go on.…'

The door opened and Hannah entered, her face filled with

vexation.

'Miss Angela, I must speak with you, I—'

'Hannah, I will be but a moment.' She turned to Lady Oxford. 'Please continue, madam. You were saying something of a family connection, although I don't believe that I recall my father speaking of a family connection with the Earl of Oxford—'

'Miss Angela, I—' Hannah interrupted once more.

Lady Oxford scowled. 'I think, perhaps, that what I have to say is best not said in the company of *a servant*.'

'I can assure you, Lady Oxford, Mrs Brown is no servant, she is my companion of long standing, and you may speak freely in front of her.'

Hannah protested, 'Miss Angela, I must warn you that your mother would never have entertained this woman for one moment.'

Lady Oxford's attitude altered immediately and she sneered, 'Ah, but her father felt differently. Very differently....'

'I must absolutely forbid you to speak of Sir Francis!' Hannah warned.

Lady Oxford persisted. 'I think what your companion does not wish me to say, Miss Coutts, is that the family connection we share in common is between my daughter Charlotte and yourself. You are ... sisters. That is to say that your father was also the father of my daughter.'

The world seemed to stop for a moment as Angela took in the words. She looked at Hannah, whose eyes were full pain.

'No, it's not possible ... I would have ...'

A flood of disgust ran through Angela's body and without warning she stood up, crossed the room and rang for the maid.

'I must ask you to leave immediately, Lady Oxford.' She gestured to the door. 'There is nothing further in this matter that we need to discuss.'

Lady Oxford remained seated.

'On the contrary, we have plenty to discuss. Your father acknowledged his obligation with a regular sum of money. I have letters to prove it. In fact the payments were for my eldest daughter, Elizabeth, also your father's child. But when I revealed to your father some time before his death that Charlotte was his child too, he made a further donation, which I have recorded here.'

She held out a small ledger. Angela turned her head away.

'Madam, I believe you have heard Miss Coutts's feeling on the matter: she has asked you to leave.'

Lady Oxford ignored Hannah's direction and continued. 'It might be very embarrassing to all if this were to become known in polite society. I really would prefer that we conclude the matter in private.'

'Lady Oxford, if what you say is true, then I am surprised that polite society receives you at all.'

Lady Charlotte stood up. 'Perhaps, Mama, we would have more success with the brother.'

Angela's eyes flashed with anger. 'You will not even be received over his doorstep!'

Hannah opened the door and indicated that the visitors should leave. Rising to her feet, Lady Oxford turned to Angela and said, 'Well, you may not have his looks, but you certainly have your father's passion, I will say that much.'

She turned to her daughter. 'This will not be the end of it, Charlotte. Your mama will see that you receive what is rightfully yours.'

The visitors were shown out by the maid and with a tremor in her voice, Angela turned to Hannah, her eyes full of resentment.

'You knew about this?'

'I'm sorry, Miss Angela, if I had taken the card at the door I would have turned her away myself immediately.'

'That is not what I asked, Hannah!'

Hannah shook her head. 'I cannot say I knew of your father's personal affairs for sure, but your mama had heard of such rumours when she was a young woman, and was devastated by them.'

'Then why did you never tell me?' Angela asked angrily. 'You knew that I was sure to find out one day!'

'I know how much you loved your father, Miss Angela, I ...'

Angela put her hands to her ears.

'... he was a changed man in the final years of his life ...'

'Please, I can't bear it. ...'

'... he tried so hard to show your mama how sorry he was for his former conduct ...'

'No more, Hannah ... No more....'

CHAPTER FIFTEEN

'You have not been at all attentive of late, Arthur. I have hardly seen you.' Angela pushed away the plate of cake which had been brought in on a tea tray to tempt her reluctant appetite.

'You know, my dear, that I have been overseeing the arrangements to receive the Queen and Prince Albert at Walmer Castle,' the duke explained. 'The building has been pulled to pieces so that it might meet with the Queen's approval.'

'It is a lot of fuss for a few weeks' visit just so that her children might have a taste of the sea air.'

'I could hardly refuse, Angela,' the duke argued. 'Besides, you know you were invited. I wrote many times and asked you to join us.'

She thought for a moment of the letters she had received from him with regularity of late and inwardly acknowledged that what he had said was true. He had expressed with great feeling how much he missed her. When she had opened his letters, pressed roses had fallen from between the sheets of the writing paper, and he had enclosed a lock of his hair entwined with hers. She had been so preoccupied with getting away from London as quickly as she could, she had not reflected upon his tenderness. She put down her cup and regretted that she had been sharp.

'I'm sorry, Arthur, I have felt so lonely without you and yet unable to enjoy the company of friends with any ease at all.'

The duke plumped up a velvet cushion behind him and, reaching for a cigar from the box on a side table by the sofa, continued,

'Then why in God's name are you hiding yourself away here?' He waved his hand disdainfully at the marble-columned room. 'It is nothing more than a gloomy mausoleum. Whatever possessed you to inhabit such a place?'

'The property was part of my inheritance. There were tenants living here until recently and I decided to occupy the place when it became vacant. I don't feel safe in Piccadilly any more. If I return to the house in Stratton Street I will be constantly looking over my shoulder, knowing that madman is free again.'

He learned forwards and said with all earnestness, 'That is natural, my dear. But if I had run away every time I had been faced with an enemy, where the devil would the country be now, I ask you? We'd all be speaking French, by Gad!'

'On, Arthur ...' She could not help but give a little laugh.

He stood up and crossed the room to the fireplace. Reaching for a taper from a pot on the mantelpiece, he lit the fire and put it to his cigar, drawing on it several times.

'It is not just that alone,' she continued, 'the business with *that woman* has depressed me further. How could my father behave in such a disreputable manner?'

Wellington, who had a colourful history of his own, found his sympathies divided. He had been unfaithful to Kitty many times over and could not in all conscience condemn Sir Francis for his infidelity. But he had noticed how Angela's vibrancy had been extinguished since learning of her father's adulterous past, and felt guilty by proxy.

He turned and replied, 'You must not judge your father too harshly, my dear. If you need a chance to regain your energy then so be it. But you must not let disappointment overcome you. And in the matter of Dunn, you must certainly never let your foe see for one instance that he has shaken you. You must carry on with your life regardless.'

She wondered again at the certainty which she always experienced in the duke's presence, as if nothing could harm or hurt her.

'Arthur? It would be so much easier if ...'

He took the cigar from his mouth. 'Yes, my dear?'

'... if you were always with me.'

There had been no mention of her earlier proposal since the trial. The duke had hoped she had given up on the idea, even though he inwardly acknowledged that he loved her with a passion. But he could not indulge his selfishness at her expense.

'Well, that is not difficult to arrange. I am never far from your side. And besides, Lord Denman warned Dunn that he would have no mercy shown to him if he appeared in your presence again.'

'You know what I mean, Arthur. You said that you would consider my proposal of marriage and yet you seem to have not given it any thought at all. In fact, you seem to have avoided the topic at every opportunity.'

His face became serious. He threw his cigar into the fire.

'You are wrong, Angela. I have passed every moment since you first made your proposal, considering your words repeatedly.' Sitting down, he took her hand. 'I think of you as I drift off to sleep and again the moment I awake.'

There was sadness in his eyes as he continued, 'You are young, and so full of vitality, my dear. And undoubtedly you have the prospect of many years of happiness ahead of you. I entreat you not to throw yourself away on a man old enough to be your father. I may be strong now, but I will certainly in time come to feel the consequences and infirmities of old age.'

She shook her head but he continued, ignoring her silent protest.

'You would be bitter at the reflection that your life had been wasted if you married me.'

'No, Arthur, you are wrong.'

'Angela, my first duty towards you is as a friend, your guardian and your protector. To become anything more than that would be a regrettable mistake.'

Her eyes were full. 'A mistake? Is that what I am to you?'

He stroked her face tenderly. 'Not at all. But a man of honour must know when to retreat and to find the courage within himself to do it. Heaven knows I was not a good husband the first time, Angela, and I fear that I would not be a good husband to you either. If you were to bear a child, I would be dead before it grew to maturity. I could not be the cause of so much grief to you. Be patient and you are certain to find someone of your own age to marry.'

'And if I do not, am I condemned to a life never knowing what it is to be loved by a man who does not simply want to marry me for my fortune?'

'I promise not to abandon you, my dear. But the moment a man appears who is worthy of you, I shall stand aside.'

With the intention of lightening the mood he slapped his hands on his knees, encouraging her to be cheerful.

'Come now, tell me of the work you have been doing in my absence.'

A playful note entered his voice, 'Oh, Angela, I dread to think what anarchy has been taking place in that little woman's refuge of yours!'

CHAPTER SIXTEEN

O'CONNOR COULD NOT remember a time in her life when she had felt sadness, but she felt it now. With the passage of years, there had been many sensations to which she had numbed herself. Sadness was the most raw and painful, and feeling it now, she remembered why she had chosen to forget. She pulled her cape about her, the wind pulling at her hair, and blinked away the tears which stung her eyes. The rain falling, Georgiana Mason, matron of Dickens's Home for Fallen Women, handed a carpet bag to O'Connor and gave a brief nod of her head in farewell.

'Hurry now, we're getting soaked. I've packed you a food parcel. Eat it before the journey gets underway. You're bound to be seasick for the first few days.'

The young woman unexpectedly cast her arms about the matron's neck and began to cry. The matron stiffened, putting her hands upon the girl's and removing them from around her neck.

'Come now, O'Connor. This is everything you have been working for, a chance to start afresh.'

'I ain't done no wrong since I came to you a year ago. I ain't never been so happy,' she pleaded. 'I'm beggin' you, let me stay.'

'It's impossible, O'Connor. Mr Dickens says that we have to give others the chance. If none of you girls ever move on, there'd be no room for anyone new.'

O'Connor looked with horror at the masts billowing in the wind. Those ghostly sheets were soon to spirit her to Port Adelaide on the other side of the world. In the past year, she had learned how to sew, cook, raise vegetables; and knew almost all of her letters now. She could find work and maybe even a husband in a land where her past was not known, the matron had told her, but nonetheless she did not want to go.

A gentleman, shrinking from the weather, touched his hat.

'May I be of assistance, ma'am? The ship is almost ready to leave. Does the young lady have a fear of the sea?' As O'Connor lifted her face to him, he observed her disfigurement and tried not to stare.

'I am the ship's doctor,' he continued. 'Doctor Lyndsey.'

'Aye, well perhaps it would be as well for her to be escorted on board by a medical man,' the matron responded. 'If you could place her in the fit company of a decent woman for the journey, I'd be grateful, sir.'

'It would be my pleasure, ma'am.'

O'Connor cast a final desperate look at the matron, hoping she might take pity on her and allow her to return.

'Goodbye, O'Connor, and remember well what you have been taught.'

The doctor gestured to the gangplank. 'Shall we board, miss? You're getting wet through.'

The last of the valuable cargoes – spices, perfumes, sugar, ivory and marble – had been unloaded and the ship was shortly to leave dock. From among the swarms of people sitting on crates, passengers carrying bundles, sailors rolling barrels, the doctor found himself violently pushed to the floor by a figure. Without warning, he felt a sharp stab of pain in his kidneys.

The matron was pushed to the ground and a pair of hands grasped O'Connor around the wrists.

'I told you I'd always find you, bitch!'

O'Connor looked into the grimy face which had haunted her life since girlhood and whispered with dread, 'How did you find me?'

'Bale knows yer smell.' He slid his tongue between his teeth, and licked his lips.

She pulled away from him, revolted. He grabbed her around the neck and reached for a knife in his pocket.

'You're my property and I can do with you what I pleases. I took yer eye once, and now I'm going to take the other. Then you won't see to go nowhere without me!'

She screamed as he sliced the knife edge across her face. Two of the ship's crew who heard her cries jumped down onto the gangplank. Bale had the girl by the hair now, blood pouring from her face. He raised the knife again, leering at the crewmen to take their chance. He did not see another sailor approach him from behind who raised an iron chain and struck Bale hard with it, felling him dead to the floor. The sailor crouched down, lifted Bale's head for signs of life and then let it fall again, his cheek wet upon the muddy ground. Crowds had gathered at the quayside, watching with horror. Blood dripped from O'Connor's face and the doctor shouted for assistance to take her on board.

She was crying loudly.

'We're taking you on board the ship, miss,' the doctor reassured, as she was lifted onto a makeshift stretcher.

He turned to assist the matron to her feet but she urged him to focus instead on the girl; the older woman was shaken but not hurt. There was no time for the matron to explain O'Connor's circumstances. If a medical man could save her life, and the boat was about to sail, so be it. She looked with concern at the girl being carried on board and wondered if she would survive. Recognizing there was nothing more that she could do, the matron turned and left the quayside.

The doctor urged the stretcher bearers to hurry, unbuttoning his jacket and rolling up his sleeves. He had not expected to find himself acting as a surgeon with the ship about to set sail.

'Set her down on the table!' he ordered as they entered his quarters.

His hands were trembling; the incident had shaken him. He knew that he could not likely save O'Connor's sight, but he possibly had the skills to stop her bleeding to death. Taking a needle from his medical bag, he tried to steady his hands and began to suture the wound. It would be an ugly result, but it would be tight and stem the bleeding quickly.

'Hold her still!' he shouted at the crewmen as he tried to work. The men held her down with difficulty. They were used to the shouts of their fellow crewmen who had to undergo medical treatment, but the cries of a woman in surgery were terrible to hear.

The doctor tied off the suture and then plunged his hands into a bowl on a nearby dresser, the water turning red. He dismissed the men and taking a bottle of whisky from the dresser, he poured a sizeable measure into a glass for his patient. What a pity there had been no time for it earlier. Scooping an arm beneath her body, he lifted her up and held the glass to her lips.

'You will have to sit up, miss,' he encouraged. 'This will help the pain and aid your rest.'

The honey-coloured alcohol trickled from the corners of her mouth: O'Connor felt as if the life was draining out of her and she welcomed the darkness.

Had O'Connor been able to see, she might have passed the first two months of the passage practising her letters or keeping a diary; there was little else to do on a ship. But she could remember little of her journey so far. The sensation of being on the sea was constant, and the doctor's voice her most familiar memory since her injury. In the darkness she lay awake to the sound of the ship creaking and the water lapping against the hull. The sound of sailor's shouts, the chatter and laughter of the passengers distinguished the day from night. There had been some occasions when she had felt a little stronger and the doctor had led her up on deck for fresh air.

With a few coins, Doctor Lyndsey had employed a woman to sit with the girl and help her to knit so that she might occupy herself. O'Connor found the woman's temper short and her touch upon her own fingers rough and impatient.

'Where is the doctor?' O'Connor asked, her fingertips deciphering the feel of the wool and the point of needles.

'He's paid me to teach you to knit an' watch over you, not to tell you where he's gone,' returned a voice, heavy with resentment.

'If you don't want to be 'ere, then go. I won't tell him you've left your post.'

The woman, who had been reminded that morning of an earlier promise she'd received from a leather-skinned seaman, eyed the young woman doubtfully.

'You'd give me away....'

'No, not if you find me somewhere to sit on deck,' O'Connor offered. 'I'm sick of being shut in 'ere.'

After a moment's hesitation, the woman made up her mind and laid the knitting to one side.

'Come along then, girl. But if you give me away, I'll tell that doctor you're a liar.'

O'Connor reached out to seek the woman's hand and got up. She allowed herself to be led up the wooden steps, and welcomed the warmth of the sun on her face as she came on deck. The darkness lifted and there were shadows before her eyes which were distinguishable now.

'Here, sit on this barrel. If you put your hands either side it will steady you, see?'

The woman helped O'Connor sit down.

'Now, don't you be talking to anyone and gettin' yerself into trouble. I'm off to find a man. When I gets to dry land, I don't want to be sent to a factory or picked at the dock fer being a servant. If I gets m'self a husband now, I'll be set up when I reach the other side of the world.'

O'Connor steadied herself and realized that with no further word from the woman she had gone. With a strong breeze on her face, the smell and taste of the sea upon her senses, she gave thought to the woman's parting words. The relief she had momentarily experienced at being outside ebbed away by degrees and was replaced by fear. She realized that everything she had learned in the Home for Fallen Women was useless to her now. Knowing her letters was pointless, she could not become a cook or a servant, and no factory would find a use for a blind girl. What would happen to her at the dock? Where would she go? How would she eat?

She was frightened. Bale, in all his vileness, had always protected her. She had never gone hungry and she had always had somewhere to sleep.

A voice broke into her thoughts.

'Now, you ain't much to look at, girl, it's true. But in the darkness, I'd say that'd be a fine body to lie next to.'

She felt the touch of a rough hand upon hers and curbed the angry desire to throw it away from her.

'I've a little cabin not far from Port Adelaide that I lets out to young ladies such as yourself. I invites me pals to visit the girls, they gives me a little bit of their earnings for rent, and the girls have a roof over their heads. Now, what do you say?'

He moved closer and she became aware of the smell of stale sweat, spices and alcohol. O'Connor hesitated for a moment. Without the Home, she'd have ended her life knowing neither kindness nor a sense of family. Perhaps she had been one of the lucky ones. Perhaps it was inevitable that her happiness should end, and that she returned to the life which circumstance had mapped out for her. What else could a penniless wastrel like her do?

She took hold of the rough hand and said, 'Yes, indeed, sir, it is a fine offer for a girl like me.'

CHAPTER SEVENTEEN

16 November 18—

We live below different stars in the same sky, separated by opposing horizons. All the pain and love I feel, like sand and dust thrown to the day, comes back to me on sad breezes. When I had looked for you everywhere, there was only one place more I could be sure that you would come to.

And I have been here every day since … waiting.

Holy Cross Church
Ramsbury

THE CURATE CAME out of the porch, carrying a large bunch of keys, and hearing the woman's footsteps, he lifted his face and smiled.

'Good day to you, ma'am. I'm sorry that there's no service in progress this morning, but you are welcome to take a moment's prayer at your leisure, naturally.' He gestured towards the church door.

The woman, shielding the sun from her eyes with a raised hand, replied, 'Thank you, sir. Actually, my parents are buried here. I came to pay my respects.'

'Ah.' The curate bowed his head respectfully.

He moved himself to one side with the purpose of taking her gaze out of the late-autumn sun.

He hesitated for a moment before enquiring, 'I hope it is not impertinent of me to ask, but am I right in thinking that you are

Miss Burdett-Coutts?'

She acknowledged his recognition with a smile.

The curate continued, 'Yes, there was a picture of you in the *Evening Chronicle*. I read about the building work that you have recently funded in Bethnal Green with Mr Dickens. It is marvellous that at last there will be respectable housing available to the working man in walking distance from the city. The church has long despaired of any good coming from the east end of London. And now to think of airy living quarters with water, drainage and gas replacing those squalid and overcrowded lodgings: it will raise the moral character of the area for a certainty.'

Angela nodded. 'Indeed I hope so, sir. Mr Dickens always argued that there was little point in reforming those leaving prison if there is no effort to improve the conditions which breed such a lifestyle.'

The curate placed his fingers together and assented. 'That is very true, ma'am. And furthermore, the church you had built in Rochester Row to honour your father's memory was a wonderful gift to the parish of Westminster.'

'It seemed a fitting tribute, but I ... I must confess that for some time I have been ill at ease over disappointing memories respecting my father. However, a dear friend of mine reminded me of my own failings and urged me to forgive.'

'That is surely a most Christian sentiment. Your friend is a very wise woman.'

'The sentiments were urged upon me by the Duke of Wellington, sir, whose death I now greatly mourn.'

The curate removed his wide-brimmed hat and holding it to his chest, bowed his head.

'As do we all, ma'am.'

Angela gave a brief nod and entered through the porch.

Her eyes scanned the expanse, adjusting to the darkness. She approached the Burdett family vault and stood in contemplation, lowering her head. Reading the inscription, her thoughts rested on the marble tablet at her feet.

'Papa?' she whispered. 'I came to make peace and to tell you that ... that I am sorry. I was very angry with you for a while. But

I realize now that I was wrong to expect you to be without fault. And that if Mama could forgive you, I should do likewise.'

Her thoughts turned to the duke.

'Arthur was so wise, Papa. He was both a friend and father to me, teaching me to live life outside of just my own understanding. He has given me confidence in myself, and I know now that I can survive alone. I know who I am....'

Angela hesitated for a moment. She thought that she had heard something.

'Hello...?' she enquired. But there was no response.

Her eyes came to rest briefly on a representation of Madonna and child, and she turned her attention back to the family vault.

'Papa,' she continued, 'would you believe that among the recent sadness there has been a moment of unexpected joy. Dear Clara, when it was no longer thought possible, has produced your first grandchild and named him Francis. If Robert remains unmarried, then you will still have an heir to carry on your name. You will be glad to know that Clara's husband, the Reverend Drummond, is an admirable man who will be a good father, and has at last instilled some sense in Clara. I only wish the same could be said of Susan and Trevanion. I tried hard to assist him in an honest living, Papa, but he and Susan have fled to Paris to escape their creditors. I doubt I shall hear from them again....'

She stopped again and turned her head to the side, imagining that she could hear breathing.

'Is there someone there?' she asked softly. 'Is that you, Curate?'

But there was nothing, and she reasoned that she had simply heard the undertone of her own whispers.

She bent down and, kissing her fingertips, she placed them gently on the tomb.

'Sleep well, Papa. I miss you, but I am confident that I can now make my way alone, with or without a husband.'

Standing up, she turned from the vault and walked towards the altar. Slipping into a pew, she took a seat and bowed her head. In her moments of reflection, she found herself recalling the ghoulish spectacle that had been the duke's funeral. His death had been sudden, with no sign of ill health in the days before. Despite his years, he had seemed to her to be immortal. He would have hated the macabre ceremony, with shops renting out their roofs and upper stories just so that spectators could gain a better view of the coffin along the funeral route. Dickens had been quite right when he had said that it was the most dreadful display of commercial greed and hypocritical morbidity that he had ever seen.

Angela acknowledged that since the duke's death, she had senselessly absorbed herself in a frenzy of intense activity which had now left her exhausted. There had been successes and failures at the Home for Fallen Women. Although some of the inhabitants had made good, it was nothing unusual for the cellar door to be prised open in the middle of the night, and alcohol shared among the most rebellious girls. Or linen, plate and cutlery stolen and sent on to former associates.

The duke had warned her repeatedly that the enterprise was a complete folly but she had refused to listen.

She had confessed her disappointment to Dickens that no word had been received from O'Connor since arriving in Australia. Enquiries had at last brought a letter from the ship's doctor, who expressed some responsibility for the girl's relapse on board. He had tried to encourage her to seek out honest employment in Port Adelaide, but the girl had stubbornly held out that her injury would hinder her progress. The doctor had done all that he could and now, in her prayer, Angela felt that she too could confess that she had done all that she could.

With her eyes still closed, she did not see a hand steal from beneath the pew, reach out and grasp her ankle. She opened her eyes with alarm and took a sharp intake of breath. Dunn slithered from his hiding place and getting swiftly to his feet, he held her fast and placed his hand across her mouth.

'Sssh ... shhh, my angel. We are together again,' he whispered into her ear. Angela struggled but Dunn continued to hold her fast, regardless.

'I knew that if I waited, you would come here eventually.... Don't struggle, my angel.... When I had looked for you everywhere, I tried to think of the one place I could be sure that you would come to.... Please don't upset yourself.... I have been here every day since. It was only a matter of time before you returned to me. What better place could there be for us to meet again, but a place where we can at last become one flesh? I will seek out the clergyman and shortly we will be wed just as you always promised me.'

Dunn looked over his shoulder. Where was that inept curate when he was needed?

'There's nothing to stand in our way now, my love. I have watched over you constantly since that first day, just as I always said I would. I have protected you from all of those false suitors who sought to taint you.'

Angela tried to free herself and sensing it, Dunn held her tighter.

'You are overcome by passion. It is understandable, but don't fight me, my angel.'

He inhaled the scent of her hair.

'Since the day that I first saw your picture, I knew that I had to have you. I have come so close to it so many times, only for you to slip away from me again. You did not know it, but I was watching you from the beginning. Watching your figure in the candlelight through the window. Watching you walk about town. Following you wherever you went.'

Angela tried to break again, but Dunn held her firmly.

'Even when you lay sleeping, I was there. I stood at your bedside and you looked so beautiful. I was tempted to wake you, but I had to be sure that you would not turn aside from me like the others. And now at last, after waiting so long, you have come to me. *You have come to* me.'

Angela felt faint, her heart drumming upon her chest. What could be the worst horror? To die here? Or to be taken from this place and held a captive?

Dunn muttered another complaint about the absence of the curate and decided that the ceremony could wait; he could not be entirely sure of the man's reliability. Taking a knife from his pocket, he pressed it against Angela's rib.

'Do not be alarmed, my love, I will never harm you, but there are those who would seek to do so and I must protect you for your own good.'

Kissing her neck he held her close to him, the sound of his footsteps scuffing against the flagstones as he pushed her in the direction of the porch door.

'Please don't do this,' Angela begged in a whisper.

'We will be home soon, my love,' he soothed. 'I have rooms nearby. You will like them very much and they will become your new home.'

They passed through the church door and Dunn guided his victim towards a carriage parked at the rear.

'It is not far. I have clothes for you. I will feed you with my own hand. I will bathe you and brush your lovely hair.'

He opened the carriage door and the impassive driver asked no questions about the woman at Dunn's side. Her face full of fear, she cowered in the corner of the seat. Dunn sat next to her, his breath so close that she could feel it upon her skin. The carriage pulled away and Angela's thoughts turned desperately to her mother and father; to the duke; to Hannah; to her grandfather, and to whether the old man could have ever known that his fortune would bring her such torture and misery.

Dunn was lost in his own madness, whispering words of passion beneath his heavy breath, looking at the world beyond the carriage window, his hand pressed against it.

Angela was crying and the sound of her tears momentarily brought him to his senses.

'Don't cry, my love. Look, I have something for you.'

He scoured an outer pocket in his jacket, searching for his journal, and putting his hand upon it, he said, 'Look, my dear, the words within are all about us. Every word, every page. It is the story of you and me and our love.'

He opened the book on his lap, his body swaying with the movement of the carriage, and began to read.

'... I was the boy ... walking in a grey mist ... searching for nowhere.... The boy was lost ... and then you found me.... Wandering inside the heart of my childhood dreams.... You were always there and my heart burned for you, hoping you would come.... The sorrow and loneliness I felt ... until I saw you on some unnamed street corner ... tied to a timepiece of stagnation which never passed the hour.... I pressed my face to the glass *as you walked away…. I opened my heart to call you … but the hand of my heart's hesitation pressed its finger to my lips … until I looked for you again and then hid when you appeared…. In dreams you came next time … and here you lingered, listening to my voice…. And I saw in the eyes of your jewels only kindness … you knew my pain and with quiet breath blew dust upon it … and the colours of the world returned … the answers came … and time began again….'*

Dunn closed his journal and said, 'Oh, my sweet love, you do not know what you have become to me.'

Angela remained silent, fearing that anything she said would incite further madness. She could not recall the route that was taken or how much time passed, but the carriage eventually drew to a stop in a narrow leafy lane with tall houses that stooped above her. Dunn opened the carriage door, and weakened by her fear, she made no attempt to resist him as he guided her up the stone steps and to a side entrance. Rain was falling in sheets and the guttering overflowed to the ground below.

Entering, they climbed the stairs, which to Angela seemed endless, until they reached the top floor and in the dim light of the corridor, Dunn tapped on a door. It was opened by Belle. She knew her master well enough not to ask any questions or to stare at the shrinking companion at his side. The wage that he had offered her far exceeded the money she had ever earned at the coffee house. She would not have another opportunity to earn such money again. Her master was silent and strange, but she had come to know his ways and learned not be disturbed by them. She had never known when or how it had happened, but in her own way she loved him: the man who was loved by no one.

Noticing Angela shiver, Dunn ordered Belle to put more logs on the fire.

'Come, my love, I will show you your room.'

Dunn opened a door leading to a bedroom and he guided Angela to sit at a dressing table in front of a mirror. He began to take the pins from her hair and as it fell, he inhaled deeply and reached for a brush on the table. Angela was crying, but he took no heed, and began to pass the brush through her hair, softly and repeatedly.

'I have imagined this moment so many times, over and over.' He was talking to himself, lost in the rhythm of the strokes. 'Your beautiful hair, passing through my hands.'

Putting the brush down, he crossed the room to a closet and taking something from it, returned with an olive-green dress with a plain ribbon trim.

He held it up to show her.

'I had another dress made for you. Exactly the same as the other one. It would please me greatly if you put it on.'

He encouraged Angela to undress; all the time she cried as he undid her clothing and he coaxed her into the dress.

'Let me see you,' he whispered, turning her around. 'You look beautiful, so beautiful.'

He stroked her face, and she turned her cheek from him in fear and repulsion.

'Don't be afraid, my love. We will be happy together and never be apart again.'

He kissed her neck and then crossed the room to the door. 'I have to return to the church so I can arrange the wedding ceremony. I won't be long.'

He took a last look at her before leaving and she heard him turn the key in the lock. Seeing the rain on the window, she crossed the room to it and tried the latch, but it was shut fast. She saw the gardens below and realized that even if she had been able to open the window, she could never have descended such heights. Among the wet foliage, Dunn's figure appeared in the darkness of the rain below and he stepped into the carriage again. Angela withdrew and watched him leave, half-hidden behind the curtain. She returned to the door hurriedly and tried it but it remained locked.

She rattled the handle and then began calling to the girl.

'Are you there? Please open the door and let me out. He is mad. He will kill me. Please let me free. Oh, have some mercy.'

Belle watched the handle moving and heard the plaintive whispers beyond. She had recognized the woman immediately. Hers had been the face which had been sketched in a hundred different ways within the pages of Dunn's journal. He had often snatched the book away from her if he had caught her looking at it, but when he had been ill, she had pored over each word, each image, finding some jealousy present in her heart.

She did not dare to open the door, and tried to block out the sound of Angela's voice. She had no notion of the woman's history, or what Dunn had planned, and she did not wish to know. The girl turned her attention back to the stew she was stirring over the fire, until the sound of the rattling doorknob ceased and she heard the sound of quiet crying from the room beyond.

Angela opened her eyes. It was dark. Dunn had returned and was asleep in a chair by the fireplace, his journal on his lap.

Angela noticed the green dress on a chair next to the bed, and looking down, realized that she was in her petticoat and chemise. She tried to recall if she had undressed herself and the precise time when Dunn had returned, but she could remember nothing. Her head ached, and seeing a glass on the bedside table, she wondered if he had drugged her.

After a moment's thought, she got up unsteadily from the bed and gently made her way towards the sleeping figure, reaching carefully for the journal on his lap.

He hardly stirred, and she began to turn the pages, immediately recognizing the strokes of the pen, the letters tall and thin, written with little spacing between them. Turning the pages over and over, she saw the horror of her years before her. Dunn's wild imaginings, his notes from the court case, sketches of her figure, face and braiding; traces of blood where he had cut himself in his maddest moments.

She turned to the final page and began to read.

'The curate is a fool and I shall murder him … just as I murdered the Duke of Wellington. The man refuses to marry us … he thinks that I am insane…. Yes! I am insane! Insane with love and jealousy for my angel…. If he will not marry us, then I cannot allow her to become anyone else's … and I shall end my life with hers, although it will break my heart to scar her lovely beauty….'

Angela's hand began to shake and she almost dropped the book in her fear. She had to escape from him before he woke. Looking at the door, she opened the journal and gently tore a page from it. She crossed the room to the dressing table from which she took a hair pin and, checking on Dunn, she returned to the door and slid the paper beneath it, leaving a part of it on the near side. She looked through the keyhole and saw the key on the other side. The girl had locked them in together just as Dunn had instructed in case Angela had tried to find the key on him while he had slept. Carefully she pushed the hair pin through the lock, easing the key loose on the other side until it fell onto the paper beneath the door. As she pulled the paper towards her, the key began to move under the door, momentarily becoming lodged. Angela checked the sleeping Dunn once more, before lifting the door slightly by the handle and easing the key on the page beneath the door again. This time it slid underneath and lay on the paper at her feet.

Steadying her hold with both hands, she put the key in the lock and gently turned it, opening the door with fear and relief. Belle was asleep beneath a blanket on a sofa. With great care Angela walked towards the door, unlocked it and hurried with the lightest footfall that she could manage down the staircase, and out through the front door. She did not dare to look up at the window or over her shoulder, but ran to a house further along the lane and banged on the door, the rain falling and soaking her underclothes.

In time a housekeeper, a candle in her hand, answered. Her eyes adjusted to the darkness outside.

'Miss, you will catch your death. What are you doing walking the lane in such a state?'

Angela begged to be let in, to ask for her carriage to be sent for, to call for the police, to escape from the constant nightmare that had been her life these past years.

When suitable clothing had been found, Angela sat by the fireside in the sitting room, waiting for the police to return and advise her of Dunn's arrest.

The policeman who arrived stood before her, not sure of how he would tell her what he had found, the woman seemed so fragile.

'Do you have him now? Did you arrest him?' she asked anxiously. 'Do you have him under lock and key?'

He hesitated a moment and then said, 'I'm so sorry, miss, but when we returned to the house, there was no one there. The rooms were empty. Only the remainder of the fire gave any hint that anyone had been there. He has gone but we have no idea where.'

'Then he is still free to torture me?'

Angela put her head in her hands and wept with despair

CHAPTER EIGHTEEN

DICKENS SAT IN the drawing room of his new house at Gad's Hill, studying a letter he had received from Cape Town. It held encouraging news from one of the two girls who had sailed there five years before. She was happily settled with her kind and practical husband, and there was a smallholding at the back of their cottage which provided what they needed. How proud she was to have been recently accepted onto the village ladies' committee.

Smiling with satisfaction, Dickens got up from his easy chair and crossing the room to his bureau, he took a small box from the drawer. Removing the lid, he placed the letter inside among a collection of others. Not all of them told the same story and he had to confess that there had been disappointments too.

It was a box which contained the many secrets of the women who had passed through the Home for Fallen Women.

His fingers lingered over the envelopes as he recalled some of the inmates. They were of no particular class; some were as young as fourteen or fifteen, others much older. Some could read well, others had no learning at all. Then there were those who had become thieves, and those whose only crime was to be poor.

He amused himself with the thought of Campbell, the girl who had no idea of her birthday and who had had her head shaved by the matron on her arrival; it had been crawling with lice. Campbell had found herself arrested after breaking windows in an empty house in order to find shelter.

She had cried like a cat when she had been made to have a bath.

Then there was the pretty girl, with the blue eyes. She had stayed out too late with friends at the theatre, and been refused entrance by her landlady on her return, only to find herself taken away by two women of disrepute.

Dickens had taken these histories and woven them into a journalistic piece for his magazine. There had been some readers who had urgently pressed him for the location of the home, on the pretext that they wished to see what good was being done there. But Dickens was wise enough to ask for their donation rather than permit their voyeurism. He replaced the lid to the box, keeping their secrets safe, and returned it to the drawer.

Seeing the morning newspaper on a side table, Dickens picked it up and settled himself back in his chair. He wished to read of the progress of the newly operational London General Omnibus Company; it would revolutionize travel across the metropolis, although he himself was personally in favour of walking whenever possible.

He shook open *The Times* and as he did a headline caught his eye.

'Well, well, well!'

He thought of the years that Miss Angela had endured Dunn in her shadow with so little assistance, and read with wonderment the report beneath the newspaper heading:

MR DUNN: A ROYAL SUITOR.

CHAPTER NINETEEN

St James's Palace
London

DUNN LINGERED IN the grounds below, his eyes scrutinizing the windows. In the breakfast room at St James's Palace, Princess Mary Adelaide of Cambridge was taking breakfast with her mother, Princess Augusta.

'I will never get used to this English weather nor this draughty English *Schloss!*' Princess Augusta complained to her daughter.

'Well, we are in England now, Mama, and guests of the Queen. We must acclimatize ourselves to our new circumstances.'

Prince Adolphus addressed his wife. 'Your daughter is a very wise young woman.' He dabbed at his mouth with a napkin. 'But I have some pleasing news that you will be glad to hear, *mein Herz.*'

Princess Augusta gave a warning glance at her daughter, who was about to take another bread roll.

'*Deine Hüfte*, Mary! Your hips, my dear!'

She turned her attention back to her husband.

'*Liebling?* You were saying?'

'The Queen has blessed us with the gift of a magnificent town house in Piccadilly, with many impressive rooms in which you will not be ashamed to entertain our guests. Then you can arrange as many balls as you wish and we will find a husband for you, Mary. It's time—'

The prince was interrupted by the arrival of the footman, who placed a silver salver bearing the morning post at the prince's elbow. He bent down and lowered his voice to his master's ear.

The prince raised his eyebrows. 'Wedged beneath the bars of the iron balustrade, you say? Why would someone do such a thing? It could have blown away!'

He took the letter from the top of the pile and frowned.

'What a singular hand.'

'*Liebling*? Who is it from?'

Princess Augusta slapped her daughter's hand, noticing she was reaching for the bread again.

The prince examined the handwriting. The strokes of the pen were tall and thin, the letters written with little spacing between them. The address on the envelope was clearly legible, as if the writer wished there to be no doubt as to who was the intended recipient.

'It is for you, Mary,' he remarked with surprise, handing it to the young princess.

'Perhaps it is an invitation!'

The princess tore open the envelope, and as she began to read the letter, her eyes passed over words which were shocking. She gave a cry of fear and revulsion.

'Who would say such things!'

Her mama took the letter from her hand and after reading a few words, hurried to the fireplace, throwing the vile insult onto the flames.

'Adolphus! That is the hand of a madman! *Es ist schreklich*! He should be found and locked up immediately.'

Outside the palace walls, Dunn paced back and forth, looking up at the windows frantically.

'Where are you? Where *are* you?' He wrung his hands anxiously.

Muttering to himself, his eyes darted repeatedly to the bushes with the belief that someone was watching him.

His eyes narrowed. 'Leave me be!' he shouted.

He returned his gaze to the palace and found it hard to focus. The solid surfaces of the walls were moving and voices jostled within his head to be heard. A bird flew unexpectedly at his face and he waved it away fearfully with his arm.

'Get away from me! Get away from me!'

Breathing heavily, he tried to compose himself.

'It's not real … it's not … real.'

Taking a set of opera glasses from his pocket, his hand shaking, he focused them on the breakfast room where Princess Mary Adelaide of Cambridge was being comforted by her mother and father.

He smiled and whispered, 'Oh, how I wish that I could see through the threads and fibres of her drapes, and look upon her heavenly form, rising and falling with each breath that she takes. How tempted I am to conceal myself in the shadows and find my way to her door. Perhaps there is a window left open, or a latch undone. If only I could stow away in her bedroom, hide myself in her armoire, then no longer would I be blighted to watch her from a distance. Through the gap in the door I would watch her and, when I was sure she was sleeping, I would steal from my hiding-place and stand at her bedside. I would place my face above hers and feel her breathing, mute and unaware. And the breath from my lips would merge with her own, and she would not know that I had been there. She would never know.…'

Prince Adolphus, comforting his wife and daughter, called for his aide and sternly instructed that the head of police be called.

The doctor stood before Dunn, whose handcuffed figure slumped in a chair.

'Do you know where you are, sir?'

Dunn shook his head, unmindful of the bare grey walls around him.

'This is the Mare Street Asylum. You were brought here from the palace after you were found trespassing in the gardens some days ago.'

Dunn lifted his eyes. 'An asylum? But I am not unwell.'

'That is what I am trying to establish, sir. Can you tell me *who* you are?' the doctor enquired.

Dunn raised his eyes and nodded with certainty. 'I am Richard Dunn, barrister-at-law, resident of the city of London.'

'And your age, sir?'

'Forty-three.'

'Are you familiar with the name of Miss Angela Burdett-Coutts?'
Dunn's face darkened.

'The woman who murdered me.'

'And the Princess Mary Adelaide?'

Dunn's air became distant, a soft smile on his face.

'The angel who brought me to life again. The cherub who gave me an unmistakable look of recognition while riding in her carriage. The heavenly one who is about to become my wife.'

The doctor nodded slowly, walked to his desk, sat down and scribbled Dunn's response on his notepad.

'And if her father were to withdraw her hand in marriage from you?'

Dunn sprang from his chair suddenly and shouted, 'Then I would slit his throat open, tear his heart from his chest, sever his head, rupture his spleen, dismember and rip him apart!'

Dunn was restrained by two of the doctor's assistants. who eased him to his chair again. He bowed his head and began to weep.

'If you try to part me from her, I will die. Do you understand? I will die.'

The doctor looked up from his desk.

'I am here to help you, Mr Dunn, I don't wish to distress you.'

'She is my beautiful princess. The one I dream of constantly, the one whose love both delights and pains me. I cannot live without her and wherever she is, there I will be also. There is nothing that can—'

Dunn was interrupted by a knock on the door and the appearance of a policeman.

'There is a lady asking to see the gentleman, doctor. She says that she is the only family that he has. She says that she is his wife, sir.'

'Very well, just for a moment,' the doctor assented.

'Agnes?' Dunn whispered.

The policeman returned with a woman at his side. She had not seen her husband in years and he was not at all the figure of the man she remembered.

'I advise you to be cautious, madam, as his mood is

unpredictable,' the doctor warned.

Agnes Dunn approached her husband and knelt before him, taking his hands.

'I came to London to visit my sister. I was staying at the Swan and came across the news of your arrest in the newspaper. I was not at all sure that it was you, but it appears that sadly I was right. I am so sorry, my love.'

Dunn was silent for a moment, taking in her appearance as if she were an apparition.

She sought his eyes and said with regret, 'I hurt you very much and caused you pain that you did not deserve. It seems that it has brought you to this place and I am responsible. Can you forgive me?'

He looked briefly at her face, which changed its appearance over and over, and then he looked past her.

'Don't you know me, Richard?' she asked.

He reached out his hand unexpectedly.

'Hello, my love, I knew you would come to me. And when I needed you most you are here.'

'Yes, I am here.' She smiled.

He frowned as if trying to piece together a puzzle.

'There is a mist that fills the space where you once were, Agnes. I have done some things which cause me regret in my calmer moments, but I cannot recall what they were now.'

'There is no rush. There will be plenty of time for us to talk when you come back with me.'

She held out her hand and he stood up to take it.

'She is here now and I am at peace.' He smiled at the doctor. 'At last I can go home.'

The doctor's assistants began to lead him away by the arm.

'There is no one there, Mr Dunn. You are quite alone,' the doctor explained.

'Alone?' Dunn looked at the figure of the woman at his side and as he did so, she loosed his hand, grew faint and began to disappear. The faces of the men at either side looked back at him.

'Agnes? Agnes!' he called.

'You need to rest, Mr Dunn,' the doctor said.

'It seems that I am always destined to be alone.' Dunn looked at the place where she had stood and asked, 'What day is it, sir?'

The doctor hesitated for a moment, wondering at the reason for Dunn's question, and then he answered him.

'The day? Why, it is a Friday, Mr Dunn....'

EPILOGUE

ANGELA SAT AT her desk in the morning room at Stratton house, dictating a letter to Hannah.

'… *if you could offer a post for destitute boys aboard a training ship, where they can learn a trade, strict discipline, and be among those who will become like a family to them …*'

Angela paused.

'If the navy can provide sufficient places on board, Hannah, then there will be at least six boys across three ships who will have a future. And who knows how many more can be placed in future months?'

'It is an admirable scheme, Miss Angela. Do you also want me to post the letter to Miss Nightingale?'

'Yes, Hannah, I wish to make a donation to her nursing efforts. Her commitment to the field has been outstanding.'

A knock at the door brought Blossom into the room with the words, 'Mr Dickens is here to see you, Miss Angela. Can you receive him?'

'Yes, of course, please show him in.'

A moment later, Dickens entered with his usual flourish.

'Miss Angela, Mrs Brown. How good to see you both. I heard that you were in London and took the opportunity to pay my respects. How are you?'

'We are well, Dickens, thank you. And how are you settling into your new house?'

'Very well, indeed. I have Mr Hans Christian Andersen as a

guest at present who is entertaining the children with his endless stories.'

'How charming!'

'And what news is there of your work with the young naval recruits?' Dickens enquired.

'I have written this very morning to three captains, all of whom expressed to the chief admiral that they would patronize my scheme. And …'

Angela paused; she had been idly scanning her morning post as she had been speaking, and her eye fell upon the handwriting of the envelope in her hand. The strokes of the pen were tall and thin, the letters written with little spacing between them. The address on the envelope was clearly legible, as if the writer wished there to be no doubt as to who was the intended recipient. Getting up from her chair, with a flood of fear, she crossed the room to the window and scanned the windows of the Gloucester Coffee House Hotel directly opposite.

'Miss Angela?'

There was no sign of anyone at the windows and looking down again at the letter in her hand, her eyes refocused and she realized that the style was not at all as she had first thought.

'Is everything in order, Miss Angela?' Dickens asked, a note of concern in his voice.

Angela sighed, and with a smile said, 'Yes, Dickens, everything is in order.' She returned to her desk with the words, 'Some old anxieties came upon me momentarily, as they do from time to time, but I seek to put the past behind me.'

'I'm pleased to hear it, ma'am. It was good news, indeed, to hear that the madman is now incarcerated. I must say how quick people are to detect madness when the Royal Family are concerned in the matter. But at least you can also rest easy now.'

'Work is a great solace, Dickens, and there are always new and worthy causes to support. I believe there is further work to be done in respect of the aboriginal peoples in Australia.'

'Indeed? To work then, Miss Angela, to work!'